SECRET IN THE
STITCHES

SECRET IN THE STITCHES

JO ANN BROWN

Guideposts
New York, New York

Thanks to Beth, Andy, and Lindsay

for making me and my words

so welcome

PATCHWORK MYSTERIES

Family Patterns

Time to Share

Muslin Mystery

Timeless Treasures

Homespun Holiday

Pieces of the Past

Threads of Truth

Secret in the Stitches

SECRET IN THE THE STITCHES

 CHAPTER ONE

*A*ntoinette held her breath. Someone was coming in. If she were to be discovered here, she would be the next to die. Light from the hall played across pale hair. It was the murderer. It was—

"Sarah? Are you home?"

Sarah Hart nearly jumped out of her rocking chair. She looked toward the partially open front door, her eyes wide. Cold night air blew in, the March chill sneaking beneath the lap quilt that covered her legs. For a moment, she couldn't pull herself out of the mystery she'd been reading.

"Sarah?" asked the same female voice again.

Sarah stood and pushed her reading glasses up on her head, sweeping back her graying blonde hair. Ella Buttonwood hobbled into the living room, all four feet, eleven-and-a-half inches of her. Her silky white hair and unsteady gait made Ella look fragile, but Sarah knew better. Not only did

1

Ella run her diner with stern efficiency, but she moderated Maple Hill town meetings without blinking an eye.

"Ella, you startled me!" Sarah set the book on the rocking chair her late husband Gerry had made for her.

"I'm sorry, Sarah. I knocked twice, but when you didn't answer I peeked in and saw a light on. The door was open, so I thought I'd see if you were home."

"Of course! I must have been so caught up in my novel I didn't hear you knocking." It was a normal occurrence for Sarah's friends and family to just walk into the house if the door was open, but Sarah was a bit surprised to see Ella walk in. They were friendly enough when they ran into each other in town, but they didn't spend much time together. "What brings you out here so late?"

"I'm sorry, but I heard you're going to Texas tomorrow, and I had to see you before you left," Ella said.

"Yes, I'm going to visit my daughter and her family."

"I just need you to look at it before you leave. Will you? I left it right outside the door on the porch."

"It?" Sarah's curiosity was piqued.

"The proof I've been searching for my whole life. Proof that my grandmother's stories about our house being a station on the Underground Railroad are true."

"Maybe you'd better start at the beginning, Ella." They both sat on the couch, knees angled toward each other. It seemed odd to see Ella without the apron she always had on at the Miss Maple, the diner she ran. Tonight, her knobby gray sweater nearly reached the knees of her khaki slacks.

"Remember last spring when everyone got water in their cellars?" Ella asked.

"Of course. Between all the rain and melting snow, I thought we'd need canoes."

"My whole cellar flooded last year. Not that I went down to check because, with this bum knee, steps are more difficult for me with every passing year. I haven't been down in the cellar in ages. We've got water again this year."

"I'm sorry. It's such a mess!"

"Actually it's been a blessing in disguise. While my nephew was cleaning up, he noticed a section of the foundation wall had begun to crumble. It must have been weakened by last year's flood, and the water this year was too much for it."

"And *that* was a blessing?" Sarah asked.

Ella laughed. "Yes. Though I don't know what I'd do without my nephew and niece. Ryan and his sister Chelsea were able to take down that section of the wall to see what repairs we'd have to make."

Sarah nodded. Ella had never married, but for the past six or seven years, she had been the guardian of her younger sister's children. Ella's sister and her husband had died in an automobile accident. The children, now teenagers, had survived and had come to live with Ella.

"And guess what we found once the wall was down?"

"I have no idea," Sarah said.

Ella stood up and took Sarah's arm as if Sarah were a child. "Come and see!"

Sarah tightened the tie on her thick bathrobe and went with Ella to the front entry. Ella opened the front door, careful not to let the wind catch the door and swing it wildly.

"Here it is," Ella said as she picked up a black garbage bag and brought it inside. It looked full. "My proof, or at least one part of it."

"What is it?" Sarah asked as she firmly shut the front door. The wind howled against the house.

Ella started to untie the top of the bag, then hesitated. "Is there anyone else here?"

Sarah shook her head. "Just us."

"Good! I don't want everyone knowing about this until you confirm it is what I think it is." Ella started walking toward the dining room. "Is it okay if I put it on your table? It won't hurt it, I promise."

"I suppose so."

Curious, Sarah turned on the overhead light. The prisms on the brass chandelier glistened brightly on the long table and the fireplace at one side of the room. She gathered up some quilting books that she'd left on the table earlier and set them in the bookcase by the door. Then she turned to watch Ella carry the bag to the table.

Whatever was in the bag must not be too heavy. Ella swung it up onto the table with ease. And it had to be soft since Sarah didn't hear any *thunk*.

Ella opened the bag and drew out a quilt, gently spreading it across the table. It wasn't large, no bigger than would cover a twin bed. The colors were mostly dark and subdued, except for one garish red fabric. Each quilt block was made up of concentric squares, a series of squares one within another. The width of each section of the squares was very narrow.

Sarah's nose wrinkled at the odor of mildew. It wasn't unusual with old quilts, but it warned that the quilt might need a lot of restoration work.

"You think this quilt is proof that your house was a stop on the Underground Railroad?" Sarah asked.

"It could be, if it's the right age." Ella looked at her hopefully. "What do you think?"

"Do you have any idea how long the wall was up?" Sarah set her reading glasses in place again. They were good enough for a quick examination. She would need to get her magnifying glass from the sewing room to do more. She slowly walked around the long table so she could view the quilt from every angle.

"A long time. I was born in that house, and nobody's ever mentioned who built that wall. This quilt must be really old, right?" Ella trailed around the table after Sarah, matching each of her steps.

"I'd need a few days and much better light to tell you that." She looked up at Ella who was appraising her as closely as Sarah was the quilt.

Sarah continued to examine the quilt, running her fingers along the fabric and the seams. She squeezed one section, then several others.

"What are you doing?" Ella asked.

"I'm trying to see what's underneath the quilt's top layer."

"With your fingers?"

"Yes." She pointed at the quilt. "Squeeze it."

"Where?"

Sarah smiled. "Anywhere. It's a way of gauging the resistance in the quilt's layers. That tells me what sort of batting might have been used."

Ella pinched the quilt. "I'm not sure what I'm looking for. What's it supposed to feel like?"

"This quilt feels a bit spongy. It doesn't have the sturdiness of a modern quilt sewn with cotton batting. Some areas are thicker than others, which could mean there's an even older quilt in the middle."

"Really? Would that quilt be more valuable?"

"Not necessarily." Sarah said. "When an old quilt is used for batting, it's usually because it's too worn for any other use. Collectors want well-preserved quilts. I could open up a seam and look at what's inside and—"

"No!" Ella shook her head in horror. "You can't rip up an antique quilt. You'd ruin it."

"I know how to do it without damaging the quilt."

"I don't want to risk it."

"Don't worry." Sarah leaned closer to look at the ties scattered through the quilt. "I wouldn't do anything to the quilt without your permission."

"I don't want the quilt damaged." Once Ella got an idea lodged in her head, she never let it go, no matter how many logical reasons anyone gave. She'd been that way since Sarah first met her in grade school.

Sarah kept looking at the quilt, ignoring Ella's hand pressed protectively on it. "The strips of fabric that create the squares are very narrow."

"Does that mean something? What about the pattern?"

"Antique quilts are often made from thin strips of fabric because material was hard to come by in the nineteenth century and earlier. This is a variation on the Log Cabin pattern, which became popular in the United States around the time of the Civil War."

"But this quilt could have been put together before the Civil War, couldn't it?" Ella asked.

"Yes, it could be an antebellum quilt." Sarah picked up one corner to get a good view of the stitching.

Ella's pressure on the quilt lessened slightly. "Do you think it could have belonged to a runaway slave?"

Sarah paused. "Why do you think it belonged to a slave?"

"Someone closed up a break in the original foundation long ago." Ella said. "We can see that a different stone was used. Maybe that was why the false wall was put up in the first place. To conceal that there'd been a hole there. If my grandmother was right, that opening was connected to a hiding place for runaway slaves."

"Wow! Wouldn't that be something?"

Ella nodded, her smile broadening. "Once I know for sure that my cellar was a station, I want to open a museum. Nothing big or fancy. A couple of exhibit spaces in the cellar. School kids can come and see what slaves endured in their flight to freedom. It's what Maple Hill needs. Stockbridge may have Alice's Restaurant and the Norman Rockwell

Museum, but we'll have the Maple Hill Underground Railroad Museum. I've already contacted a couple of experts to come look at the house and give me their opinions."

"That would be a wonderful thing for Maple Hill," Sarah said. "But I can't be certain that this quilt is old enough to fit that time period until I look at it more closely. There are a lot of things I need to check. Would you be willing to leave it here so I can look at it when I get back from Texas?"

Ella shook her head. "I need to show it to the experts tomorrow."

"They're coming so soon?"

"If the house is truly a previously unknown Underground Railroad site, it's a major find." She began to stuff the quilt into her garbage bag.

Sarah winced and reached out a hand to halt her. "Do you mind if I take some photos of it?"

"Go ahead if it'll help you."

Ella smoothed out the quilt on the table while Sarah got her camera. Sarah retraced her steps around the table, taking a dozen shots of the quilt's pattern and stitching. She turned the quilt over and snapped as many of the bottom. A quick check of the photos told her that she could see the details of the pattern and the stitching. She put the camera on the fireplace mantel.

"Those will really help, Ella," Sarah said. "I'm glad you brought it over."

"Now you can see why I couldn't wait to show this to you." Ella began to roll up the quilt.

"I'll need to spend a lot more time checking out the stitching and the knots and the fabric. Then I'll need to compare it to already dated quilts. After that, I should be able to put an approximate date on your quilt.

Ella tied the bag closed. "But you think it's old, and that's enough for me right now."

"When can you bring it back so I can get to work on dating it more accurately?"

"I'm not sure. I can't promise anything until I know what's going on. I've contacted the Elijah Burt House in Longmeadow and the Seth Hunt House in Northampton. They're both Underground Railroad sites, and they're both sending out someone to look at my house. They're almost as excited as I am." She chuckled, "If that's possible."

Sarah walked with Ella into the foyer. Ella reached for the door, and Sarah wrapped her arms around herself. Even her thick robe wouldn't stop that icy wind. "I hope they can confirm your house as a station. It'd be such a great thing for Maple Hill and for your family."

Ella smiled and opened the front door. "I'll let them know what you've told me about the quilt."

"I can't wait to go over it in detail. I'm sure it's got lots of secrets to share with us."

CHAPTER TWO

arah had never guessed two weeks could fly by so quickly. She had spent every second with either her daughter Jenna or the rest of the family. She and Jenna had gone shopping several times, once at a craft sale at her grandson Thomas's grade school. Jenna had teased Sarah each time she stopped to admire a different quilt. The patterns used in Texas weren't very different from the ones in Massachusetts, but Sarah never missed a chance to speak to a quilter and talk shop. Jenna enjoyed listening for a while, then wandered away to look at other tables. By the time they'd left, Sarah had purchased a new carry bag for her quilting and beautiful Fair Isle knit sweaters for Jenna, her husband, and the boys.

And that had been one of the quieter days. Both Jenna and David had taken a long weekend from their jobs, so the five of them could visit some must-see sites in central Texas. They had tried to cram a year's worth of experiences into two weeks. Though Sarah was exhausted, she had loved every minute of her visit. It hadn't mattered whether she was sitting on the floor with Thomas and Jonathan playing with their toy cars, or wandering through a historical site with the whole family.

She had returned to Maple Hill last night, and now it seemed as if she'd never been gone. Except that she was exhausted from the long trip home, and she had a lot of errands to run. All the things she had put off until she got home now needed to be done.

The top items on her list of things to do included picking up the mail at the post office and buying groceries to fill her empty fridge. But Sarah was also anxious to call Ella to find out what the experts had said about her cellar and the quilt. She was eager to examine the quilt in more detail and research what she discovered.

She also wanted to catch up with her best friend Martha Maplethorpe. Maybe they'd get together this afternoon for a nice warm drink over at Liam's café on the village green.

She put her shopping list in her purse and pulled on her coat, then buttoned it up and flung a scarf around her neck. She had gotten spoiled with the warm weather in Texas, while winter seemed unwilling to give up control of the Berkshires.

The grocery store's parking lot was half full, but Sarah found a spot not far from the door. She hurried into the store to escape the cold. She pulled out a cart and began to work her way through her shopping list.

"Sarah!" called a familiar voice. "How was your visit with Jenna and her family?"

She smiled as she saw Pastor John Peabody reaching for a bag of onions. "It was wonderful. I swear the boys have grown half a foot since I saw them at Thanksgiving."

The pastor of the Bridge Street Church set the onions in his cart next to a carton of milk. The silver in his hair glistened in the glare of the supermarket lights.

"You've missed a lot of excitement," John said. "Things are really buzzing over at Ella Buttonwood's house."

"Did the experts confirm her house was part of the Underground Railroad?"

"Must be. Plans for a museum are moving forward. Dave Diamond has been hired to oversee the construction work to finish the cellar and put in a new entrance for visitors. Funding for the museum is on tonight's town meeting agenda, and there's a big fund-raiser planned for it out at the diner tomorrow night."

"Oh my. I never guessed it would move this quickly."

Sarah heard her name from behind her. She looked back to see two women coming toward her. She recognized one as Mandy Maplethorpe, Martha's daughter-in-law. She walked slowly because her third child was due in only a few weeks.

"Mandy! You look beautiful. How are you feeling?" Sarah asked.

"Huge." She put her hand on her stomach. "Have you spoken to Mom yet?"

"Not yet. I plan to call her when I get done with my errands."

"Oh good. I know she's missed your company."

"Mrs. Hart," said the other woman, who appeared to be close in age to Mandy, "I have a question for you."

"Sure," Sarah said. "I don't believe we've met. I'm Sarah Hart."

"I know. I wanted to ask you a question about quilts." The woman kept going, neglecting to offer her own name. "Where would I find out about patchwork patterns from before the Civil War?"

Sarah was used to talking about quilts, but not often in the vegetable aisle of the supermarket. "I can suggest a couple of good basic books." She started to give the titles, then paused to ask, "Do you want to write these down?"

"I'll remember them!" The woman beamed.

Sarah gave her two titles and was surprised when another woman across the display of potatoes asked her to repeat them while she scribbled on the back of a piece of paper. Then a man walked up to ask her a question about colors for antebellum quilts. She realized a crowd was gathering around her. Everyone had questions and anecdotes about quilts in their attic or hanging on their mother's wall. She answered most of them and suggested books or Web sites for further information. It was a delight to talk about her passion for historical quilts, but once or twice she glanced down at her unfinished shopping list.

The crowd finally wandered away to do their own shopping, each one thanking her.

Sarah glanced at Pastor John and smiled. "Are all these questions about quilts because of the one Ella found?"

"It's been the talk of the town. There's a tremendous amount of excitement about having an Underground Railroad site here in Maple Hill." His eyes focused over her shoulder. "Looks like you're about to get a few more. I'll see you on Sunday, Sarah. Good luck!"

Sarah quickly found herself giving many of the same answers again. She finally had to excuse herself to go find the rest of the items on her list before the milk and eggs in her cart got too warm.

After her shopping was done, she stopped at the post office, and the situation was almost identical. Patrons waiting in line asked about quilts. People checking their mailboxes came over to listen and ask questions of their own while she signed for the package of seedlings she'd ordered. One of the mail carriers came out from behind the window to get her opinion on a discussion about quilts he'd had with his wife the night before. She had never guessed that a single quilt would create such a hubbub.

Sarah went to her car and opened the door of her silver Grand Prix. A gust of icy wind almost pulled it out of her hands.

"Let me help you, ma'am," said a pleasant male voice. A broad, gloved hand steadied the door.

"Thank you." She looked at the man. He was tall and thin, and probably close to her son's age though his blond hair was already thinning on top. His wrinkled pants looked as if they'd been packed in a suitcase during a very long trip.

She set her mail on the passenger seat and settled herself behind the wheel. She reached for the door, but realized the man still held it.

"I heard you answering all the questions inside," he said with a smile. "Are you Sarah Hart by any chance?"

"Yes I am."

"I'm George Krause. I've got a question of my own…if you don't mind."

"Sure. I'll answer it if I can," Sarah said.

He leaned down a bit, ducking his head away from the brisk wind. "Is there a connection between quilts and the Underground Railroad in Massachusetts?"

Sarah considered the question for a moment, then shook her head. "I really don't know. That's one of the things I hope to find out when I do more research on Ella Buttonwood's quilt."

"Why don't I give you a couple of days and then call you? Would that be okay?"

"Of course. My number's in the book."

"Great. Thanks." He closed the door firmly, then, waving, walked away.

Sarah pondered the question as she drove home and carried her shopping bags into the house. Of course she'd learned about the Underground Railroad in school. But even in her extensive research in the course of restoring antique quilts, she had seen only a passing reference or two to quilts and the Underground Railroad.

After putting the perishables in the fridge, she hurried into her sewing room where she kept her computer on a desk near the window. She turned the computer on, then picked up the stack of photos she'd left on top of the printer two weeks ago.

She paged through the shots of Ella's quilt. They were clear enough to show the stitching, but it wasn't the same as being able to view the quilt itself. She found Ella's phone number and called. It rang and rang before the answering machine picked up.

"I'm sorry we're unable to take your call right now," said a female voice that wasn't Ella's. It must be her niece's. "If you're calling with questions about the Maple Hill Underground Railroad Museum project or wish to make a contribution, please leave your number, and we'll call back as soon as we can."

Sarah waited for the beep, then said, "Ella, it's Sarah Hart. I'm home from my trip, and I'd love to have a chance to inspect the quilt again. I know today might not be a good time with the town meeting tonight, but can you let me know when I can come over? Thanks." She left her home number, then hung up the phone.

She turned back to the computer. Launching her Web browser, she sat down and typed in *Underground Railroad*. The number of available sites with information about the Underground Railroad was over two million.

She needed to get a bit more specific. Next, she typed in *Underground Railroad quilt*.

More than sixty-two thousand sites came up on this search. Sixty-two thousand was much better than two million, but still bit overwhelming. Her eyes scanned the offerings on the first page of results.

Sarah's breath caught when she read "Underground Railroad Quilt Code." She clicked on the link and began to read. It was a municipal site from a Canadian city, and it said that slaves who could not read and write conveyed secret messages to each other through the patterns in quilts. It listed several quilt designs, including the Log Cabin, as patterns used by slaves to show when it was safe to flee north. Other quilt patterns were used to give directions to havens along the Underground Railroad route.

The more Sarah read, the more she wanted to know. It could be a great topic to feature in her column on quilts and quilting in *Country Cottage* magazine. She went back to the links page and clicked the next one. It was an excerpt from a book repudiating the whole idea of a quilt code used by fugitives escaping via the Underground Railroad.

She folded her arms on the edge of her desk and read. The story began in 1993 when the writer was approached by an older woman at a street market in Charleston, South Carolina. The woman was selling quilts and hinted that a history passed down through her family revealed that slave quilts were used for more than keeping warm. The writer was intrigued and asked questions, even though it took several years to convince the older woman to open up to her again. The woman told the story that was the basis for the quilt code theory. She claimed that quilts placed in a certain order and in specific places conveyed secret messages to slaves on their escape north.

But, the Web site went on to say, none of the claims could be corroborated. The site's author began to pick apart the story and the research behind it with the intensity of a quilter pulling out each stitch of a wrongly sewn seam.

Sarah scanned through more sites. Some accepted every detail of the quilt code story. Others refuted it. None of them went into as much detail as the second site Sarah had visited. And none of them suggested that quilts were used by the Underground Railroad in New England.

Sarah knew she needed to find out more if she wanted to determine whether Ella's Log Cabin quilt had anything to do with the rumored quilt code. She decided to read the book that had started the whole quilt code debate and judge for herself.

She first called the public library to see if they had a copy. They didn't. Next, she called Liam to find out if he had it in his bookstore.

"Sorry, Sarah," he said with his charming Irish accent. "I don't stock it, and my distributor lists it as taking a week or more to get here. If you want it before then, you could check online and see if anyone can get it to you more quickly."

Sarah thanked him and returned to the computer. She quickly found the book online. The listing stated that it would be delivered in two to three days, so she ordered a copy. She couldn't wait to read it.

The high school auditorium was more crowded than usual for a town meeting. Sarah was used to seeing half of the chairs for residents empty.

She looked around but didn't see Ella. No doubt Ella was busy with last-minute details. The town meeting moderator was responsible for almost every aspect of the meeting, from making sure that copies of the questions to be discussed were available to ensuring every legal and parliamentary requirement was met. Sarah hoped to have a chance to talk to her later.

She smiled when Martha Maplethorpe waved from the second row. She looked ready for spring in her bright green cable cardigan. Sarah made her way up to Martha, through the other chairs at the front of the auditorium that faced the podium where Ella would run the meeting. Behind the podium was the table where the Board of Selectmen and the Finance Committee sat during the twice-yearly meetings. Anyone who wasn't a registered voter in Maple Hill had to sit on the bleachers at the back. The Board of Selectmen met every other week to handle day-to-day issues of the town, but town meeting was a uniquely New England form of democracy that allowed residents to vote directly on town issues. Two times each year, or more often if a special meeting was called, the residents gathered to discuss and vote on the annual budget and decide how that money would be spent. Sarah always tried to get to town meeting, even if she didn't speak to any issues that night.

"Welcome back," Martha gave Sarah a hug. "Sit down and tell me about your trip."

She sat, but asked, "Isn't Ernie coming?"

Martha's smile faltered. "He's not feeling great tonight, so he decided to stay home."

"I'm sorry to hear that." Martha often had just as tough a time dealing with her husband's Parkinson's disease as Ernie himself did.

"How was your trip?" Martha asked.

"It was wonderful. I loved having time with Jenna's family. Wait till I show you the pictures I took."

"I can't wait to see them. Did you catch up on hugs and kisses?"

"Almost." She laughed. "You're lucky to have all your grandchildren living nearby."

"And now you've come back to quilt fever! Mandy told me that you were mobbed at the grocery store today."

Sarah chuckled. "Quilt fever? That's the perfect name for it. Everybody I talked to wanted to know everything about quilts."

"And I'm sure you could tell them what they needed to know."

"All but one. I'm doing some research on that." She didn't want to explain further until she had a few more facts.

"Really?" asked Martha. "I thought you knew everything about quilts."

"Me too," said a woman in the front row who turned to face them. Abby McCormick wore her dark hair cut in a bob, which suited her square face. She was tall and rawboned, and though her features were severe, when she smiled, they softened and made her easily approachable.

"No one knows everything," Sarah said. "You probably know that better than most, Abby." Abby was a reporter for the *Maple Hill Monitor* and took her job seriously. Her articles focused on town meetings and the various volunteer committees that kept the town running. Abby had a reputation for getting the facts and writing about them fairly.

"What do you know about the project over at the Buttonwood house?" Abby asked.

"Not much. I got a quick glimpse of the quilt before I left to visit family."

"That's more than most people have gotten," Abby said, a smile easing her stern expression. "What do you think about the idea of a museum at Ella's house? I suppose you're pleased."

"I'm pleased that the quilt may be an important find," Sarah said. "But you don't sound very pleased."

"I'm not." Standing, she called to a tall, thin man with dark hair who sat across the aisle. "Fred, can you come over here for a second?"

He did. "What's up, Abby? Oh hi, Mrs. Hart. Mrs. Maplethorpe. Everyone here for their twice a year civics lesson?" Fred Daniels, who had graduated with Jason, was now a history teacher at the high school.

"Wouldn't miss it," Sarah said.

Abby sat and draped her arm over the back of her chair. "Fred, tell them what you told me about losing out on your Cultural Council grant."

Fred frowned. "How come?"

"I thought these ladies would be interested."

Sarah looked from one to the other, saying nothing. Beside her, Martha was also silent. Fred and Abby stared at each other.

The teacher relented first. "Okay, okay. I was granted some Cultural Council funds for a speaker for my AP history class. Then I was asked to relinquish the funds so they could go to the museum project. It wasn't a big deal. In the long run, the museum will be good for Maple Hill."

"That's very generous of you, Fred," Sarah said.

"I'm trying to be a good loser." He chuckled as he stuck his hands in his pockets. "I don't know if my kids will agree when I put them to work researching the Underground Railroad to help the museum instead of listening to the speaker I'd planned to hire."

Martha asked, "What will they be doing for the museum?"

"I volunteered them to gather the data and photos for the information boards that will be set up at the Buttonwood house. It'll give them an opportunity to be involved, and I can always try to get the speaker in for my class later in the semester. Well, you ladies enjoy the meeting." Fred returned to his seat as the Board of Selectmen began to sit at the table up front.

"That's what bothers me about this museum project," Abby said. "Everything else is being trampled on in an effort to get it up and running."

"Maybe it would have been better," Martha said, "for the Cultural Council money to be discussed tonight at the town meeting. That way, everyone could have had a say in how it was spent."

"Cultural Council funds are disbursed by a town committee. It's always been that way." Abby shrugged. "Changing traditions in Maple Hill is about as easy as shoving rain back into the clouds."

Sarah smiled. "You're right about that."

More voices echoed in the auditorium as the chairs filled up. Most of them belonged to familiar faces. Abby was right. Things in Maple Hill seldom changed, but when they did it was often for the better. Sarah smiled and waved when she saw her son and his wife walk in. This was their first real town meeting, and they'd been excited to attend. They waved back and turned to talk to some of the friends they'd made since they'd moved from California.

"I'm not the only one," Abby said, pulling Sarah back into the conversation, "who's been trying to get the committee members to open their eyes and reconsider how the money can best be used. Not for another class at the library or cleaning a statue down at Patriot Park. The committee members act as if the funds are manna from heaven that they have to use up before they vanish."

"Don't the funds revert to the state if they aren't used?" Sarah asked.

"Yes, but not two seconds after the money is granted to the town." Abby flipped open her notebook and took out a pen as the Finance Committee members came out to take their seats at the table. "There would be plenty of time to do a thorough investigation of the Buttonwood house and the materials found in the cellar before the money is allocated."

"And then you'd be fine with the money going to the exhibit?" Martha asked.

"Not every penny of it." She lowered her voice. "I really care about Maple Hill, and that's why I don't like Cultural Council funds being put into someone's private house. It doesn't seem right. What if Ella decides to sell her house the day after the museum opens?"

Sarah nodded. Ella selling her home wasn't likely; the house had been in the Buttonwood family for generations, but there should be some written agreement. She'd ask Jason about it. Her son would know about the legalities.

"And now she's placed a question for more money on tonight's town meeting warrant." Abby frowned as she scanned her notes. "I'm not sure how she managed to do that in such a short time. I need to check into that."

"Ella always follows the rules," Martha said.

Abby's smile returned. "I didn't mean she did anything wrong. I'm just curious about how she got approval in such a short time. That's something everyone should know."

A gavel sounded against the podium, and Sarah looked past Abby, who quickly faced forward, to see Ella standing behind the podium. Ella wore a simple navy dress with a strand of pearls. She always wore something similar to town meetings, and always with the pearls.

Ella ran the meeting with the skill her father had displayed during his long tenure as town meeting moderator. She introduced herself and the people at the table, even though everyone in attendance knew who they were. She also pointed out the reporters who sat in the front row on either side of the center aisle. Procedural matters like establishing a quorum were quickly dealt with. The first three items to be brought to the town residents were each read aloud, and Ella asked if the Selectmen and the Finance Committee members approved of them. Then the floor was opened for town residents to give their opinions or ask questions. As all three involved shifting money from one town account to another to cover the winter's snow removal and repairs on the Bridge Street bridge, there was little discussion before the vote was taken to approve the transfer.

Even so, if anyone spoke longer than their allotted time, Ella firmly cut them off, citing the rule that everyone must have a chance to speak. No one could doubt that Ella liked to be in charge. It was one of the reasons Sarah had never been especially close to her old schoolmate. It always had to be Ella's way, whether she was right or wrong. Sarah preferred working with others as a team.

"Here we go," said Martha as Ella announced the fourth and final item. It concerned approving the town's provision of funds for the Underground Railroad museum. The amount would be an exact match of what was raised by the fund-raiser combined with the Cultural Council funds.

Ella stepped aside to allow Jack Handelman, the chairman of the Board of Selectmen, to take the podium. "We don't want any suggestion of conflict of interest," she said.

Sarah tried to catch Ella's eye, but Ella focused on Jack as he read the item and announced that both the Board of

Selectmen and the Finance Committee had approved bringing it to town meeting. When he called for debate, Sarah was astonished there wasn't any. That made her uneasy. Even the items about snow removal money had elicited a couple of comments.

It had to be quilt fever.

Sarah's surprise must have shown on her face because Martha asked, "What's wrong?"

"I thought *someone* would protest giving money to the museum. I hope we're not jumping into this too quickly."

"Trust Ella," Martha said, settling back in her chair. "She wouldn't do anything that wasn't for the benefit of Maple Hill."

The vote was taken by a voice vote. Sarah didn't hear anyone vote no. Not even Abby who was scribbling frantically in her notebook.

The meeting was then adjourned. Sarah tried to speak with Ella, but there was such a crowd around her that Sarah couldn't get close. All Sarah got was a wave and "I'll see you at the fund-raiser tomorrow night." Ella hurried out with the Selectmen and reporters following. Sarah could hear their excitement.

But that hint of disquiet remained behind. Sarah couldn't get Abby's words about the museum out of her mind: *Everything else is being trampled on in an effort to get it up and running.*

CHAPTER THREE

The next night, Sarah rode to the Miss Maple diner with her son Jason and his wife Maggie. Their twelve-year-old twins had decided not to come and were at home watching a movie. Sarah was glad to get away from the computer. She had spent much of the day chasing down links to find out more about the elusive quilt code and slave quilts. She'd learned a lot though much of it was contradictory.

"You must be really excited to examine that quilt again," Maggie said as Jason turned the car onto Morton Street, a twisting road that led toward the mountains. Here the snowbanks were higher than in the center of town.

"I really am. I've stared at the photos again and again, but it's not the same as looking at the real thing. I tried calling Ella again this morning," Sarah said, "but didn't hear back. I even tried again this afternoon." She laughed. "To be honest, I began to feel like a stalker by the third time I left a message.

I know she's busy, but I'd hoped she'd give me her okay to start getting a solid date for the age of the quilt."

"I'm sure you'll see her tonight." Looking over her shoulder at Sarah in the back seat, Maggie smiled. "When my donation is raffled off, I can call both of you up to help me hand the prize to the winner." Maggie had given a complete set of antique china from her store for the fund-raiser.

"I don't think that would be the best time to say I want to see the quilt *now*." Sarah laughed along with her daughter-in-law. "I know it'll be worth the wait."

Jason had to park along the road because the diner's lot was full. He found a spot where the snow had receded enough to let him get the car off the road. As they walked toward the diner, Maggie picked her way around a puddle, not wanting to ruin the heels that made her even taller. She was very elegant with her auburn hair in a French twist and wearing a tailored cream suit. Jason wore a navy jacket over khakis, more casual than he would have been when he represented a client in court.

"You seem distracted," Sarah said to her son. The cold wind threatened to suck her breath out with every word.

"Thinking about a case I'm taking on." He chuckled. "I'm trying to come up with some precedent that might help. Even though I'm here with you, my brain is paging through law books."

"Sounds painful."

"Only when I can't recall what I need." He gave Sarah a grin when they reached the diner.

Wide windows ran along the front of the Miss Maple, except where a door was set in a small porch. A double set of concrete steps led up to the door. It was larger than most area diners and was popular with tourists traveling to Vermont's Green Mountains.

Jason opened the door and ushered them in. Someone handed Sarah a piece of paper. She didn't have a chance to look at it as she was thrust by the crowd behind her into the diner.

The space was packed with people eager to help raise money for the museum. The Miss Maple came straight out of the fifties, and Sarah guessed not an inch had been redecorated in the past sixty years. Its walls were covered with stainless steel, and the counter was topped by white laminate with gold speckles. The booths, the freestanding tables, and the stools by the long counter were a bright red that went perfectly with their chrome edging. Gone were the checkered tablecloths, the baskets with mustard and ketchup, and the vases that usually held flowers. Both the booths and the counter were being used to display items for sale or to be raffled. At the far end of the counter was a coffee urn instead of the usual pie cabinet. Big posters announced the most valuable item being raffled: a new car donated by a local dealer. Other items were on display throughout the diner.

Sarah shrugged off her coat. She saw a big basket filled with books in the closest booth. A small placard on the table said it was a donation from The Spotted Dog Bookstore and

Café. Liam had even arranged for several books to be signed by the authors.

Sarah glanced down at the paper and saw it was a flyer listing all the contributors to the evening's raffle. She was amazed. A lot of people must have worked hard to bring this together in such a short time.

On the left side of the page was the drawing of a map with a road heading toward a line labeled Canada. She guessed it was meant to be a route on the Underground Railroad— Maple Hill was marked with a star. Above the line at the top was the figure ten thousand dollars, the amount she guessed was needed to get the museum built and open to the public. A sliver of the road had been inked in. It was a clever way to show how much money had been raised so far. With all the items to be raffled off tonight, she guessed several more inches of the road would be filled in, and the fund-raising well on its way.

When she looked up, Jason and Maggie were gone, swallowed by the crowd trying to see all the auction items. She hadn't seen which way they'd gone so she decided to look around herself. Maybe she would get a chance to speak with Ella and nail down a time to look at the quilt.

Someone bumped into Sarah and began to apologize, then said, "Sarah! It's good to see you."

Sarah had time to smile at Irene Stuart before she was jostled again and had to step forward to keep her balance. Right onto Irene's right foot.

"Oh Irene. I'm sorry," Sarah said. "That's not a very friendly greeting!"

The man who had run into Sarah said, "Excuse me. I wasn't watching where I was going."

"George Krause," Irene asked, "have you met Sarah Hart?"

He smiled. "Yes. At the post office yesterday."

"He stumped me with a quilting question." Sarah shook Mr. Krause's hand. "I'm looking for your answer. So far, I've found more questions than answers, but I'll keep looking."

"Great." His cell phone, which hung off his belt, started to ring, but he ignored it. "Irene will tell you that I'm sticking my nose into every part of the exhibit."

"George is in town to help design the Underground Railroad exhibit at the Buttonwood house," Irene explained. "He's using the back room at the historical society for his office. That gives him easy access to our records, but he's over at Ella's most of the time."

"Are you a historian?" Sarah asked, edging aside to let someone past her. If possible, the diner seemed to be even more overflowing with people than a few minutes ago.

"No," Mr. Krause said. "I'm a consultant. I specialize in historical nonprofits, helping them get underway and making sure they file the proper paperwork with the Commonwealth and the federal government." He gave her a warm smile. "I'm looking forward to working with you. Miss Buttonwood is lucky that you were able to recognize her quilt was something special."

"I hope to examine it further soon. I can't be certain about its age until I've had a chance to really dig in."

"Of course, you must," Mr. Krause said. "For an exhibit this important, we can't have anything that isn't unquestionably accurate."

Sarah smiled. "I'm glad you understand."

"I do. Once we confirm the age of the quilt and the other things we've found in the cellar, I know where we can get more grant money that will help the museum promote itself and bring in visitors." His cell rang again. "If you'll excuse me...."

He was gone before Sarah could reply.

"What else have they found?" Sarah asked.

Irene's eyes lit up. "Some carvings that could be maps to the Canadian border. Runaway slaves may have left them for the others still to come."

"Really? That's amazing!"

"Like the quilt, we've got to be sure that everything is the real deal. But that's the fun part, right?"

When Irene went to buy some raffle tickets, Sarah again tried to look for Ella. Sarah took three steps along the counter and bumped into five people. Everyone laughed and good-naturedly apologized before bouncing off someone else. Voices rose as people tried to be heard. It was like being inside a pinball machine—bright lights, lots of noise, and ricocheting from one thing to the next.

"Excuse me," she said again and again. Was she wasting her time looking for Ella? At some point, she guessed Ella would help with drawing the winners of the various prizes.

Waiting last night hadn't worked, but how could she find one specific person in this crowd?

"Sarah, I'm glad you're here." That sounded like Ella, but Sarah couldn't be sure with all the noise.

She turned to see Ella right behind her. She couldn't help staring. Ella wore a light blue linen suit, and her hair had a new stylish cut. Her pearl necklace fell over the front of her navy blouse.

"You look lovely, Ella," she said.

"What?" Ella cupped her ear.

Sarah stepped behind the counter to a calm pool in the crazy current. "Come over here so we can talk. Or try to." As soon as Ella had slipped behind the counter, Sarah repeated her compliment and added, "The pearls are beautiful too."

"My great-grandmother wore them at her wedding and so did my grandmother and mother." Ella fingered the strand. "My sister did too. Someday maybe my niece will wear them at her wedding. In the meantime, I get to enjoy them. If anything happened to them, I don't know what I'd do." She hesitated, but then pasted on a smile. "Isn't it a wonderful turnout?" Ella leaned back against a freezer door. "I keep pinching myself. It's like a dream."

"If you've really found a previously undiscovered Underground Railroad site," Sarah said, "then it's a dream come true for all of Maple Hill."

"It is! Did you hear that we've found carvings in the wood beams that supported the fake wall?"

"Yes, Irene told me. She said one might be a map."

Ella's eyes twinkled. "I'll leave that to the experts. They look like squiggly lines to me."

"I'd love to examine the quilt more closely. I've found something online that might connect. A quilt code used by slaves escaping on the Underground Railroad. One of the patterns is the Log Cabin pattern."

"Wow!" she said. "If that's true—"

"Well," Sarah said, "that's the problem. Some people don't believe there was a quilt code. And even if there was, it might not have been used in New England. I'm still doing some research, but it'd help a lot if I could get my hands on the quilt again."

"You wouldn't have to take it apart, would you?"

"I wouldn't without your permission." Sarah reminded her. "But I want to examine it inch by inch."

"Can you give me a couple of days? It's been a whirlwind for the past two weeks. Why don't you come over Thursday afternoon? I think no one's around that afternoon."

"I could take the quilt over to my house. Then I'd have all my quilting supplies and resources with me if I need to look something up."

Ella shook her head and folded her arms over her chest. "It shouldn't leave my house. That's what I was told. I know it's safe when it's at my house. I'd be a fool to let it out of my sight now."

Sarah pressed her lips together. Ella still refused to believe Sarah's promise not to open up the quilt.

Ella continued, "Let me double-check with my niece and see if Thursday works." She looked past Sarah. "Here's Chelsea now." She raised her voice. "Honey, come here and tell Mrs. Hart if Thursday is okay for her to come over and look at the quilt."

A beautiful young woman in her late teens came over. She had perfect blonde hair that couldn't have come out of a bottle, and her eyes were wide and a deep, rich brown. She was tall and slim, and her graceful motions seemed to belong on a fashion walkway. She wore a little too much makeup, but Sarah knew that kids needed to experiment to find what worked for them. Her only imperfection, which Sarah barely noticed, was a tiny scar, a small crescent above her left eyebrow.

"Chelsea, this is Sarah Hart, the lady who is our quilt expert," Ella said. "Sarah, my niece Chelsea Palladino."

"Hello," Chelsea said, staring at Sarah's shoes. "Nice to meet you."

"And you too." Sarah never would have guessed that tiny Ella Buttonwood would have such a statuesque niece.

"Is Thursday afternoon open for Mrs. Hart to come over and look at the quilt?" Ella asked.

Chelsea nodded. "I think so, but I'm not sure what time. I'll have to check when we get home. Aunt Ella, they're asking if you'll come over by the door because they want you to get people to buy more raffle tickets for the donated car."

"Got to go." Ella squeezed Sarah's arm. "We'll talk later."

Chelsea and Ella edged around the table and into the crowd. Thursday was the day after tomorrow. Sarah could hardly wait to see the quilt again.

The next morning, Sarah carried that day's edition of the *Maple Hill Monitor* into her kitchen. The cold, bright sunshine gleamed off the kitchen's cranberry walls and pale cabinets. She left the paper on the table while she made breakfast. When she opened the paper after she had taken her first few bites of cereal and sips of coffee, she noticed that a photo took up half of the front page. Ella beamed as she stood next to a clear container filled with cash and coins. The Board of Selectmen was arranged around her, and she held a giant check for fifty thousand dollars. It—according to the caption—represented the Cultural Council funds as well as the money raised thus far by the residents of Maple Hill. The article under Abby's byline told that the matching funds would be disbursed later, but this first payment was to pay the consultant, George Krause, and begin the initial construction work in the cellar of the Buttonwood house. None of Abby's concerns about the museum had seeped into the article.

Putting the newspaper on the kitchen table, Sarah folded her hands on her lap. *Dear Lord, please be with Ella and her family and guide them through these astounding experiences. Help me help them by using all I have learned.*

The house suddenly seemed too empty. She trusted in God to hear her prayer, but she wished she could talk this over with Gerry too. Her late husband had always had a way of seeing through the fog that confused other people.

They deserve the truth. She could almost hear Gerry's strong voice telling her what she knew in her heart.

Sarah finished her breakfast, put the dishes in the dishwasher, and then went to get her coat. She'd spent enough time on the computer. The book about the quilt code should be arriving soon, but maybe she could find something else at the public library that would help her learn more about the Underground Railroad and quilts. She wanted to be prepared for examining the quilt tomorrow afternoon. She'd been caught up in quilt fever, but now it was time to get to work.

 CHAPTER FOUR

The imposing Maple Hill Library dominated one end of the town green. On this chilly morning, not many people were out visiting the shops on either side of the green. The storefronts' striped awnings were bright patches of color against the dirty snow while the maple trees reached thin fingers into the bright blue sky. Even so, Sarah was stopped twice before she reached the library. She offered quick answers to the quilt questions, because it was too cold to stand outside and chat.

Sarah rushed into the library. Its stone front and large arched window were over a hundred years old, and it wore its age with quiet dignity. The reading tables were empty, but Sarah heard hushed voices from between the bookshelves that jutted out from the side walls.

After walking against the chilly wind swirling around the green, Sarah was too warm in the library. She pulled off her gloves and stuffed them in her coat pockets. She unzipped her coat as she headed for the history section that was about halfway back.

She walked past European history and stopped in front of the shelves holding American history books. She scanned the section, starting with books about events after the Revolutionary War. She frowned when she reached books about settling the western United States without finding a single book on the Underground Railroad. She began again, this time more slowly. She made sure she read each title. If it wasn't clear on the spine, she pulled out the book to look at the title on the front cover or the title page inside. She found books on the Mexican War and on the California gold rush. There were books about the campaign of 1860 when Abraham Lincoln was elected president. After that there were dozens of books on the Civil War.

She couldn't believe that the library had no books about the Underground Railroad. She decided to check with the librarian, Spencer Hewitt.

Spencer stood behind the circulation desk, staring at his computer. He gave Sarah a warm smile. "Good morning, Sarah. How can I help you today?"

"I was hoping to find some books on the Underground Railroad, but I must have been looking in the wrong place because I couldn't find any in American history."

He sat on his chair and folded his arms over the papers on the desk. "You might as well ask for the holy grail or a map to El Dorado. Books about the Underground Railroad have become scarce around here since word got around about Miss Buttonwood's find. It's become everybody's favorite topic, and I can't keep a book on the subject in the library—not on the adult side or in the children's library. The holds list for the books is a mile long." He chuckled. "Not that I'm complaining. I like when books are out being read."

Sarah wasn't all that surprised. With all the quilt fever she'd seen, there was bound to be even more interest in the Underground Railroad. "I'd really like to get some books about the Underground Railroad. I've ordered a book about the Underground Railroad quilt code, but I was hoping to find some other information. How about the other libraries in western Massachusetts? If I get on the computer and find some books in one of the other libraries, can you get it for me?"

"I could, but you'd be on a waiting list with those libraries too. Once all our books on the subject were checked out, other libraries got tapped too." He looked past her toward the library's three computers. "Your best bet for information right now is probably the Internet."

"I'm researching online too, but no one seems to agree about slaves and quilts and the Underground Railroad. I don't know whom to believe."

"I'll be glad to put your name on the waiting lists for the books. Don't count on getting one any time soon. Like I said, the waiting lists are pretty long. If you need the books fast, you can see what Liam's got at the store."

Sarah nodded. "I will, but I think I'll add my name to the holds lists for a few books here too. I'll let you know if I find the answers somewhere else."

"That's probably the best plan." He went back to his computer and looked up Sarah's account. "I'll put your name on the list for the most popular books. Okay?"

Thanking him, Sarah left the library and headed through the blustery wind toward Liam's. She pulled her scarf up around her nose and mouth. The sun was bright, but it felt as cold as January. Knowing that spring was only weeks away somehow made the chill even harder to take.

Traffic moved slowly around the green. A friendly honk kept one car from backing out into another. Sarah nodded to people she passed but didn't try to speak through the scarf that covered the lower half of her face.

Her phone rang, and she winced. She should have turned it off before going into the library. Fishing it out of her bag, she flipped it open as she hurried along the street.

"Good morning," came Martha's cheery voice in her ear. "How much longer am I going to have to wait to see pictures of your grandsons?"

Sarah laughed. "I'm on my way to Liam's. Why don't you meet me there? I've got some of the photos with me."

"Be right there. Order me a slice of coconut cream pie, if he's got some."

Just the sound of her friend's voice eased Sarah's frustration about bumping up against walls in her research. She always felt better once she'd talked to her best friend. Martha was a good sounding board, and she had practical ideas as well as a lively curiosity. Sarah couldn't imagine anything else better in a best friend.

Liam waved from the café when Sarah entered. He always had a friendly smile for his patrons, whether they were interested in a book or something to eat. His hair was more silver than red these days, and his green eyes twinkled as he asked, "Your regular?"

"In a minute, when Martha gets here." She shoved her gloves back into her pockets. "You know I have a weakness for your spiced chai lattes, but first I wanted to look for some books."

He came around the counter and into the cozy area where bookshelves jutted out from the walls. He paused to let Murphy, his small black-and-white dog and the namesake of the shop and café, walk past to lie down in the sun by a well-worn sofa. "Did you find a copy of the other book you wanted?"

"I did. Online. It should be in today's mail or tomorrow's. Now I'm looking for some more books about slaves and quilts at the time of the Underground Railroad."

He picked up a stack of books and began shelving them in the proper sections. "I can't keep books on the Underground Railroad on the shelves. As soon as they come in, someone buys them." He winked as he added, "Not that I'm complaining about good business."

"Can you order some for me?"

"Sure." He went to the table where he had his cash register. He took out a notepad and a pen. "Write down the titles. If you've got the authors' names, that would be even better."

"I don't have either."

Liam pulled the pad and pen back toward himself. "Well, I'd be happy to suggest some of the titles that have been popular the past couple of weeks. But I'm not sure if they'll really touch on the quilting information you're looking for."

Sarah undid her coat and slipped it off. "Thanks, Liam, but I'll find some book titles. I've been reading a bunch of Web sites, and some of them have bibliographies. I'll drop off a list once I've put it together."

"Sounds good. Let me shelve these books, and I'll be right in to take your order."

"No hurry. Martha won't be here for a few minutes." As she turned to go into the café, she added, "She asked me to check if you have any of your world-famous coconut cream pie."

"She's in luck." He gave her a jaunty grin as he picked up another stack of books. "There are a couple of pieces left."

Sarah smiled as she went to her favorite table by the window. The café wasn't full at this hour, only a couple of the tables were in use. She leaned back in her chair and watched the wind dance shadows across the green.

If only she could be examining the quilt *now*. She was casting about in the dark without any specific direction. Once she looked it over, she'd have definite questions. She could focus her research and not miss the information she sought.

A chill rushed through the café as the door opened, but Martha's warm smile swept it aside. She gave Sarah a hug before shrugging off her coat and sitting at the table.

"I can't believe we haven't had a chance to get together even for a cup of coffee since you got home from Texas," Martha said. "Life just gets busier and busier, doesn't it?"

Sarah's answer was interrupted when Liam came over to take their order. Martha had regular coffee along with her piece of pie, and Sarah asked for a cranberry-orange muffin to go with her spiced chai latte.

Pulling out the half dozen photos she'd printed, Sarah handed them to Martha who oohed and aahed, and smiled at a particularly silly picture of Sarah and the boys making goofy faces.

"We were on the Riverwalk in San Antonio then," Sarah said. "We'd just visited the Alamo, and the boys were so excited by all they'd seen that we half-expected them to end up in the water."

"They're cuties, Sarah. You must miss them and Jenna and David so much."

"I do. I—"

"Excuse me?" asked a woman who came to stand by their table. "Are you Sarah Hart, the quilter?"

Sarah exchanged a wry glance with Martha, then looked at the tall woman. "Yes, I am."

"Can you settle an argument my friend and I are having?" She gestured toward another woman who sat at a table closer to the counter. "She thinks that there is some kind of quilt called a yo-yo, but I think she's making it up."

"Actually you're both right," Sarah said. "There's something called a yo-yo quilt, but it's not a true quilt. It's only a single layer of round scraps sewn together, and it's used as a throw or over another blanket. Mostly for decoration."

The woman nodded, thanked Sarah, and walked back to her table.

Martha chuckled under her breath. "I think she's disappointed you didn't tell her that her friend was wrong."

"I feel like I'm playing some trivia game with everyone trying to find the most obscure questions about quilts."

Martha set the photos on the table. "You can't blame folks for being excited."

"I don't. I'm excited too."

"Y'know," Martha said as she fanned the pictures across the table, "I used to worry after Gerry died that you'd move to Texas or California. I was so happy when I heard Jason and Maggie and the twins were coming here to live because I knew you'd stay in Maple Hill."

Liam carefully set their drinks and food on the table and glanced at the photos. "Are those handsome lads your grandsons, Sarah?"

"Yes. Thomas is six, and Jonathan just turned four." She let pride fill her voice. "I think they're pretty special, but I'm a wee bit prejudiced."

"A wee bit?" He laughed. "You're their grandmother. You should think they are special. Next time they visit Maple Hill, bring them by. Murphy has been moping around, and he could use some lads to play with." He walked back to the counter as the door opened again, and some more customers came in.

Sarah put the photos away, then picked up her cup. The steam and spices swirled around her, and she drew in a deep breath. "I craved one of Liam's spiced chais while I was in Texas." Taking a drink, she set it down. "How's Ernie today?"

"Doing better." Martha dug her fork into the pie and smiled as she tasted it. "So what have you found out about Ella's quilt?"

"About the quilt? Nothing because I haven't had a chance to look at it yet. I'm going over tomorrow."

Martha's brow furrowed with her puzzled frown. "As excited as Ella's been, I would have guessed she'd drag you over to the house the second you set foot in Maple Hill. The museum plans must be taking up more of her time than I'd realized. So you haven't found out anything about it?"

"Not the quilt itself, but listen to what I discovered on the Internet." Sarah shared what she'd learned about the Underground Railroad quilt code.

Martha listened, her eyes growing wider with each fact Sarah shared. "That's amazing! And now we've got an Underground Railroad quilt right here in Maple Hill."

"Whoa! I didn't say that."

A man cleared his throat as he came over to their table. Sarah wasn't surprised when he had a question about quilts. He was followed by several other people, each one eager to ask what he or she believed was a unique question.

"I'm sorry," Sarah said after they were interrupted for the fifth time.

"You don't need to apologize, but you're answering the same questions over and over," Martha said, pushing her empty plate aside. "Why don't you talk to the newspaper and do a FAQ article or something? That might help."

"What a fine idea."

Martha glanced at her watch. "I need to get home. Give me a call after you examine the quilt. I can't wait to hear what you find."

"I will." Sarah drained the last of the chai out of her cup as Martha got up.

After they had paid their bill, Liam said," Sarah, I heard all those questions people were asking you about quilting. Would you be interested in doing a talk on quilts here at the shop?"

Sarah smiled. "That's a great idea."

His brogue deepened when he said, "My dear colleen, I decided long ago that I would save my brain power and only have great ideas."

Sarah laughed, tickled by the cadence of his Irish accent in full force. She waved good-bye as she headed out the door to go back home. She'd have the whole afternoon to compile a list of books and prepare for tomorrow, when she would finally have another chance to examine the quilt.

Sarah printed out the information from the Web site she had just read. It was one that accepted the idea of a quilt code. The site's author had gone into great detail about how the various quilt patterns were used to help fleeing slaves. Even the knots on a quilt's ties were important because the placement of the knots would show the distance between safe houses. The quilter who shared the quilt code suggested that there were usually five knots on each tie.

Sarah pushed back from her desk. Waiting until tomorrow to tell Ella more about the quilt code seemed silly.

Her back muscles creaked as she stood. She looked at her watch. It was past four. She'd been surfing the Web most of the afternoon. She collected the pages she'd printed from the last site. The pile was substantial, but she guessed Ella would be interested in all the information she had uncovered.

Sarah picked up her camera. She might want to take more photos if she had the chance to see the quilt.

Snow drifted in the air as Sarah left her house and got into her car. She couldn't remember ever visiting Ella in her home. She hadn't driven past the Buttonwood house in years because it was on the other side of Maple Hill.

Sarah parked her car as close as she could get to the curb. She got out and paused by the sidewalk that was packed with snow. She stared at the Buttonwood house through the thickening twilight.

It could have been the set of an old scary movie. The few shutters still attached to the house hung at strange crooked angles, and only a few spots of paint remained. The clapboards had weathered to a brownish-gray and more than half the spindles were missing or broken on the porch railing. One corner of a leaning barn was visible along a driveway that led around to the back of the house.

The steps didn't creak, Sarah was glad to discover, as she climbed them. She crossed the porch to the front door. It was a slab of thick oak, darkened by years of storms, with etched glass sidelights on either side. She looked for a doorbell button. She pressed it and heard nothing. She tried again, but with the same result. She guessed, from the appearance of the rest of the house, that it was broken.

She knocked.

No answer came.

Disappointed, Sarah turned to leave. She paused when a beat-up car covered with mud and salt stains pulled into the driveway. Was that Ella?

The car stopped, and Chelsea got out. Her movements, while she picked her way around the snowbanks, were as graceful as they'd been when Sarah saw her at the diner. She stopped at the bottom of the porch steps.

"Mrs. Hart?" she asked. "I thought you were coming here tomorrow."

"I found some information that I wanted to share with your aunt, but I guess she isn't home."

Chelsea came up the steps. "She's supposed to be. She planned to take a nap this afternoon."

"Doesn't she have people working down in the cellar?"

"Aunt Ella figured she'd be exhausted after the fundraiser last night, so she asked everyone to take the afternoon off. That way she could nap if she wanted to." She went to the door that was almost lost in the darkness. "C'mon. I'll let Aunt Ella know you're here."

Sarah was surprised Ella would have taken the afternoon off when she had refused to let Sarah look at the quilt until tomorrow. Then again, Ella *did* always insist on doing things her way.

Dusky shadows hung like a curtain over the once grand foyer. She heard Chelsea's footsteps on the staircase to the left of the door. The stairs took a sharp turn at a landing close to the top. Sarah knew it was called a coffin corner. It was a tradition in old New England homes, for it allowed families to bring a coffin down the stairs.

The thought sent a shiver through her as she glanced to her right. Pocket doors closed off what Sarah guessed would be a parlor behind them. A door beneath the stairs could have led to another room or the cellar.

"Aunt Ella, are you awake?" Chelsea's voice filtered down from upstairs.

Sarah didn't hear an answer. Instead more doors opened and closed, and Chelsea continued to call her aunt's name.

Chelsea floated down the stairs. "She's not up there. Maybe she's down in the cellar. Will you look in the dining room and kitchen?" She pointed along the hallway toward the back of the house, then threw open the door under the stairs and went downstairs.

Sarah found the light switch in the dining room by groping along the wallpaper. She flipped it, and about half of the lights on an ornate crystal chandelier lit. The pale cream wallpaper had been in style when Sarah was Chelsea's age.

"Ella?" Sarah went between a round oak table and a computer desk toward the door she guessed led into the kitchen.

It didn't. It opened into a butler's pantry. The etched glass on the upper cupboards revealed that nothing was stored in them. Wide drawers and four cabinet doors were set beneath the counters on either side. One of the doors was open.

Sarah knelt to see what was inside. It was too dark. She put her hand on the door as she stood, but she halted halfway up. The interior of the door wasn't wood. It was metal.

"Mrs. Hart?" Chelsea came into the dining room. "Did you find Aunt Ella?"

"No, but I found this." She pointed to the metal door. "What's this for?"

Chelsea pushed past her and dropped to her knees. She reached into the space. "It's empty!"

"What is it?" asked Sarah.

"My aunt's safe. It's empty. Where's the money?"

"What money?" Sarah feared she already knew the answer.

"The money for the museum."

"Maybe your aunt took it to the bank," Sarah said.

"I'll check online." Chelsea jumped to her feet and ran to the computer. She moved the mouse, and the computer screen came to life. She quickly accessed her aunt's bank accounts. She paged through them. "No deposits today."

"If she deposited it at an ATM, it might not be posted yet."

Chelsea turned to her. "She couldn't have used an ATM. There were a lot of coins."

Sarah recalled the newspaper photo and all the coins in the clear container. "Try her cell."

Chelsea did. "Voice mail. But she always has her cell on." Without another word, she ran out of the dining room.

Sarah went after her. Chelsea raced up the stairs and into a front room. By the time Sarah reached the door, Chelsea stood by a nightstand. She had a cell phone in her hand.

"Your aunt's?" Sarah asked.

"Yeah. Why would she leave it here?" Chelsea rushed to the closet and began pushing clothes and shoes aside. "Her suitcase is gone!" She went to the wide dresser and yanked out the top drawer. Stockings and underwear flew onto the bed until she had emptied the drawer. She pulled the drawer out, tilted it upside down, and shook it. She threw it on the bed too, then looked into the space where the drawer had been. "Her pearls are gone."

"Pearls?"

"She's gone. The money's gone. The pearls are gone." She sank to the floor and covered her face with her hands. "She took the money and her pearls and left us."

Sarah sank to the floor and wrapped one arm around the distraught teenager. With the other hand, she slipped her own cell phone out of her pocket and called the police.

CHAPTER FIVE

S arah stayed with Chelsea until the police arrived. She offered to sit with her while the police interviewed her, but Officer Hopkins asked Sarah to come with him.

"Take me through the events that brought you here today," he said.

She explained how she'd come over to see the quilt and had met Chelsea on the porch. While he took notes, he had her physically retrace her steps through the house. They paused at the door of the butler's pantry while she pointed to the open safe.

"Did you see anything out of the ordinary upstairs?" he asked when they returned to the foyer.

Low voices came through the closed pocket doors, so Sarah assumed Chelsea was with another officer in the room behind them.

"I've never been here before," Sarah said.

He noted that and said, "All right. I think that's all I have for you right now. Give us a call if you think of anything you forgot. Thank you."

Sarah glanced at the closed pocket doors.

"We've called Miss Palladino's brother," Officer Hopkins said. "He's on his way. She won't be alone. Plus, the next-door neighbors have agreed to check on the kids later tonight."

"I'm glad."

He opened the door. "Thanks again, Mrs. Hart."

As soon as Sarah had stepped out onto the porch, the door closed behind her. She guessed Officer Hopkins was eager to continue his investigation.

Another police car pulled up behind the one parked in the street. Two more police officers got out and passed by Sarah on the walk. They nodded when she greeted them but didn't slow down.

Sarah's cell rang as she was shutting her car door. She pawed through her purse, knocking her camera to the floor in the process. She grabbed it and tossed it on the passenger seat as she flipped open her phone.

It was Martha. "Hi, Sarah! I forgot to ask you—"

"Ella is missing!" Sarah blurted out the words, unable to halt herself.

"What?"

Sarah explained, then said, "I can hardly believe what I'm saying. Ella and I had an appointment for me to see the quilt tomorrow."

"What if something awful happened to her?" Martha asked.

Sarah's hand tightened on the phone. "There weren't any signs that she didn't leave the house of her own free will."

"Well, that's good, but…," Martha sighed. "Are you okay? Where are you?"

"In front of Ella's house. I'm heading home."

"Why don't I come over? I'm warming up leftover spaghetti and meatballs for supper. I'll bring a plate over."

Sarah wanted to reach right through the phone and hug her friend. "Thank you. I'll see you in a few minutes."

She didn't take off her coat when she got home. Instead she went into the living room and picked up the newspaper. She scanned the article under the big picture at the top of the first page. Fifty thousand dollars!

Now it was missing. All of it? Sarah tried to concentrate, but her thoughts were a jumble. She tried to sort out what had happened. Why had Ella gone and taken the money with her?

Sarah decided to find out as much as she could about the new museum project. She made a call to Dave Diamond, who'd been hired to do the actual construction for the exhibit space in the cellar.

"Hi, Sarah," Dave said when he answered the phone. "Your timing's perfect. I just finished putting Sheetrock up on a ceiling and needed a break. What can I do for you?"

"I was told you're going to work on the museum at the Buttonwood house."

"Yes. It's exciting, isn't it? I'm going to get started over there as soon as I finish up this job."

Sarah hesitated at asking such a personal question, then plunged in. "Dave, could you tell me about the arrangements you made with Ella for payment on the project?"

There was a pause, and she guessed Dave was unsure how to answer.

"I'm not sure what you mean, Sarah," he said. "My clients usually pay me one-third up front and I order the materials needed to get the job going. They pay another third when the job is ninety percent complete; then the final third within ninety days of its completion."

"Do you ever take payment in cash?"

"Sometimes, but usually with a major remodel like this, the homeowner pays with a check."

"Did Ella ask you whether you'd prefer to be paid by check or cash?"

"No, but I assumed she'd pay me by check since there's money coming from the town and the state. She did complain that some of the people involved wanted cash payments and that would complicate everything."

"Did she say who?"

"If she did, I didn't pay attention." He chuckled. "I was concentrating on getting measurements so I knew how many two-by-fours and how much Sheetrock to order. It was delivered yesterday, so this morning I took over the invoice. She told me she'd get me a check before the end of the week."

"You didn't ask for up-front money from her?"

"No, because I knew she wouldn't have the money until yesterday, and I needed to get the supplies ordered before then." He paused again, then asked, "What's up, Sarah? You sound worried."

Sarah chose her words carefully. "I saw the photo in the paper of Ella with that cash, and I was curious how she was handling payments. I couldn't reach her, and I figured you'd know. Thanks, Dave."

"You're welcome." He sounded confused as Sarah told him good-bye.

She hung up the phone. Dave must think she was a raving loony with those questions. She wondered if one of the experts had wanted cash payments. Sarah went into the kitchen and put on the kettle. She got out two cups and tea bags, put them on the table along with plates and silverware, and then went back into the hall just in time to see Martha's car slowing in front of the house.

She opened the door as the frigid wind blew Martha up the sidewalk. Her friend's cheeks were bright red with the cold.

Martha's hands shook as she handed Sarah a warm casserole dish and took off her brown coat. "You know, Sarah, I can't believe this either," she said as if there'd been no break in their conversation. "I've known Ella Buttonwood so long that I can't remember when we first met."

"I remember. It was in grade school, the year you were in Miss Warner's class and I had Miss Atkins. You were so impressed when Ella brought in her father's gavel to show it off to the class that you couldn't talk about anything else for days." Putting her arm around her friend's shoulders, Sarah steered her toward the kitchen.

Sarah nuked the spaghetti, which had lost some of its heat on the way over from Martha's house.

Martha sat at the table. "I know you and Ella aren't close, Sarah, but she's been my friend for years. She isn't the sort of person to steal money."

"I agree. Once, when I was at the diner, Ella found a twenty dollar bill on the floor by the cash register. She set it aside, sure a customer had dropped it." The microwave beeped. She opened it and took out the casserole. Setting it on the table, she said, "One of her regulars came in and mentioned he'd lost twenty bucks. Ella handed it over, no questions asked."

"See? That's not a woman who'd steal from her neighbors."

"Which makes this so puzzling."

Sarah poured hot water into the cups and returned the kettle to the stove. The motions gave her a chance to gather her thoughts. She forced her eyes to close while Martha said grace. But the women returned to full speed as soon as Sarah said, "Amen."

"One question keeps running through my head," Sarah said. "Why did Ella have all the cash from the fund-raiser at the house? She's a smart businesswoman. She'd know better than to keep that much money in her house. She would have put it in the bank."

Martha put spaghetti on their plates. "She must have had a good reason not to."

"Her reason could have been that she planned to run off with it right from the beginning."

"I can't believe Ella would do something like that."

Sarah picked up her fork but didn't take a bite. "I don't want to believe it, Martha, but she's gone and the money's gone. She left her cell at the house. As if she doesn't want to chance using it and letting someone figure out where she is."

"Or she forgot it when she left."

"That's possible. She did take her pearl necklace with her. Discovering that really upset Chelsea."

Martha dropped her fork. "You didn't mention that before." She pushed away her plate. "Sarah, that changes everything. She treasures that pearl necklace. If she planned to come back, she wouldn't have taken it."

"But she did."

"I know she did, Sarah." Martha took a breath, then said, "I'm sorry to snap at you. I'm upset." It was a moment before Martha spoke again. "Do you really think she took the money and ran?"

"I don't know, but I'm not assuming anything until I have more answers."

With a faint smile, Martha sipped her tea. "I'm glad to hear that, Sarah. I knew you wouldn't jump to conclusions."

"I'd rather try to figure out what facts we have and look at them and see if we can find the truth."

"All right. What do we know?"

"Ella believes that her cellar was used as a stop on the Underground Railroad," Sarah said. "She hopes to open an exhibit there, and Maple Hill is donating money to the project and holding fund-raisers."

"And having quilt fever."

Sarah stared at her friend. How could she have forgotten the quilt? Now she wondered where the quilt was. Had Ella taken it with her too?

"Is the quilt the real deal?" asked Martha.

"I haven't had the chance to give it a proper examination."

"But you were the one who told Ella it was really old, right?"

Sarah flinched, even though Martha's words weren't meant to be an accusation. They just felt that way. "I told her it could be old. Before she even showed it to me, she'd convinced herself it'd belonged to a runaway slave." She closed her eyes. "Why didn't I stand up at town meeting and say that the quilt needed more study?"

"You didn't want to embarrass Ella."

"But this is far worse than embarrassing her. She's always had a great reputation in Maple Hill. Nobody in town can imagine anyone but a Buttonwood being the town meeting moderator."

"Don't blame yourself, Sarah. We all got carried away."

Sarah heard knocking at the front door. Excusing herself, she went out to see who was there.

Her eyes widened when she saw Nate Webber, Maple Hill's chief of police. She quickly ushered him in from the cold. He was a big man, hardened by his decade as a military policeman and his service on the Maple Hill Police Department. His dark hair glistened with gray, and he wore his usual uniform of a blue shirt and black trousers under his thick winter coat.

"Good evening, Mrs. Hart." His deep voice rumbled through the foyer. "I hope I'm not disturbing your supper."

"Not at all. Can I get you some tea or coffee? Martha and I were just chatting in the kitchen."

"Thanks. I could use a cup of coffee."

She nodded, then led the way into the kitchen. Martha got up to greet Chief Webber. He waited until Martha sat back down, then took the chair next to her.

When Sarah deposited a cup of instant coffee in front of him and pulled out another chair, he said, "I'm sure you know why I'm here."

"About Ella supposedly leaving town with all the cash from the fund-raiser," Martha said.

"I'm glad you said supposedly. For all we know, Miss Buttonwood's forgotten to leave a message about her plans, and she has a legitimate reason for both her and the money being gone at this time."

"But you don't believe that," Sarah said.

He shook his head as he pulled out a small notebook. "It's not what I *believe* that counts. My stock in trade are facts."

He glanced at Sarah. "Mind if I take some notes while we talk?"

"Not at all."

Martha nodded her agreement.

"Officer Hopkins has your statement about what you did and observed at the Buttonwood house, Mrs. Hart, but I want to ask you about the quilt Miss Buttonwood found in her cellar," Chief Webber said. "She brought it over here for you to look at about two weeks ago. Is that right?"

"Yes," Sarah said. "Is the quilt gone too?"

He ignored the question. "What did you tell her about the quilt?"

"I said it might be an antique quilt because the pattern seemed to be of the antebellum period, but I needed time to examine it more carefully."

Chief Webber wrote down her answer even as he asked, "How did Miss Buttonwood act when she came over here that night?"

"She was as excited as a kid with a new toy."

"Which one of you first brought up the Underground Railroad?"

"Ella did, and I have to admit her excitement was contagious. I thought it'd be great if Maple Hill played a small part in the abolitionist movement."

He jotted down a few more words, took another drink of his coffee, then asked, "And who first spoke about the quilt belonging to a runaway slave?"

"That was Ella too," Sarah said. "But since then, I've been researching slave quilts, and I've read a lot about what's called the quilt code."

"Tell me about it."

She did, then said, "But a lot of researchers don't believe it's true. Even if it is, it might not have anything to do with this quilt. I told Ella that."

"Did she listen?" Chief Webber asked.

"I don't think so. She was the first one who caught quilt fever."

"Quilt fever?" He chuckled. "That's the perfect name for it."

"Martha's the one who came up with it," Sarah said, smiling at her friend.

"Can I ask a question now?" asked Martha, her eyes shimmering with tears.

"I can't promise you an answer." His smile softened his response.

Martha toyed with her fork. "What if someone knew Ella had that money and kidnapped her?"

"We are looking at this from every possible angle." He gave them a sympathetic smile. "As I'm sure Mrs. Hart told you, there weren't any signs of a forced entry or any violence at the house."

"But the front door was unlocked," Sarah said.

"Are you sure?"

She thought about it for a moment, then nodded. "When Chelsea came home, she didn't unlock the door. She turned the knob and went in."

"Miss Palladino said she had to unlock the door. So think about it again please, Mrs. Hart. Are you sure?"

Sarah got up from the table, picked up Chief Webber's cup, and walked over to the stove. She refilled it with water and spooned in more coffee.

What had she seen Chelsea do at the door? It'd been growing pretty dark, so she hadn't *seen* Chelsea unlock the door. That didn't mean Chelsea hadn't. As she replayed the murky scene in her mind, she became less and less certain of what she'd seen.

Neither Chief Webber nor Martha spoke until Sarah came back to the table with the cup. She set it in front of the police officer, and he thanked her.

Sarah sat again. "I guess I'm not really sure if the door was locked, Chief Webber. I thought it was unlocked, but if Chelsea says she had to use her key, then there's no reason not to believe her."

"Actually, Mrs. Hart, that's a good thing because it means that no one broke in."

"Thank God," murmured Sarah, repeating the words that came straight from her heart.

Martha leaned forward. "Has anyone said why Ella didn't just deposit the fund-raiser money right away?"

"Jack Handelman gave her the cash because he knew she had a safe at the house where she keeps the money from the diner overnight. Apparently Miss Buttonwood had the safe put in the house when the kids moved in and she had to start doing her bookkeeping at home after they went to bed. She didn't tell anyone until the fund-raiser came up."

"And everyone trusted her," Sarah said. "I spoke with Dave, and he ordered supplies for finishing the cellar without asking for any money from Ella."

"We do tend to stick by that 'innocent until proven guilty' aspect of our justice system." He smiled again as he took another deep drink of coffee.

"Well," Martha said, picking up her own cup, "if you want to know my opinion, even though I know it doesn't matter to your investigation, I don't believe Ella would do such a thing."

"I know." Chief Webber became somber again. "Miss Buttonwood is someone you've probably known a long time."

"Most of my life," Martha said.

"Are you friends?"

"Yes."

He looked at Sarah. "And you and Miss Buttonwood? Are you friends too?"

"Not exactly. We're more friendly acquaintances."

"Please don't be offended when I ask you if you can be completely unbiased as to Miss Buttonwood's guilt or innocence when you help us. I need your expertise with quilts, Mrs. Hart. We're going to need to have Miss Buttonwood's quilt authenticated as soon as possible. It's important to know exactly how old that quilt is and where it came from."

Sarah was surprised that the police chief had asked her to help him. He had often reminded her in the past of the importance of allowing the police to conduct an investigation without the worry of some well-intentioned citizen interfering.

"So Ella didn't take the quilt?" asked Martha.

Chief Webber shook his head as he closed his notebook and put it in his pocket. "We found it at the house."

"Where?"

"Mrs. Maplethorpe," he said with the same gentle, but stern tone he'd used with Sarah, "you know better than to ask me questions like that about an active investigation. I can tell you that the quilt is now at the police station. If possible, Mrs. Hart, we'd like you to look it over tomorrow."

"Of course I'll help."

He pushed back his chair and stood. "Thanks, Mrs. Hart."

"How are the kids?" she asked, getting up too.

"They're pretty shook up by their aunt's disappearance."

"Are they going to be okay alone?" asked Martha.

Chief Webber nodded. "Chelsea is eighteen, so we don't have to alert the Department of Children and Families. A next-door neighbor offered to stay with them tonight. We'll keep an eye on them, and if they need help, we'll bring in a social worker. Thanks for the coffee, Mrs. Hart." He walked toward the door. "I'll see you tomorrow at the police station. Any time after nine."

Martha didn't say anything until the front door closed. Looking Sarah squarely in the eyes, she said, "I need to ask you a big favor, Sarah."

"You know you can ask anything."

"I want you to help me find Ella." She held up her hand when Sarah started to answer. "I know Ella can be annoying. She always has been, but you told Chief Webber you'd help get to the truth."

"You may not like the truth."

"I don't believe she took the money. Will you help me find out who did?" Martha asked.

Sarah hadn't hesitated when Chief Webber asked her. She wouldn't now that her closest friend was asking. "All right. I'll do my best."

CHAPTER SIX

arah wanted to skip breakfast, she was so eager to get to the police station and look over the quilt. But she didn't. Chief Webber had said specifically that she could come in after nine. She suspected that he wanted to be present since the quilt might be evidence if Ella was brought to trial for taking the money.

Keeping to her regular routine would be best. Sarah reminded herself of that as she made coffee and toast and instant oatmeal. It was a good breakfast for a cold day.

She thanked God for her breakfast and for the sun outside, then added, *Lord, you know what's in all our hearts. Please reach out to Ella and help her find her way. Please watch over Chelsea and Ryan and remind them that they're never alone. Bring them the comfort they need during this stressful time. They've endured so much in losing their parents. Now they need you more than ever when they're without their aunt. Bring them closer to those who can help them.*

As she whispered amen, Sarah knew that she was someone who could help. She hurried through her breakfast and went to her sewing room to get what she would need when she examined the quilt.

She got one of her brightly colored quilting bags from the closet. Into it, she put a pincushion bristling with straight pins, a cloth measuring tape, her best magnifying glass, and her quilt notebook. While she analyzed the quilt, she would make notes in the book to read and consider later. She also packed the pages she had copied off the Internet. She wanted the information on both antebellum quilts and quilts sewn by slaves to be readily available.

Her eye was caught by sunlight on the metal end of a seam ripper. She reached for it, then paused. There was no way that Chief Webber would allow her to undo any seams on the quilt, and right now, the quilt she guessed had been used for the lining wasn't the focus.

She carried the bag out into the hall. She got a couple of her best reference books from the dining room bookcase and put them in the bag, making sure they didn't break her magnifying glass. Pulling on her coat and gloves, she picked up the bag. It was heavier than she'd expected. She couldn't risk not having something she'd need while she worked to figure out the age of the quilt. Plus, she wasn't sure if Chief Webber would allow her access to the quilt again.

Sarah opened the door and stepped back when she saw someone walking up the porch stairs—an old and very dear friend. Phyllis Dobkin's smile hadn't changed since she and

Sarah had played together as children when their mothers had been good friends. Phyllis was now tall and wore stylish glasses that went perfectly with her tight silver curls.

"Phyllis, I didn't realize you were back in Maple Hill," Sarah said, giving her friend a hug. She hadn't seen Phyllis since her friend had moved to Chicago more than a decade ago. "How's your family? How are the kids and the grand-kids?"

"All doing well." Phyllis's voice was as warm as her smile.

"How long are you here in Maple Hill?"

Phyllis glanced into the house. "May I come in?"

Sarah was torn. She wanted to see her friend, and she wanted to get to the police station. Sarah reminded herself that the quilt wasn't going anywhere, and Chief Webber had told her that she could come to the station any time after nine.

"Of course." She held the door open for her friend.

Phyllis glanced around the foyer. "Sarah, you and Gerry worked wonders on this house. I remember when you first bought it, and you weren't sure if it would stand up long enough for you two to remodel." She walked over to the banister and ran her hand along the smooth wood. "How long did it take you to get the paint off this?"

"A long time. There were about a dozen coats." Sarah smiled at the memory of Gerry and her taking turns with the paint remover and the putty knife. They'd slowly and carefully removed all those layers until they reached the bare wood.

"You're on your way out," Phyllis said, "and I can't stay long. I just wanted to stop in and say hi. I'm supposed to meet Jason in about half an hour."

"He'll be so happy to see you too."

"He was friendly when I called him last week." Phyllis smiled at Sarah's confused look. "Didn't Jason tell you? I hired him to help us."

"Jason doesn't usually talk about whom he's representing. Client-attorney privilege."

Phyllis nodded. "But I wouldn't have minded him telling you. He's going to help us find my mother's lost sisters."

Sarah remembered the day she'd found out that Phyllis had two aunts who had been given up for adoption. It had been shortly after Phyllis's grandmother's death, and her friend had just learned the truth herself. Since then, Phyllis had been determined to find her aunts and reunite the family. She'd been searching for almost forty years.

Giving Phyllis another hug, Sarah said, "I'm happy to hear that. Jason will do everything he can to help you. I know that."

"I do too. When I was looking for a local lawyer to help me, I saw his name listed and I knew your son would know the value of family. Imagine! I used to change his diapers, and now he may be able to change my life—and the lives of the rest of my family."

"I'm having dinner with Jason and his family tonight. Why don't you come too? I'll check with Maggie, but I'm sure she wouldn't mind."

Phyllis smiled and shook her head. "Thanks, but as soon as I finish meeting with Jason this morning, I'm heading to Boston to visit my sister and her children. Jason has already told me it'll take at least a week to get the ball rolling on having the adoption files unsealed. I'll be back in Maple Hill Monday or Tuesday."

"Call me when you get back and we'll have lunch. I can't wait!"

"Me neither." With another hug, Phyllis went out and down the front steps. She waved to Sarah before getting in her bright blue car.

Sarah followed close behind, pausing only to lock her door. She stared at her key as she withdrew it from the lock. *Had she missed Chelsea unlocking the door last evening?* Chelsea had told the police that she had unlocked the door, and they didn't doubt her. Sarah wished she could reconcile that one small fact with what she remembered.

A loud voice met Sarah when she entered the Maple Hill Police Department. A man was arguing vehemently and banging his fist on the counter atop a half wall. It was near the center of the large space. The policewoman standing behind the wall listened without comment until the ranting man took a breath.

"Mr. Langley," the policewoman said in a calm voice, "you were picked up on radar doing sixty in a school zone. If you wish to fight the ticket in traffic court, you are welcome to do so."

That wasn't the answer he wanted because he began shouting at her again. Another cop came over from his desk by the tall windows, but the policewoman had the situation in control. She let Mr. Langley continue until he had to draw in another deep breath.

"Mr. Langley," she said in the same calm tone, "I'm sure Chief Webber will be glad to speak with you about the matter. However, he has a very full schedule this morning. I can't guarantee when he'll have time. If you'd like to make an appointment—"

"I'll wait!"

"If that's what you want. You can sit there on the bench, and as soon as the chief has an opening in his schedule, I'll let him know you're waiting." To the other officer, she said, "Dan, please get Mr. Langley some coffee if he'd like any."

The angry man stomped over to the bench, but accepted the offer for a cup of coffee. He glared at everyone in the station, including Sarah.

The policewoman motioned for Sarah to come forward. "How can I help you, ma'am?"

"I'm Sarah Hart. Chief Webber is expecting me." She spoke quietly, not wanting to set off Mr. Langley again.

"Come with me."

Sarah had been in the police department before, but she was always amazed by the contrast between the old building with its worn marble floors and the modern equipment.

Each desk had a state-of-the-art computer, and closed-circuit cameras watched from near the ceiling.

The policewoman knocked on an open door, "Mrs. Hart is here, Chief." She smiled at Sarah and went back to her post.

Chief Webber's office looked like the "after" picture of a natural disaster. Papers and books were stacked everywhere, but Sarah had been there before and had seen that he could lay his hand on any specific item he wished. She couldn't have gotten anything done in such chaos, but it seemed to work for him.

He glanced at the clock on the wall. "It's half past nine. I'm surprised you held out this long."

"I had a surprise visitor," Sarah said with a smile.

"How surprising?"

"Not Ella, if that's what you're asking."

Standing, he chuckled. "One of these days, we'll have a case that solves itself so simply." He opened a drawer and pulled out a set of keys. "I'll have to record your time with the quilt, so no defense attorney can claim you tampered with it."

"I understand. I hope the room where the quilt is has good natural light."

"There aren't any windows in the room. Windows can be opened, and open windows let in dust and other materials that can contaminate evidence."

Sarah went with Chief Webber to the room he'd set aside for her to use. It was painted a dull tan. The only thing on the wall was the camera. A red light blinked on as they entered, a sign the camera was recording. There were two tables and two metal chairs. On one table the quilt was neatly spread out.

"Don't put anything you've brought with you on the quilt's table," he said. "Leave your things on the other table."

"Can I use a measuring tape on the quilt?"

"Try to hold it above the fabric, not on it. No tools of any kind on the quilt. Your fingerprints are probably already on it, but you'll need to wear gloves today." He sat, crossing one leg over the other knee.

Feeling self-conscious, Sarah carried her bag to the other table. She set the bag next to an open box of gloves. She should have guessed that Chief Webber or one of his officers would be present the whole time she was studying the quilt.

Sarah undid the tie at the top of the bag, then carefully drew out the reference materials, her notepad, and her sewing tools. She left her camera in the bag. Chief Webber wouldn't allow her to take photos of the quilt now that it was possible evidence in a crime.

She picked up one of her books and paged through until she found photos of antebellum quilts. She compared the style of those quilts to the one spread out across the table.

At first glance, they seemed similar, but Sarah knew the importance of not making any assumptions. Stepping back, she appraised the quilt as if she'd never seen it before. Whoever had sewn this quilt had chosen dark and somber colors, except for the loud red fabric. It caught her eye and drew it to each repetition of the fabric.

She picked up the pages she'd printed from Web sites. The ten patterns in the quilt code were supposed to have been used in a specific order. Monkey Wrench, Wagon Wheel, Bear's Paw, Crossroads, Log Cabin, Shoofly, Bow Tie, Flying Geese, Drunkard's Path, and Star.

Sarah decided to measure next. Usually she pinned one end of the cloth tape to a corner and drew it along the edge. She couldn't do that. Maybe if she laid the tape on the table beside the quilt.... That didn't work because the tape moved every time she did.

"Can I help with that?" asked Chief Webber.

"Yes. Thanks." She handed him one end of the measuring tape. "Hold the tape by the far corner, please."

Sarah measured each side. It took longer than it usually did, because she had to walk back to the other table to write the dimensions in her notebook. Five feet wide and seven feet long. She thanked Chief Webber. As he sat again, she wound up her measuring tape and set it aside.

She drew on a pair of the gloves, which made her feel clumsy. She'd do her best. Using her thumb and forefinger, she pinched the quilt in various locations and wiggled her fingers. As she'd discovered before, some sections were denser than others. There wasn't a feel of modern batting, but she couldn't be completely sure what was inside without taking the quilt apart.

She returned to the other table and scanned through the pages she'd copied from a Web site on slave quilts. The quilts used for the quilt code were said to be the best ones, because they wouldn't wear out from constant use. It also suggested that the spacing of the ties and the number of knots in each tie were clues.

The quilt in front of her hadn't been used regularly. The fabric, even though it stank of mildew, showed little sign of wear. Sarah examined the fabric itself. It was cotton. Many antebellum quilts had linen as a backing, but cotton had been growing more popular during that period. It could be a transitional quilt. But, even though the quilt looked as if it had been washed several times, the fabric seemed too shiny for antique cotton.

Sarah frowned as she looked at the quilt again as a whole. The repetitions of the pattern and the colors were perfect. Many nineteenth-century quilters put intentional "mistakes" in their quilts, because they believed only God could and should make something perfect. Not having a mistake in the pattern didn't mean the quilt couldn't be antebellum. Nor did a mistake mean the quilt was old, because any careless quilter could make an error and not realize it until the quilt was completed. It was simply another aspect of a quilt that helped her determine its age and origins.

The fabric had been both quilted and tied. Sarah decided to start with the ties. They were knotted with thick thread. Slaves, it was believed, used hemp when tacking their quilts.

The larger knots made directions for the quilt code easier to see from a distance. Even quilts made for everyday use might be tied together with hemp, which was more readily available to slaves than thread.

Taking care not to loosen any individual fibers, she examined the ties. There didn't seem to be any pattern to the number of square knots holding them in place. Most had two, but some had only one. The number of knots appeared to have more to do with the depth of the area being tied than anything else. She noted that in her book.

Sarah picked up her magnifying glass and positioned it over one tie. Peering through, she traced the quilting line beside it. The line was smooth, as was the cotton thread. Too smooth for handspun thread. That meant the quilt couldn't be older than the late eighteenth century when the first textile mills were established in New England. The thread was mottled with age, but Sarah knew there were several ways that thread could be "aged," including the simplest method of dying the thread with tea.

She had seen several examples of this alternate Log Cabin pattern in her quilting books. It was a legitimate style for the early nineteenth century, even though one of the Web sites that tried to debunk the quilt code claimed that the Log Cabin pattern hadn't been around until Lincoln's presidency. Examples had been found as far as back ancient Egypt.

Her forehead furrowed with concentration as she ran her fingers along the quilting line again.

"We may have a problem," Sarah said as she straightened.

"What's that?" Chief Webber came over to the table.

"See how the quilting line follows the contours of the fabric exactly, no matter whether the layers are thin or bulky."

He peered at the quilt. "I think so."

"Look here and here." She pointed at two places on the quilt. "Many quilts from the antebellum period have breaks in the quilting pattern because quilters couldn't sew accurately through thicker sections. Quilters often sewed alongside those areas instead, but these quilting lines don't have any breaks."

"So does that mean it's a fake?" he asked.

"Let me check something else before I answer that."

Sarah moved to a different section of the quilt. The arched pattern was squared off. It resembled block patterns that were still in use. Again she looked through her magnifying glass. Again she saw an anachronism.

"Look here, Chief. See how the quilting stitches follow the pattern of the blocks exactly? In antebellum quilts, the quilting doesn't always follow the block pattern. Sometimes the quilting lines go around the blocks. Sometimes they go right across at odd angles."

"More proof it's a fake?"

She pulled off the gloves and kneaded her lower back that ached from bending over the quilt for so long. "I'm seeing some discrepancies, but I'd like to go over my notes and check out a few more parts of the quilt before I give you a definite answer."

Chief Webber nodded. "I appreciate your being so careful. If I have to go to court, I want to be a hundred percent sure I'm right when I swear this quilt is a fake. How long will it take you to give me a definite answer?"

"Not more than a day or two at the absolute longest."

"Good. Let me know as soon as you know, and if you need more time, let me know that too."

Sarah began putting her books and equipment back in her bag. "If I need to see the quilt again, will that be possible?"

"Maybe. We want to handle it as little as possible."

Closing the top of the bag, she said, "I want to speak with Vanessa Sawyer. She knows more about fabrics than anyone else I know. Is that okay?"

"Yes."

"And I'd like to talk to the Palladino kids about what I've found. Just in case they altered the quilt in any way while they had it. They might have loosened knots in the ties, for example, or retied them."

He didn't give her a quick answer this time. After thinking about it, he said, "Let me check with the DA and see if she's okay with that."

"All right. Just let me know, please."

"I will. As long as you let me know as soon as you find out anything I can swear to in court, Mrs. Hart."

"You'll be the first."

CHAPTER SEVEN

ıllllllllllllllllllllllllllllllllllllllllllllllllllllllllllllllllllllllllllllllllllllllllllllllllllllllllllllllllllllllllllllllllllllllllllllllllllllll

S arah walked out of the police station and along the street that followed the contour of the town green. She had to wait for several cars to pass before she could cross the street, though there weren't many people walking about. She wanted Vanessa's opinion on the fabrics used in the quilt, so she would stop at the Wild Goose Chase before she headed home. She hadn't visited the fabric store since she had returned from Texas.

She had other questions for Vanessa as well. Her friend enjoyed historical quilts as much as Sarah did, and she'd grown up down South among women who loved needle-work. As an African-American, Vanessa might have heard stories from her family about the quilts slaves made.

Vanessa wasn't behind the counter, but her assistant Kathy Earhart was. Bright-eyed and cheerful, Kathy always reminded Sarah of the little lost gosling chasing the others in the mural over the tall shelves. Yet when Kathy looked up at Sarah, her expression was grim.

"Are you okay?" Sarah asked.

Kathy gave up the effort to smile. "I'm mad." Her brow deepened into a V. "No, I'm furious. You must be too, after getting taken in by Ella Buttonwood and her scheme. I spent over a hundred dollars on raffle tickets because I wanted to help. Now she has all the money. How could we all have been so stupid?"

"No one was stupid. We wanted to believe something wonderful was happening for Maple Hill."

Kathy barely let Sarah finish her sentence before she burst out again. "Maybe not stupid. But gullible. You should have heard the talk over at Liam's this morning. People are mad, but they also feel like Ella's stabbed us in the back. She was our neighbor, and she stole from us. Even little kids donated. How could she steal from little kids?"

Sarah waited until Kathy was finished before saying, "Well, the police aren't sure that Ella actually stole the money. We should wait and see if she and the money turn up. I just hope Ella's not in some kind of trouble."

"You didn't come in here to listen to me complain." Kathy acted as if she hadn't even heard Sarah. This time her smile seemed more genuine. "What can I do for you?"

"I was looking for Vanessa."

"She's gone to Albany to see a new line of sewing supplies. She'll be back tomorrow. Anything I can help you with?"

"I have some antique fabric questions."

"You'll definitely have to wait to ask Vanessa." Kathy said. "She knows more about fabrics than I'll ever learn."

Sarah thanked her and left. She was disappointed, but tomorrow she would bring in the photos she'd printed. It was easier to see the fabric and the quilting details in the photos than on the screen of the digital camera. It would work out for the best. She had to believe that.

The book on the quilt code had been delivered while Sarah was at the police station. She took homemade soup out of the freezer, heated it up, and sat at the kitchen table to read. She was fascinated by how the proponents of the quilt code drew on many aspects of African society to explain why the quilt code had developed in the first place. The book went into depth about secret societies and coded messages in West Africa, where many slaves had been captured.

Most of the information specific to the quilt code Sarah had already found online. Not that it mattered if Ella's quilt was a replica.

The phone rang and Sarah was surprised to hear Chief Webber's voice.

"I spoke to the DA," he said, "and she's okay with your talking to Chelsea and Ryan Palladino about the quilt. We'd prefer you didn't tell them it might be a fake until you've confirmed that."

"All right." That was a fair compromise. She thanked him.

She would have to guard every word she spoke. The kids had been broadsided by their aunt's disappearance barely twenty-four hours before. She needed to ask them about the quilt as gently as possible. She smiled as she thought of what Gerry would have said. *Think before you speak, then say what you would wish to hear.*

It was good advice, and she intended to follow it.

The air was surprisingly mild when Sarah drove to Ella's house later that afternoon. Not warm, but the bite was gone. A sure sign of spring. Yet spring was fickle in the Berkshires. It would flirt, then disappear while winter returned with snow in April and even May.

Sarah parked behind a bright yellow Volkswagen Beetle on Ella's street. On such a sunny day, the Buttonwood house didn't look as dilapidated. There were old apple trees near where the driveway curved around the back. Their contorted branches soon would be a perfect white cloud.

The battered car that Chelsea had been driving yesterday was parked near the trees, but when Sarah knocked, she got no answer. She rapped again, harder this time. She waited, but nobody came to the door.

She considered leaving but glanced at the car in the driveway. It would be a shame to leave if the kids were inside and simply hadn't realized someone was at the door.

Sarah looked through one of the door's sidelights. She squinted into the dimness of the interior of the house, and she saw someone moving inside. She knocked again on the door. Louder and hard enough to make her knuckles sting.

Still no answer.

But she'd seen someone inside.

She tapped on the sidelight window, then went to a larger window to the right of the door. She peered inside, feeling like a Peeping Tom.

The furniture in the parlor was threadbare, but clean. Quilts hung over every piece of furniture. Their colors came to life in the sunny room. On the back of the sofa was a Basket of Flowers quilt with bright yellow blossoms. A Star of Bethlehem quilt, all the tiny pieces of the huge star in red, white, and a very faded blue, draped half over it. The quilt on a chair facing the front window had a circular pattern done in sedate blues and gray. The bursts coming out of the circles had the sharply pointed ends of a Snowflake quilt. Two more quilts were folded on a table beneath the window. The top one was a Double Wedding Ring in pinks and blues on a black background, but the bottom one was hidden.

Who had made so many beautiful quilts? She must ask Chelsea if she could look at them. Every quilter left unique clues behind in her stitching style or her color choice or some other aspect of quilting. If Sarah could see similarities between the quilt from the cellar and these, that might give her some information to share with Chief Webber.

She scanned the rest of the parlor. Plants by the side windows drooped sadly, looking like they needed water. Magazines were scattered across a coffee table in front of the sofa, and a large TV commanded one corner.

Sarah moved back to the door and rapped again. "Hello? Anyone home?"

The door swung open, and something flashed, momentarily blinding her.

Someone stepped out onto the porch, carrying a camera.

"Abby!" Sarah cried.

"Sarah!" the reporter said at the same time. "What are you doing here?"

Sarah calmed her rapidly beating heart and blinked away the spots in front of her eyes. "I stopped by to see Ella's niece and nephew. Are Chelsea and Ryan home?"

Abby hesitated, then said, "No. Ella told me to come over whenever I wanted." She locked the door and slipped the key into her purse.

Sarah couldn't imagine why Ella had given Abby free run of her house, especially when Ella had so much money under her roof.

Abby faced her. "I can think of only one reason you're over here, Sarah. You must have discovered something interesting about the quilt." She smiled. "Don't look surprised. Chief Webber told me that he was having an expert look it over. Who else would that be but you?"

"He did ask me to take a look."

"What did you find?"

"I'm not sure yet, and I promised Chief Webber that he'd be the first to know anything." That *was* the truth, so Sarah felt better about hedging.

"All right," Abby said, disappointed. "I'll wait until the official report."

"What were you photographing this afternoon? Besides me?"

Abby eyed her as if searching for something Sarah hid. "I came over to take photos of where the quilt was found. I wanted some to go with the story about Ella's disappearance."

"I'd like to see the cellar too."

"You can't." Her mouth straightened. "I can't. The cellar door is locked, and it doesn't open with the key Ella gave me. I don't know why."

"The police might want to keep everyone away from the scene of the crime."

"You sound like Chief Webber."

"Thanks. I'll take that as a compliment." Sarah smiled, hoping to ease the tension between them.

Abby walked over to the steps. "You'll have to come back later. Chelsea and Ryan aren't here. They're probably hanging out with their friends." Abby rushed down the steps and to her yellow Beetle.

Sarah watched her drive away. At the town meeting, Abby had acted as if Sarah was a trusted confidante. Now Abby took everything Sarah said as an accusation.

She wondered if Abby was looking solely for information to satisfy her editor. Abby had been given the key before Ella and the money disappeared. Could the reporter be mixed up in Ella's disappearance? She had been very upset about every penny of the Cultural Council funds going to the quilt exhibit.

Abby had been eager to put a halt to the quilt project. She had a key to Ella's house and Ella's permission to come in whenever she wanted. Or so she said. Without Ella around, Sarah couldn't know whether Abby had been given permission to look around the house or not.

CHAPTER EIGHT

Walking into Jason and Maggie's house was such a pleasant change from being at Ella's. Her son's home was freshly painted and glowed with welcoming light. Sarah reminded herself how much renovation Jason and Maggie had done. Not too many months ago, plaster had hung loosely from the walls and the lights had blinked out time and again when fuses blew. Now it was warm and inviting.

But it wasn't only how the house looked. Aromas of roast beef and chocolate cake wafted through the entry hall. Soft music drifted along with the delicious scents. It felt like a happy home.

Sarah called out, "Anyone home?"

"In here, Grandma," came Audrey's voice from the right.

The twelve-year-old twins were stretched out on the living room floor between the camelback sofa and the piano. Each held a cell phone and was texting rapidly.

"Hi, girls," Sarah said.

"Hi!" the blonde twins replied, getting to their feet and coming over to give her a hug.

"How's school?"

Audrey rolled her eyes. "Don't ask."

"Terrible," Amy said at the same time. "I hate it! My brain is going to explode if this keeps up."

"What's wrong?" Sarah took off her coat.

They both gave her a look that suggested she was completely out of touch.

Audrey said, "Grandma, it's March!"

"I know that." She tried not to smile at their poses of indignation and irritation that suggested no one had ever suffered as they were. "Do you have spring fever?"

"I wish we were sick," Audrey said. "Then we wouldn't have to go to school."

Amy dropped with a thump to sit on the stairs. "What good would that do? If we miss the tests, we'll have to make them up. I hate the MCAS tests."

"Ah, now I understand," Sarah said. The statewide assessment tests were done each spring.

"I don't!" Audrey flopped onto the steps next to her sister. "First our teachers tell us that each of us is special and unique, and then they force us to take standardized tests. So what are we supposed to be? Unique or exactly like everyone else?"

Sarah recognized the stubborn tilt of her granddaughter's chin. She'd seen it on Gerry's face enough times.

"That's something you'll need to decide for yourself," Sarah said.

"That's what Mom said." Amy grimaced. "That's parent-speak for I don't have an answer."

Nothing she said about the MCAS would ease the girls' frustration. "Are you both still up for staying over at my house on Saturday night?"

The twins grinned, and Amy said, "We can't wait! Can we make popcorn and pancakes?"

Sarah laughed. "Popcorn *and* pancakes? I hope you're not planning on cooking them together."

"Grandma!" Audrey said with a groan. "Don't be silly!"

Both phones chirped, and their attention focused on new text messages appearing on their screens. They tapped back quick answers as Sarah walked through the dining room and into the country kitchen where her daughter-in-law stood in a small mountain of paper. More paper was scattered across the granite countertop of the kitchen island and the wide-board pine floors. A chocolate layer cake sat at the far end of the counter, away from the flurry of paper. From the oven came the luscious scents of roast beef and onions.

"Come in, Sarah," Maggie said. "Don't mind the mess."

"What are you doing?"

"Unpacking. I made a rule that if something was still in a box a year after we moved in and we hadn't missed it, we don't need it any longer." She smiled. "Which means I have to go through the boxes I've been ignoring."

"You've still got a few months."

She reached deep into the box and pulled out another paper-wrapped item. As she undid the paper, she laughed. "Now I know where Audrey's favorite hairbrush went to."

She set it on the counter. "She'll be glad to get it back, but I wonder how it got in here. This stuff was in the garage in Los Angeles."

"Can I help?" Sarah asked.

"This box is empty, thank goodness. It's the last one I'm doing today. Only a couple dozen more to go." She pointed to another box set by the door that opened onto the backstairs. "Most of what I'm unpacking is there. We're going to donate it to the next yard sale at church. Roller blades that are too small for Amy, Jason's old golf clubs."

"That's a good idea."

"I hope Jason thinks so. He hates getting rid of any of his golf things."

"Like father, like son." Sarah poured herself a cup of coffee from the pot on the counter. "Gerry never threw out any of the kids' sports equipment. It used to drive me crazy, but now I'm glad, because the girls use it when they come over."

Maggie paused as she reached for handfuls of paper. "Are you okay?"

"I'm fine," Sarah said.

"Are you sure? I heard about Ella."

"Yes. I never expected that." Sarah took a sip of coffee and set the cup back on the counter.

"Neither did anyone else. It was all my customers wanted to talk about today." She stuffed the discarded paper into the empty box. "Have the police questioned you about the quilt yet?"

"Yes. I'm working to get an idea of how old it really is."

"I wonder why Ella picked the Underground Railroad for her scheme." Maggie folded down the top on the box.

"She said that her grandmother told her stories about the house being a station on the Underground Railroad." Sarah leaned her elbows on the kitchen island and stared at the blinking numbers on the oven timer. "Martha doesn't believe that Ella took the money."

"But you do?" Maggie gathered up more paper.

"Everything points to Ella taking the money, but I trust Martha's gut feeling. I hope friendship isn't blinding her, and I hope the fact that I've never been particularly close to Ella isn't keeping me from seeing the truth."

Maggie dropped the paper back onto the floor and gave Sarah a quick hug. "This must be difficult for you."

"I just wish I could make some of the pieces fit together." Sarah smiled. "That's me. The quilter. Always wanting the pieces to make a logical pattern."

"Now I know where Jason gets that."

"Gets what?" asked Jason as he walked into the kitchen, a piece of paper crunching beneath his feet. Giving his wife and then Sarah a kiss, he helped Maggie put the last of the paper into the box.

"The need to have everything in logical and proper order," Maggie said with a grin before she called for Amy and Audrey to set the table.

The twins came into the kitchen to get the dishes while Jason lit a fire in the dining room hearth. The comfortable noise was a pleasure after Sarah's too quiet house. She hoped the bedrooms she rented to boarders wouldn't stay empty too much longer.

The meat was quickly sliced, the gravy made, and the potatoes mashed. Everyone helped carry the platters and bowls to the table. They glistened in the light from the antique chandelier. The fire crackled merrily in the fireplace, and its reflection flickered in the windows.

"Mom, would you like to say grace?" Jason asked as soon as they were seated around the table.

"Thank you. I would." Sarah waited until everyone had bowed their heads. "Heavenly Father, we ask you to bless this food and those who are about to enjoy it together. We ask, too, that you bless those who are far from their families tonight. Bring them comfort in knowing your love and guidance. Amen."

More amens echoed around the table.

Maggie asked, "How's the case?"

"Not good," he said, and motioned to the twins to serve themselves and start passing the bowls around the table.

"More roadblocks?" asked Maggie.

"Of course. That's how family law works." He smiled at Sarah. "I started working on a new case a week or so ago."

"And this is the first night since that he's been home on time," Maggie said.

"It sounds like a tough one," Sarah said.

"Long hours of digging in old records going back over fifty years." He took a generous serving of mashed potatoes out of the bowl, then passed it to Amy. "Some are still handwritten, so I've got to translate someone's chicken scratch into words."

Sarah took the gravy from Audrey. As she spooned it on the potatoes and beef, she asked, "Are you doing all of this for Phyllis Dobkin?"

"How did you know?" he asked.

"She stopped by this morning to say hello, and she told me that she'd asked you to help find her mother's two sisters. Do you think you can help her? She's been searching for years."

"I hope so." He toyed with his roast beef. "Adoption is a touchy subject. Records are sealed when the adoption is finalized. Getting those records unsealed isn't easy, especially under these circumstances."

"What circumstances?"

"You probably didn't know, Mom, but Mrs. Dobkin's grandmother was charged with child abuse."

"Jason, that can't be true!" Sarah took a deep breath. "I remember Phyllis's Grandma Bennett. She wouldn't have hurt her children."

Jason reached across the table to pat her hand. "I'm going to try to convince a judge of that, Mom. Maybe he'll listen to the fact that the Bennetts were hit hard by the Depression and couldn't afford to feed their kids. It wasn't that uncommon. Some children were placed out with relatives who could put them to work and would feed them in return."

"They made them work for their meals?" asked Amy in astonishment.

"Those were the lucky ones," Jason said. "They had family to help. Others didn't have anyone to help. Phyllis's mother's family was one of those that wasn't so lucky. They had a fire that killed most of their milking cows, and they almost lost their farm. I suspect someone contacted the state hoping to get help for the family. Instead, the state stepped in and took the youngest two children and put them up for adoption because no relatives could afford to feed them. But the state had to have a reason, so they claimed abuse. Unfortunately, breaking apart families wasn't that uncommon then either."

"That's lying." Audrey said. "Like telling us we're special and then making us take the MCAS tests."

Maggie gave a good "mom look." "Girls, we've heard enough complaints about those tests."

"But, Mom…"

Sarah didn't hear the rest of Audrey's protest. Her thoughts drifted to how Chief Webber had said he would bring in a social worker for the Palladino kids if necessary. Chelsea was eighteen, but if Ryan was taken away because their aunt had abandoned them and was accused of a felony, the kids could be separated.

More than ever, Sarah was certain that like the quilt, the mysteries of the vanished money and Ella's disappearance weren't what they appeared. At first glance, what had happened seemed obvious, but a closer look might make every assumption collapse like a house of cards.

Right now, the quilt was her best guide. First thing in the morning, she would go to the Wild Goose Chase. Maybe Vanessa could lead her to a clue that would help Sarah keep another family from being torn apart.

CHAPTER NINE

Lights shone through the front windows when Sarah stopped again at the Buttonwood house later that evening. This time when she knocked, the door was opened by a very tall, gawky teenager she guessed was Ryan Palladino. He wore jeans and a bright green Boston Celtics basketball shirt. He didn't share his sister's spectacular good looks, but the features beneath his light brown hair were pleasant.

"I'm Sarah Hart," Sarah said. "I wanted to speak with Chelsea about the quilt you found in the cellar."

He hesitated, then said, "All right. Come in." He didn't meet her eyes. In fact, he looked everywhere but at her. She wasn't sure if he was shy or trying to hide something. It could be either with an adolescent boy.

"Are you Ryan?"

"Yes."

"How are you doing, Ryan?"

"Okay." He turned and walked into the front parlor, motioning for Sarah to follow. "Hey, Chelsea, Mrs. Hart is here about Aunt Ella's quilt."

Chelsea, who was wrapped in a crazy quilt in various shades of red and green, glanced away from the TV as Sarah entered. "Did it tell you anything about where our aunt is, Mrs. Hart?"

"No, I'm sorry." Sarah said, glancing at the show though she didn't recognize which one it was. Several slim, very pretty women stood in a line in pretty gowns. It must be some sort of reality show. "I was wondering if I could borrow a few of the quilts here."

"These old things?" Ryan's eyes widened as if he were shocked that he'd spoken. He quickly looked away when Sarah met his gaze.

Sarah explained about how finding similarities could help her learn more about the quilt and the quilter. "If these quilts have the same sort of ties holding them together, for example, it would tell me that the same person made both quilts. Do you know who made these?"

Chelsea said, "Grandma McEvoy. Aunt Ella's great-grandmother or great-great or something like that. You can look at them if you want." She tossed one side of the crazy quilt over the back of the sofa.

Sarah said nothing as she ran her fingers along the quilt. The pieces sewn together like an insane jigsaw puzzle showed wear consistent with a well-used quilt. She calculated quickly and realized the quilt could be almost a hundred years old.

"Because of its age, this quilt should be handled more gently," Sarah said.

"We've got so many of them," Ryan said, "that Aunt Ella doesn't care how they get used."

"Will you let me borrow a few?" Sarah asked. "I'll bring them back in a couple of days."

"What do you think, Chelsea?" Ryan asked, clearly not wanting to be the one to decide.

"Doesn't matter to me," Chelsea said, still staring at the TV, "but I don't see how that's going to get Aunt Ella or the money back."

Sarah thought of the hysterical girl who'd discovered her aunt was gone and the money missing. Chelsea now acted as if every bit of emotion had been wrung out of her. Was the girl in shock or simply trying to hide her fury and fear?

There was no sign of either emotion as Chelsea picked up a piece of brownie from a plastic microwave container, then settled back, never looking away from the TV.

Sarah noticed other plastic dishes next to a stack of textbooks on the coffee table. The teens must have nuked frozen dinners for the past two nights. A trash basket on the far side of the sofa was overflowing with other plastic plates. She wondered if they always ate in front of the TV or if they were taking advantage of having no adult in the house. She couldn't believe that a woman who made her living cooking for others would let her niece and nephew eat frozen dinners every night.

"What are you watching?" Sarah asked, hoping to get through to Chelsea somehow.

Ryan answered, "Reality shows!" He grimaced. "That's all she ever watches."

"You do too," Chelsea said without taking her eyes from the screen. "Football and baseball and basketball and hockey.

"But they're *real!*" Ryan said. "Not like *Runway Model Stars* and *Hollywood Hopefuls* and the other silly shows you watch."

Chelsea muttered something as she picked up the clicker. She turned up the sound and focused again on the TV.

Sarah looked at Ryan. "Does your aunt ever watch TV too? She probably doesn't have much time."

"She watches in the winter. The rest of the year she's too busy working." Ryan's smile faded. "I wonder if there's a TV where she's at now."

Sarah wanted to put her arms around the gangly boy and give him a hug. He was trying to hide how upset he was. Even when he smiled, there was a shadow in his eyes. He was clearly haunted by his aunt's disappearance—unlike his sister, who seemed unmoved by the events going on around her.

"I'd like to see where you found the quilt in the cellar, if I could," Sarah said.

"I figured as much. Everyone wants to see it." Ryan said, "Chelsea, it's your turn to do the tour." He pointed to the books on the coffee table. "I've still got two more chapters to read before my English test tomorrow."

Chelsea nodded. "Okay, Mrs. Hart. C'mon. I'll take you to the cellar."

"Thank you," Sarah said.

Chelsea got up and led the way to the door under the staircase. Every motion was graceful, even as Chelsea turned the knob on the cellar door. Sarah asked, "Did you unlock it when you came home?"

"Why would I need to unlock the cellar door?"

Abby had told her that the cellar door was locked. Someone was lying. Sarah couldn't accuse either Abby or Chelsea when she had never checked to see if the door was actually locked.

"I assumed that with the exhibit . . . that is, I wasn't sure if you kept anything valuable . . . ," Sarah paused. She sounded silly. "Never mind."

Chelsea opened the door. "Make sure you duck your head. It's really low in spots. Don't touch the stone walls. They're wicked gross." She pulled a string to turn on a light and hurried down the steps.

Sarah went more slowly. The risers in an old house could be uneven, and this was one of the oldest houses in Maple Hill. The damp air tickled her nose as she slid her foot cautiously to the edge of each riser before lowering it to the next.

The stench of mold and mildew filled every breath she took. She glanced around the cellar. Insulation wrapped around pipes was torn, and damp spots littered the floor. Years ago, Maple Hill had been awarded a grant to clear out asbestos and other dangerous materials from older houses. She and Gerry had had the old pipe insulation removed, but Ella must not have. She wanted to hold her breath on the chance there were asbestos fibers in the air, but she hurried after Chelsea toward the front of the house.

"I told you it was wicked gross," Chelsea said as she stepped around a puddle. "We don't have rats only because the spiders are so big that they scare the rats away."

Sarah didn't answer, not wanting to insult Ella and her family. The whole house needed some TLC. Yet jars of preserves were neatly labeled and arranged on wide wood shelves against the stone foundation. She couldn't help wondering when Ella had time to do canning while busy with the diner and raising two kids.

Building supplies were stacked beyond the shelves. Sheetrock, boxes of screws and nails, and two-by-fours. Those must have been the materials Dave ordered. The thought of Dave made her wonder again who had asked to be paid in cash. She considered asking Chelsea, but doubted the girl would know.

"Over here," called Chelsea.

"Over where?" Sarah couldn't see where the girl had gone.

A bulb flickered on, and Chelsea waved from beyond the huge furnace that looked as big as a car. "Watch where you step. The cement floor ends beside the furnace, and we've got some big potholes that were left after the flood drained away."

Sarah appreciated Chelsea's warning. She inched her way along the uneven floor. Dirt squished beneath her shoes, and she knew the water hadn't seeped completely out of the cellar yet.

"They were planning to put the exhibit back here?" Sarah asked as she edged around the furnace and into the cramped space behind it.

Chelsea took a half step to the side to give Sarah some room. "Part of the money was for moving and updating this old fuel oil furnace. This whole section of the cellar was supposed to be redone and opened to the public." She laughed without a hint of humor. "My aunt had grand plans after a couple of you experts gave the go-ahead."

Sarah asked, "Why don't you show me where you found the quilt?"

"Over there." Chelsea gestured to a pile of stones. "You'll need this." She held out a flashlight.

Sarah switched on the flashlight and stepped over fallen rocks. The cellar odors grew stronger as she walked closer to where the fake wall had been. Now there was only a row of water-stained two-by-fours. She wondered why a stone wall had needed studs behind it. Beyond them was the original foundation. Pieces of mortar had crumbled onto the floor, and she saw droppings and chewed acorns left by squirrels. It would be the perfect haven for them in the winter. Out of sight and warm from the heat off the large furnace.

She looked at the patched foundation wall. She didn't know enough about masonry to guess why or when the work had been done.

"Your aunt mentioned there were some symbols carved into the wall," said Sarah. "Where are they?"

"Actually they're on the studs," Chelsea said. "The ones on the floor."

Sarah focused the light along the board and saw some lines gouged out of the wood. She shifted so her own shadow didn't hide the lines. They were hard to see. Reaching out to run her finger along the carvings, she froze when Chelsea spoke sharply.

"The guy from the Underground Railroad house told us not to touch or move anything," Chelsea said.

"Other than the quilt?" Sarah straightened and backed away from the stud wall.

"Yeah, he was pretty annoyed about that."

"Where did you find the quilt?"

Chelsea pointed toward the foundation wall. "There. Pieces of a wooden crate were beneath it. The wood must have rotted in the damp dirt, but enough was left to protect the quilt."

Sarah stepped past the stud wall and turned off her flashlight. "Aren't you curious about how the quilt came to be in that space?"

"It must have gotten left behind by mistake. That's what a woman from one of the Underground Railroad houses said. Mr. Krause agreed. Mr. Krause is the guy the town brought in to help set up the exhibit."

"I've met him."

"Mr. Krause and the woman joked that we wouldn't know much about the past if everyone had recycled instead of leaving their garbage behind. They were really eager to find out more about the carvings. The historian was supposed to come out today. He was charging a bundle, so I guess someone canceled the visit. What's the point now?"

Sarah didn't try to answer the question as she glanced around the rest of the cellar. It was dusty and filled with clutter. Nothing unusual in it. "Did any of you find anything else?"

"Nothing, but if there'd really been fugitives, they wouldn't have had much with them."

"Do *you* believe this was a station on the Underground Railroad?"

"No one's telling Ryan or me anything." Chelsea looked at the stairs, obviously ready to go. "Before Aunt Ella left, we had lots of people coming down here. They debated every detail."

"Like who?"

Chelsea led the way back to the center of the cellar. Counting off on her fingers, she said, "Oh let's see. That guy doing the construction in the cellar. Abby McCormick was here almost every day, especially if someone else was here. She wanted to get a sound bite or a quote or whatever you call it with newspapers from every possible person. Mr. Daniels came over to measure for the information boards his classes were supposed to work on. He spent a lot of time alone down here trying to figure out the best way to display them. And then there was Mr. Krause. He's been here so much that I thought it'd be easier for Aunt Ella to let him have his own room."

"How about your aunt?" Sarah asked.

"She came down a lot at first; then her knee began to act up again. She had to stop."

"And who's been here since you called the police to report your aunt missing?"

"Just you. Oh, and Ms. McCormick said she was going to drop by, but I haven't seen her. That doesn't mean anything because Aunt Ella gave her a key."

Sarah was relieved that Chelsea knew that Abby had a key. "How are you and Ryan doing?"

"Okay, I guess. Good enough to keep the Department of Children and Families from coming in and taking Ryan to a foster home. It's not like we have any other relatives for DCF to send us to. Aunt Ella was the only one after Mom and Dad died."

"How's everyone treating you at school?"

She shrugged. "The kids and the teachers are being really nice. They don't blame us for Aunt Ella stealing their money."

"Do you have any idea at all where your aunt might be?"

"No." She raised her eyes and said, "And I don't really care. I'm tired of her lying to us."

Sarah didn't say anything, letting the girl get it off her chest.

Chelsea flung out her hand. "All this Underground Railroad baloney." She walked toward the stairs. "I mean, I understand why she did it."

"Really?"

"My aunt is a workaholic." She walked up the steps, looking over her shoulder to make sure Sarah was following. "She runs the diner from spring through leaf-peeper season in October. Once she closes the diner after tourist season, she works in November and December at a hunting camp higher up in the mountains. She cooks for the hunters and keeps the cabin clean. She used to drag Ryan and me up there to the middle of nowhere, but for the past couple of years, we've convinced her to let us stay in town. By Christmas, she's done there, but as soon as the holidays are over, she begins working on getting the diner ready to open in April. Oh, and don't forget the spring and fall town meetings."

No wonder Ella didn't have time to maintain her house. She was too busy with her other jobs. And Chelsea hadn't even mentioned the most difficult one: raising two teenagers when Ella was at an age to bounce grandchildren on her knee.

Closing the cellar door behind her, Sarah said, "That makes me wonder even more why she'd leave when she should be opening the diner next month."

"She isn't this year," Chelsea said.

"She isn't what?" asked Sarah.

"She isn't going to open the diner this spring."

"I hadn't heard that." Not having the Miss Maple open on April first was like saying the sun wasn't coming up tomorrow.

"She didn't want to make any announcement," Ryan said as he sat on the arm of the couch. He looked at his sister. She nodded, and he said, "If she had made an announcement, then she'd have had to admit that she didn't have the money to open the diner. Now that she's got the money, I guess she didn't want to be tied down with us any longer."

"I'm sure she still cares about you," Sarah said.

Neither teen replied. Then Chelsea picked up the television remote and changed the channel. She sat on the couch, leaving Ryan and Sarah in an uncomfortable silence.

"Could I take a few of the quilts?" Sarah asked when she couldn't think of anything else to say.

"Yeah. I got some for you." Ryan walked over to the table and picked up the quilts stacked there.

Chelsea glanced over at the four quilts he'd folded on the table. "Not the one on top."

Again brother and sister stared at each other. If some message passed between them, Sarah couldn't guess what it was.

Then Chelsea shrugged as she had before. "Okay, take those four."

Sarah took the quilts and thanked Ryan. She called a good-bye to Chelsea but didn't know if the girl heard her or not. Chelsea was engrossed in the TV once more.

It didn't take Sarah long to be certain that Ella's great-grandmother hadn't made the quilt found in the cellar. Mrs. McEvoy must have enjoyed quilting to make so many quilts, but there were a lot of mistakes in the patterns and stitching. The quilt Ella had brought over two weeks ago was close to perfection. Mrs. McEvoy's quilts were signed with a red acorn embroidered at the bottom right-hand corner, but Ella's quilt hadn't had that symbol on it.

Sarah's feet dragged as she climbed the stairs. She was exhausted after her long day, and she couldn't help wishing—just once—this puzzle would be easy to solve.

After readying herself for bed, she sat in the comfortable chair in her bedroom. She took down her Bible and opened it to a verse in Timothy that Pastor John had preached on only a few weeks ago.

"And having food and raiment, let us be therewith content. But they that will be rich fall into temptation and a snare, and into many foolish and hurtful lusts, which drown men in destruction and perdition. For the love of money is the root of all evil: which while some coveted after, they have erred from the faith, and pierced themselves through with many sorrows."

Sarah closed the Bible and folded her hands on it. She prayed for Ella and her family. Chelsea, who seemed to switch her emotions on and off as easily as she did the TV.

Ryan, who couldn't hide how hurt and fearful he was, and who looked to his older sister for help with every decision.

She hoped Gerry was listening in too. He was always good with kids. Their house had been filled with them while Jason and Jenna grew up. Slumber parties, baseball games, tea parties, summer carnivals, pizza parties. The sound of young laughter had lasted until Jenna went off to college.

That was the way a home with teenagers should be, not quiet and filled with despair. If Ella could be found, maybe she would have the answer to where the money was.

Or maybe she wouldn't.

Chelsea had spoken of how often George Krause had been to the house. Fred Daniels and Dave Diamond had been there too. Abby McCormick even had a key. Any of them could have known where Ella had put the money. Any of them could have taken it.

But why?

As Sarah turned off the lamp and climbed into bed, she vowed that in the morning she was going to get some answers.

 CHAPTER TEN

T he front page of Friday's paper was devoted entirely to the missing money and Ella's disappearance. Sarah read every word, hoping someone had discovered information she hadn't. Chief Webber was characteristically tight-lipped, and his comments were generic. Abby, who'd written the primary article, hadn't quoted anyone else. It was a rehash of what Sarah already knew.

When Sarah went into the town center after breakfast, she had to search for a parking spot. Everyone must have decided to take advantage of the break in the cold weather. She found a spot two blocks from the Wild Goose Chase. Liam's café was full, and she smiled and nodded to people she passed along the sidewalk.

The lights were still off at the fabric store. A sign hung on the door. *Back at 10:00* AM.

She looked at her watch. That was about half an hour from now. She considered stopping in at Liam's for a chai to pass the time, but decided she'd save that treat for later. She needed to keep searching, so she decided to visit the historical society and speak with Irene.

Sarah continued along the sidewalk. The air was warm for the first time since fall. She loved walking downtown on a spring morning. It wouldn't be long before crocuses were budding, promising an explosion of white and purple in the coming weeks.

A bell rang over the door as Sarah walked into the Maple Hill Historical Society. Inside it was quiet, but she noticed a pile of papers ready to be passed out to visiting students. Irene often prepared scavenger hunts and other fun learning games for elementary and middle school field trips. A fire burned on the large hearth where colonial cooking classes were held. Shelves held histories of the town and Berkshire County. Comfortable chairs were set in front of the fireplace, offering visitors a place to read. Glass cases contained a rotating exhibit of artifacts from various eras in Maple Hill history. This month, clay pipes and cracked cups filled the main case.

Sarah walked to the counter. She smiled when the office door opened and Irene came out. Her trim navy skirt and bright pink blouse suited her perfectly, bringing out the rose in her cheeks. Her charm bracelet glistened in the light from the hearth.

"Sarah! Exactly the person I wanted to see," Irene said with a smile. She pointed to her necklace. "Look! I won this necklace at the raffle."

"I'm glad someone's happy about this mess." Sarah didn't realize how bitter her words sounded until Irene's smile faded. "I'm sorry, Irene. I didn't mean that the way it sounded."

"I know you didn't. What have you found out about Ella and the money?"

Sarah was confused. Had she told Irene that Martha had asked her to help find out what happened to Ella?

Irene's smile was a prelude to a healthy laugh. "It was just a guess. But I'm like you, Sarah. I like looking at pieces and seeing the completed puzzle. It must come from my amateur archeology digs and trying to get those shards back into their original shape. When I see a mystery and you, I know that the two of you must be linked somehow."

"What do you think, Irene?" Sarah asked. "Could the Buttonwood house have been a stop on the Underground Railroad?"

"I don't think it's likely that any house in Maple Hill was used by the Underground Railroad. We're smack dab in the middle of the Berkshires. South of us are the Taconic Mountains. North are the Green Mountains. Most known escape routes to Canada followed river valleys. Walking was easier, and so was the weather."

"That's true."

Irene kept talking. "But it's more than that. Cities and larger towns lie along river valleys. In small towns, a stranger or a group of strangers would be quickly noted. It's easier to get lost in a crowd. That's why cities like Cincinnati and Detroit and Boston and Philadelphia were very busy stations along the Underground Railroad. Anywhere where there was a river crossing between slave states and freedom, the Railroad ran. Mostly we hear about the routes north, but some slaves escaped across the Rio Grande into Mexico." She laughed. "Listen to me rambling on. Not that it matters now. This is such a sad situation for everyone in Maple Hill."

"You're a great resource, Irene." Sarah put her purse on the counter. "And you've found out more about the Underground Railroad than I've found out about Ella and the missing money. Maybe you can help me."

"Tell me what you need, and I'll try."

"Okay. Do you know anything about this supposed quilt code? I've read Web sites and the original book that started it all. Nobody seems to agree on much of anything to do with it. Do you think it's real or simply a great story?"

Irene came around the curved counter and went to the hearth. She put on another log as she said, "The short answer is: I don't know. I've read some articles about the Underground Railroad quilt code in professional journals, but there's no consensus there either. Did you check with Spencer? He might have more information than I do."

"Every book about the Underground Railroad in every library in the county has been checked out."

A few jabs with the poker made the fire burn brighter as Irene said, "They'll be back soon. I doubt many people are interested in the Underground Railroad any longer. A few days ago, you couldn't take two steps in town without hearing someone talking about the museum planned for Ella's house. Now there's just a lot of anger and disappointment."

"Tell me about it." Sarah sighed. "The sooner I can get to the truth about Ella and the money and the quilt, the happier I'll be."

Irene stood and wiped pieces of bark from her hands. "What have you found out so far?"

Sarah drew a page of her notes out of her purse. Irene took it and began to read.

"I've found out," Sarah said, "that the idea of quilts being used to guide the slaves is a story that's been handed down through the generations. It's a pretty specific story, and it names ten different quilt patterns and explains how the square knots in the ties that hold the quilts together are also a map for runaways. But I've found just as many articles saying the quilt code is an urban legend."

"No surprise there." Irene handed the page back to Sarah as she sat on a chair. "Both sides of the quilt code argument hold fervently to their beliefs. We only know that slaves did have help escaping to the north. Unfortunately too much else is conjecture. Historians are suspicious of oral history, and few slaves left written records. Not only would it be dangerous, but it was illegal to teach slaves to read and write."

"So all we have is oral history." Sarah snuck a look at her watch. It was almost ten. She should head over to speak with Vanessa. "Well, thanks for talking through it with me, Irene."

"Of course. I'm sure there's such a problem with finding proof for the quilt code since quilts wear out and are thrown away. Especially quilts made by slaves because their materials were of low quality, and the quilts would have gotten a lot of use."

Sarah picked up her purse. "True. If any quilts were made using the patterns and special knots of the quilting code, not many of them would have survived."

"If one did," Irene said with a smile, "that would quiet the critics. The truth is probably as well hidden as an escaped slave was. Do you know how the Underground Railroad got its name?"

Sarah shook her head.

Irene didn't seem to notice that Sarah was still edging toward the door. "One man was chasing a slave who was fleeing across the Ohio River. The fugitive vanished. The man chasing him said the slave seemed to disappear as if a railroad took him underground. The story was repeated enough that the term was adopted by abolitionists." Irene smiled. "The kids always get a big kick out of that story."

Sarah chuckled, mostly at Irene's enthusiasm, then said, "Thanks again, Irene." Before she could say good-bye, the office phone rang.

Irene sighed. "Here we go. They're starting late this morning."

"Who's starting what late?"

The phone stopped, then began ringing again.

"These calls." Irene waved a hand in the phone's direction. "Ignore it. I try to. It's probably for George. When the phone rings lately, it's always for George."

"George Krause?" Sarah had assumed that Mr. Krause had left Maple Hill now that the money was missing. Why would the museum consultant hang around?

"Yes. He gets phone calls here all the time." She slapped her hand on the chair's arm. A cloud of dust rose, which Irene waved away. "From a lot of angry people who demand to speak to him *now*."

"Why don't they call him on his cell?"

"I think they do, because whenever he's around, that's always going off too."

Sarah started to say something, but the phone rang again.

"I'd better check," Irene said, "in case it's not for George."

"I've got to go," Sarah said.

"See you later." Irene rushed into her office.

Sarah turned to the door just as it opened and Mr. Krause himself walked in. He wore a wrinkled black coat with an open-neck shirt and dark trousers under it. He pulled a suitcase behind him.

"Good morning, Mr. Krause," she said.

He smiled. "Why don't you call me George and I'll call you Sarah?" Without waiting for her reply, he said, "The museum didn't turn out quite as we'd hoped, did it?"

"I wish Ella had waited for confirmation on the quilt's age before she contacted you."

"I agree, but we know now that wasn't her plan, don't we?"

"I don't know what her plan truly was," Sarah said. "I'd like a few more answers before I make any assumptions."

His brows rose. "Forgive me. I didn't realize she was your friend."

"It has more to do with the truth." She looked at his suitcase. "I hope your next job turns out better."

"I hope so too. My next big job won't start until next month, but I found some stopgap work here in Maple Hill." He leaned the suitcase against the counter. "Irene mentioned that you took in boarders, Sarah. I'm looking for a place to stay that's cheaper than the hotel." He shrugged. "I'd planned to be collecting my consulting fee by now."

"I'm sorry. I only take in women."

"Do you know somewhere I might get a room?"

"I'd try the Shady Lawn first. It's a B and B, but I'm sure they'd be thrilled to get someone who wants a longer rental."

He shook his head. "I stopped there on my way here. To stay there more than a week, I'd need to give them a credit card. I don't like plastic. Too easy to spend what you don't have. Cash is easier in the long run."

Sarah couldn't imagine how a man who traveled to different sites to help get small museums established could do business without a credit card. Her breath caught. Ella had complained about someone wanting to be paid in cash. It could be George.

"Can you suggest somewhere else?" George asked. "Somewhere cheap where I don't have to jump through all sorts of hoops."

"You mean signing a lease agreement? That's pretty standard. That and a credit check."

A flush erupted up his face. "I don't want to go through the hassle for only a couple of weeks while I'm still in Maple Hill." He walked over to the hearth and bent to stir the embers.

Could George be in some sort of financial trouble? Enough trouble that he'd steal the museum's money?

The phone began ringing again in the office, and George's shoulders tensed. A moment later, Irene came out of her office. "Sarah, I thought you were leaving. Do you need something else?"

"No. I was talking to George."

Irene scanned the room until she found him by the hearth. "George, I took a call from a Mr. Rogers."

"Rogers?" He tensed even more. "What did you tell him?"

"What I tell everyone who calls and demands to speak to you. To call your cell."

As if on cue, his phone rang. He flinched, but quickly excused himself to take his call in the back room. He went in and closed the door. Sarah heard his raised voice, but couldn't discern any words.

"Well, I need to get going and pick Vanessa's brain about Ella's quilt," Sarah said.

"If this is all a mistake, Ella better hurry back home," Irene said. "She's going to be heartbroken when she loses her town meeting moderator post."

"What's that?"

"A recall petition's been started."

"Who started a recall petition?" Sarah asked.

"Mr. Daniels's history class at the high school."

Fred Daniels. Sarah didn't know Fred well, but he had a reputation as a good teacher and a nice guy. Fred had seemed fine with the Cultural Council funds being earmarked for the quilt exhibit. He had even offered to have his classes help with research and building the exhibit. Was he being a good teacher by helping his students learn about the recall process, or was he being vindictive because he had lost out on getting the funds?

Last night, Chelsea had said that Fred had been over to the house. Sarah wished she could ignore the thought that Fred was using the petitions to focus suspicion on Ella instead of himself.

George Krause. Fred Daniels. Had one of them taken the money?

CHAPTER ELEVEN

Sarah opened the door to the Wild Goose Chase. Vanessa was waiting on a woman who wore a blue scarf over her blonde curls. They were discussing which thread was the closer match to the swatch the woman had set on the counter.

Vanessa would give her customer all the time she needed to make her selection. She enjoyed helping others. Sarah admired how she balanced running the shop and being a single mother to a young son and daughter.

"Hi, Sarah. I'll be with you next." Vanessa smiled in her direction, then concentrated on her customer who compared one thread, then the other, then the first again to her original piece of fabric.

"No hurry," Sarah said, even though she couldn't wait to get Vanessa's thoughts on the quilt.

"Maybe if we go over to the natural light by the window," Vanessa said to her customer, "it'll be easier to decide." She picked up the spools and the cloth sample and led the woman toward the front window.

Sarah went to the back of the shop where Vanessa welcomed friends and customers to enjoy tea and talk. Setting her purse next to her favorite chair, she poured herself a cup of fragrant jasmine tea.

Sarah sat and picked up a quilting magazine. She loved to look at what other quilters were doing. She was reading the instructions for a new modification of a Mariner's Compass quilt pattern when she saw Vanessa walking toward her.

"Sorry to keep you waiting, Sarah." She refilled her own cup. "Sometimes I wish there weren't so many choices of thread color. Then white would be white and not cream and ivory and too many others."

Sarah chuckled. "But where would the fun be in that?"

"Which quilt are you looking at?" She peered over Sarah's shoulder. "That's a complex pattern. Circles and points in each compass as well as in the border. Are you going to try that one next?"

"Well, I've got some complex issues with a quilt I'm looking at right now, and I could use your help." Sarah gestured for Vanessa to sit in the chair right next to her. "I need advice to help me nail down the age of a quilt." She reached for her purse and pulled out the pictures of Ella's quilt.

Vanessa took the offered photos and flipped through them all quickly, then started back at the beginning, this time more slowly.

"I know about quilting designs and quilt patterns, but I need your expert advice about the fabric," Sarah said. "The quilt is made of cotton, which could be accurate for its time, but, to me, the fabric doesn't feel old enough. It's almost like there's still sizing in it, but how could that be in an antique quilt?"

"Do you have the quilt at home?"

"No, just photos."

Vanessa stopped halfway through the stack of photos. "Is this the quilt I think it is?"

"Yes, it's the one found in Ella's cellar. The one she believed was made by a fugitive using the Underground Railroad. Chief Webber asked me to put a date on it, and I could use your help."

"I don't think I can help you. Sorry."

Sarah was surprised at her friend's lack of enthusiasm. Any other time she had questions for Vanessa, she had been eager to help her as much as possible. Sarah didn't understand her unwillingness.

"I know it's a lot to ask, trying to help just by looking at the pictures, but would you give it a shot please?" Sarah asked.

Vanessa got up and walked toward the table where she cut fabric to her customers' specifications. "Let's look at those pictures here where the light is better."

Vanessa was silent as she studied each one. She pulled a magnifying glass from beneath the table to focus on a photo with mostly red fabric. "Huh."

"What is it?" asked Sarah.

"See this?" She pointed to a "log" made of the garish fabric that seemed out of place with the somber colors. The bright red was sprinkled with pale cream flowers. "This is a new fabric. Very new. I remember it because I was surprised the sales rep from the fabric supplier even showed it to me. I don't usually order such gaudy fabrics."

"How new is the fabric?"

"He started selling it about six months ago." She ran her finger along the edge of the photo. "Maybe a little longer, because the deeper colors are usually available in the fall."

Sarah looked from the photos to Vanessa. "Well, that settles it, doesn't it? The quilt can't be an antique."

"Unless someone used some modern fabric to fix a ruined spot on the quilt. As far as I know, Ella isn't a quilter, so I doubt she could have fixed the quilt this nicely."

Reaching across the table, Sarah pointed to two other photos. "The same fabric is used throughout the quilt. Always in the same part of the pattern."

"Then unless the quilt suffered massive damage in the same spot in each repetition, this quilt can't be more than about six months old." Vanessa looked up at Sarah. "You don't seem surprised."

"There are enough other things wrong with it. If the quilt had been brought to me by a client, I wouldn't have hesitated to say this was only a replica of an antique quilt. However, because it's part of a criminal investigation, I wanted to be doubly sure." Sarah pointed at the red flowered fabric. "You've never had any of this in the shop?"

"I knew I'd be wasting my money to bring it in," Vanessa said. "I doubt many stores in this area ordered any."

"How do you know?"

"The sales rep didn't have it in his sample book when he stopped in last week. He's not going to tote around fabrics that don't sell."

Sarah considered what Vanessa had said. Whoever had used the brand-new material for a quilt that they wanted to pass off as an antique either didn't know any better, or they thought no one else would. That made no sense. They should have known that eventually Maple Hill would want proof that the quilt was a true antique.

"Do you think," Sarah asked, "that the sales rep would be willing to tell you where he sold this flowered fabric?"

"I'm sure he would. It's not unusual for one store to need fabric that's no longer available and to contact other shops to see if they've got some left. I'll call him and leave a message. He may not get back to me until after the weekend, but I'll tell him it's really important."

"That would be great, Vanessa. In the meantime, I'll let Chief Webber know the quilt is a fake." She gathered up the photos. "I appreciate your help."

"You're welcome." Vanessa stayed at the table as Sarah gathered her things and headed out.

Sarah opened the door and called a "See you later!" over her shoulder. As she shut the door, she looked back through the glass into the store.

Vanessa was staring at the mural near the ceiling of the flight of geese with one small gosling trying to catch up. Her fingers were on her forehead as if she had a headache.

Sarah debated going back into the store. Perhaps Vanessa was getting a little tired of "quilt fever" too. Sarah realized she hadn't really asked Vanessa about how she was doing, or how her kids were liking school. Sarah turned away, deciding to do something special soon for Vanessa to say thank you for helping with the quilt. Friends were much more important than any old quilt, after all.

CHAPTER TWELVE

A thin line of bright green grass was visible along the sidewalk leading to the Bradford Manor Nursing Home, the snow slowly beginning to melt. The red bricks and white columns glistened in the sunshine. It looked like a calendar photo of spring about to be sprung.

Sarah tried to go to the nursing home at least once a week. Her father had moved to Bradford Manor after the death of Sarah's mother Ruth. Sarah had hoped he would come to live with her and Gerry, because both men had enjoyed sports and a very serious game of checkers. But her father had refused to burden them, even though Sarah had reassured him that he would never be a burden. As the years passed and she'd seen the excellent care he received at the nursing home, as well as the friends he'd made, she knew that things had worked out just the way they were supposed to.

The serenity of the expansive view of the mountains was exactly what Sarah needed after her hectic morning. She'd stopped at the police station after leaving Vanessa's store. Chief Webber's reaction when she told him that she was certain the quilt was a fake had been typically low-key.

"I guessed that," he'd said after she had been shown into his office, "after watching you with the quilt yesterday. You looked more and more annoyed that it didn't hold up to your scrutiny."

"Someone must have made it to defraud Maple Hill. And then they snuck it into Ella's cellar."

He shook his head as he sat on a corner of his desk. "We can't assume that."

"But they didn't know the quilt was there until the wall came down."

"So we've been told. You know better than to take anything at face value, Mrs. Hart. Ella or her niece or nephew may not be completely honest about being surprised by discovering the quilt. One of them might have bought the quilt legitimately. We'd need to know who made it to follow that lead."

"I'm checking into that."

His eyes narrowed, and she suddenly felt like a bug pinned to a piece of cardboard. "You are? When were you going to mention that to me, Mrs. Hart?"

"Now?" she said in a whisper.

"Mrs. Hart, when I asked you to help as an expert on quilts, I thought you understood that your opinion on the quilt's age was all I was looking for. I didn't invite you to participate in the other aspects of the investigation."

Sarah clasped her hands in her lap. "Chief Webber, I wanted to be sure of my facts before I brought them to you. So far I've found out only that one fabric in the quilt has been available for only the past six months. It felt too new to me, so I went to ask Vanessa Sawyer about it. She's checking with one of her sales reps to see if she can find out where around here the fabric was sold."

He absorbed the information, then asked, "Anything else?"

She hesitated before saying, "Chief Webber, I'm almost certain there's another quilt inside the outer layers. Maybe there's something about that quilt that will identify who made it. If I could open a couple of the seams, I could examine it too."

"That can't happen without the DA's approval," he said, "and I can guarantee she won't give it simply because you're *pretty* sure. I know you've got good intentions, Mrs. Hart, but good intentions and evidence usually don't mix. I'll mention your suspicions to the DA, but that's all I can do." Sarah had thanked him and left. He hadn't told her anything she didn't expect, but it was still frustrating.

Sarah opened the nursing home's front door and walked past the birdcages where parakeets were chirping with excitement. They must suspect, too, that spring was coming.

With a wave for the nurse at the nursing station, Sarah stopped to sign in as a guest. She turned toward her father's room, hoping he would be himself today. Himself in this time and place. He was only three years from celebrating his hundredth birthday, and sometimes he became lost in the past. In *his* past where her mother was still alive or even further back to his childhood. She was glad he had wonderful memories to cherish, but she couldn't help being a bit sad that she was losing him more with each passing day.

Because the weather was still too cold for using the patio, many of the residents had gathered in the TV room. A few looked up as Sarah walked past, but most continued to watch the movie that was on or doze in their chairs.

She thought many of the residents watching TV looked similar to Chelsea—they wore the vacant stare she had directed at the television last night. Her mind began to turn the clues over and over, trying to find something that would lead her to discover who had made the quilt.

Now wasn't the time to be thinking of the quilt or the missing money and Ella. Now was for visiting her father. But the puzzle wouldn't let her go. While she'd spent the morning trying to sort out the clues, she hadn't paid any attention to the nagging feeling that she was overlooking something. She'd been able to suppress it while she spoke with Irene and with Vanessa. Now, it demanded her attention. She *had* seen something that would help her, but she couldn't put her finger on what it was.

Sarah arrived at the open door of her father's room. The walls were painted a pleasant light green, and there was room for a single bed and a bedside table. A plant thrived on the deep windowsill.

Rapping on the door frame, she said, "Knock, knock. Anyone home?"

Her father looked up from where he sat in his wheelchair close to the window. White hair wisped around his head, and his face was deeply lined from the many smiles and laughs he'd shared during his long life. He wore a dark green plaid flannel shirt, one of his favorites. He motioned with a quivering hand for her to come in.

She went in and kissed his cheek.

He smiled. "Sarah! You look pretty today."

"Thanks, Dad." She glanced down at her red sweater. "I like bright colors." She sat on the chair by his bed. "Something I inherited from my father."

"You can't blame me for wanting to wear something dandy after spending the whole day in my postal uniform."

"I remember how in December you used to wear that tie with the tiny Christmas tree ornaments hanging off it. When I was a teenager, I was mortified every time I thought about how everyone in Maple Hill saw my father in that silly tie."

His gnarled fingers reached out to take her hand. "Yet you bought me another one when that tie wore out."

"Because, by then, I wasn't a teen who thought everything her parents did was embarrassing." She laughed. "Of course, Jason and Jenna probably found everything *I* did appalling. Dad, how have you been since I last saw you?"

"You went away." He rubbed his chin. "Where?"

"To Texas. I went to visit Jenna and her family."

"Jenna is in Texas."

"Would you like to see some pictures?" Sarah asked, knowing what his answer would be. Her father loved looking at photos of his grandchildren and their children.

"When is Jenna coming to visit?" he asked.

"She hopes the whole family will come up this summer. It's going to depend on whether she and David can get time off at the same time. Between her work at the marketing agency and David's dental practice, it's difficult for them to get away for more than a few days at a time."

"I miss her." His voice became forlorn.

She squeezed his hand gently. "I do too. But let me get out the pictures I took when I was in Texas. Wait until you see how much the boys have grown."

She moved the chair closer to his wheelchair and pulled the packet of photos she'd taken in Texas out of her purse. She handed each one to her father, pointing out Jenna, her husband David, and their sons Thomas and Jonathan. Her father crowed with laughter to see them making silly faces on the Riverwalk in San Antonio, and he pretended to be annoyed at the photo of the family at the new Dallas Cowboys Stadium. His loyalties were completely with the New England Patriots.

"Where's my great-granddaughter?" her father asked abruptly.

"Which one?"

"Amy! Spring training is underway, and I need to persuade her that the Red Sox are the team to watch this year."

Sarah put the photos back in her purse and smiled. "It's Friday, Dad. Amy is in school."

He nodded. "That's right. The days sort of blend together here."

"Even though you know when every Red Sox game is."

"I couldn't forget something that important." He gave her a wink. "One of these days, I'm going to convince Amy to become a Red Sox fan."

"I'm sure you will, Dad." Sarah smiled.

Amy liked all sports, but baseball wasn't one of her favorites. Even so, she'd spent a lot of time on the Internet learning the statistics of the various teams. She wanted to be able to hold her own in any conversation about baseball with her great-grandfather. They teased each other about Amy's supposed dedication to the Los Angeles Angels, a team she'd chosen because they were rivals of the Red Sox.

"How is that son of yours?" her father asked.

"Busy." Sarah was glad to be able to say that. Only a few months ago, Jason had been anxious about building his law practice in Maple Hill. Now he was well on his way to being a success.

"That's good. It'll keep him out of trouble."

Sarah smiled, even though she wasn't sure if her father was growing confused again and thought Jason was a child. She couldn't be sure when his mind would start wandering through time.

"Dad, do you remember Grace Bennett? She was Phyllis Dobkin's grandmother."

"Poor Grace," he said, and paused for a moment. Sarah knew to give him time to go back and remember. "It was such a sad thing. Those little girls were taken away, and that was the last any of us ever saw of them." He stared at something Sarah couldn't see. "She came to the post office every day for the rest of her life, hoping for some word from them."

"Jason is hoping he can find a way to get Phyllis's family back together again." When her father didn't respond, Sarah hesitated, then decided to ask. "Do you remember Ella Buttonwood, Dad?"

"Yes, and I hear she's in big trouble."

Sarah was surprised. Usually her father didn't pay attention to news other than the box scores. "It seems that way."

"Hard to believe a Buttonwood would do anything like that. Her father and her grandfather were among the best men I've ever known. Those Buttonwoods squeezed every penny until it cried for mercy. No fancy house or fancy cars for them. That's why they've always been our town meeting moderators. Everyone knows that they'll watch over Maple Hill's funds as closely as they do their own."

Sarah had heard about the Buttonwoods' frugality too. It was a trait of proud old Yankee families, but maybe it had skipped Ella's generation. She wondered if Chief Webber had investigated Ella's financial accounts. Most likely he had. She wondered if he'd found proof that Ella needed the money that had disappeared. Sarah's promise to Martha could be keeping her from seeing the truth about Ella. But too many other people had been in and out of the house and had had a chance to steal the money.

Yet if Ella was innocent, where was she?

CHAPTER THIRTEEN

That's what I've learned so far," Sarah said as she sat in Martha's cozy living room later that afternoon. The Pennsylvania-Dutch style furniture was perfect for having a comfortable chat. She'd come over to the Maplethorpe's snug Cape Cod after leaving the nursing home. She hoped bringing Martha up-to-date on her day would allow Martha to see something vital that she had missed. "I've learned a lot about the quilt and the Underground Railroad but not a lot about where Ella or the money might be."

Martha's crochet hook dipped and danced in vivid green yarn. She was making another small afghan to donate to Project Linus. The group provided the donated blankets to sick children in hospitals, giving them a gift to brighten their hospital room and to take home. Martha had lost track of how many she had made, but she'd kept every thank-you letter written by a grateful child or parent.

"You've found out a bunch in a short time," Martha said. "Do you think we can put a halt to those petitions to recall Ella?"

"Irene told me about them, but I was hoping they were only a school project."

Martha shook her head. "I was asked to sign one when I stopped at the pharmacy. I refused. I'm going to call Fred Daniels and get to the bottom of why he started these petitions. While I do that, Sarah, you've got to find Ella before this gets even more out of hand."

"But I've hit a brick wall. The quilt isn't an antebellum quilt, and until I hear from Vanessa about where that red flowered fabric has been sold, I'm at a dead end. The Palladino kids—" Sarah sank deeper in the comfy chair. "Oh dear. I should call them to tell them that the quilt was a fake. They should be home from school soon. I don't want to leave *that* message on their machine."

"So what are you going to do next?" Martha put down her crochet hook and set the small afghan in the wooden yarn basket by her chair. "Is there somewhere else we can check?"

"I've been to Ella's house, even down in the cellar. That didn't help me." She frowned. "Hmm…the cellar."

"What about it?" asked Martha.

Sarah stood and began to pace between the TV and the sofa. "I've got this nagging thought that I noticed something important, something I overlooked, something that could help me figure this out. Maybe it was in the cellar."

Martha went out to the coat closet and opened the door. "Why don't we check out Ella's usual haunts? She might be in one of them, not even realizing that everyone is looking for her. Plus, it will take your mind off whatever's been bothering you. I can't tell you how many times I've remembered something once I stopped thinking about it."

"Martha." Sarah walked over to her friend and put her hand on Martha's shoulder. "What if we find something that proves that Ella did take the money?"

"We won't." Martha smiled as she took her coat out of the closet. "The obvious place to start is the diner. We'll need a key to get in there."

"Let's call the kids. Maybe they're home from school by now."

She tapped the number into her cell. It rang twice, then she heard, "Hello?"

"Chelsea, this is Mrs. Hart," she said. "I'm glad you're home from school already."

"Oh I didn't feel like going to school today. I needed some time alone."

"So is Ryan there?"

"No. He should be home in about half an hour. I'll tell him you called."

"Actually you can help me," Sarah said before Chelsea could hang up. "I was wondering if you had a key to the diner."

"Why?"

Sarah hesitated, then realized that not being up-front with Chelsea would not make sense. Most teens had radar that let them know when adults weren't being honest with them.

"I want to look around to see if there's anything that explains where your aunt is. Could I stop by and pick up a key? I can drop off your quilts too. I'm finished with them." Sarah would tell Chelsea that Ella's quilt was a fake then. Face-to-face.

"I don't know where the diner keys are. Aunt Ella must have taken them."

"Is there a second set of keys?"

"Not that I know of."

"Will you look around and see if you can find them?" Sarah asked.

"I'll look around, but don't hold your breath. Aunt Ella isn't great about holding onto things." Chelsea's voice grew icy. "Like money."

Sarah started to offer her some consoling words, but Chelsea said good-bye. Clicking her phone off, Sarah sighed.

"That doesn't sound good," Martha said.

"Chelsea doesn't know where the keys to the diner are, so we can't get in."

"Another brick wall." Martha shook her head.

"Not necessarily. Why don't we check out the camp where Ella cooks during hunting season? That would be the perfect hideout."

"The police must have thought about that too."

"True," Sarah said, "but why don't we drive up and see what we can see? I'm sure the police went there first thing, but it's been a couple of days since Ella went missing."

"Then let's go. What do we have to lose?"

Half an hour later, Sarah was afraid what she had to lose was a wheel or two on her car.

"Can you find any road between the potholes?" Martha grabbed the door as the Grand Prix jounced into another deep rut.

"I'm trying." Sarah winced when the passenger side tires dropped into an even deeper hole. "My poor little car. It's never going to be the same after this."

Sarah spun the wheel to the left and barely managed to avoid another pothole. The dirt road was narrow, and she hoped they didn't meet another car for fear she'd have to back up the entire way they'd already driven in. Thick trunked trees grew at the very edges of the road. Under their branches, which rocked in the rising wind, snow piled up. She guessed if she hit one of those piles, it would be as hard as ice.

She put her foot on the brake and slowed the car until it was creeping up the steadily sloping road. Her car wasn't made for a road like this one.

Martha carefully touched the top of her head. It had hit the car's roof. "Maybe this wasn't such a good idea."

Sarah wished she'd borrowed Maggie's Tahoe. Her daughter-in-law used the big vehicle to transport large items for her antique store. Sarah didn't need its size, but she could have used its four-wheel drive.

Sarah slowed again when she saw a gate ahead. On the wooden crosspieces were two signs. *Private Property* and *No Trespassing*. She exchanged a glance with Martha when she noticed the gate was partially open.

Her friend smiled and opened her door. "I'll pull the gate aside. You drive through, and I'll close it after us."

Sarah laughed and waited for Martha to open the gate far enough to squeeze her car through. She parked on the other side while Martha latched the gate. Her friend grinned like a naughty child as she slid back into the passenger seat.

"Let's hope we don't get caught," Martha said, "like we did when we snuck into the Turnquists' garden and picked their tomatoes."

"Martha, we were ten years old then. We didn't know any better."

"Sure we did, just like we do now, but isn't this fun?"

Sarah eased the car around a sharp turn, then looked at her grinning friend. "To think my mother used to believe you were a good influence on me."

"I was ... and I am." She laughed. "Aren't you having fun too?"

Sarah had to admit that she was. It was exciting to be tracking down a clue that might lead to the solution to this puzzle, and it was *fun* to chase it with Martha.

The road became even narrower, and Sarah was determined to be down off the mountain before it was dark. She didn't want to depend on headlights to pick her way along this winding road that was only wide enough for one car.

There were still almost three hours before full dark. They had plenty of time to look around and return to Maple Hill.

Suddenly the road widened into a small clearing. She drove toward a cabin set to one side. No other vehicles were in sight.

"Here we are," Sarah said.

"Talk about the ends of the earth." Martha got out and went around the car to where Sarah stood.

It was much colder up here on the mountain than down in Maple Hill. Wind swirled around the clearing, but they bent their heads into it and headed for the cabin. Its logs had weathered to the color of the bare maple branches. Moss was growing on the sheltered side, and the caulk between the logs had turned a soft brown.

"It's bigger than I'd guessed," Martha said.

"Shall we see if anyone's home?"

Martha's eyes dimmed with worry. "I hope no one is. I don't want Ella to be holed up with the money like a Wild West bandit."

Sarah nodded, sad that her friend's faith in Ella was being tested over and over. She hurried to keep up as Martha climbed the steps to the porch. When Martha knocked on the door, Sarah held her breath. She wasn't sure if she hoped Ella was inside or that she wouldn't be.

Nobody answered Martha's knock.

"Let's look in the windows," Martha said. "Just in case."

The first floor was one large room. A kitchen counter could be seen in the rear right corner opposite a staircase.

In the center was a huge fireplace. The fieldstone chimney rose two floors before it disappeared into the roof. Slate floors were dull in the shadows. Two draped canvases leaned against an easel.

"See anything or anyone?" asked Martha from where she was peering through a different window.

"Nothing."

Martha stepped back from the window. "Everything is covered with sheets. If Ella has been here—"

Sarah grasped her friend's arm and whispered, "Shh!"

"What is it?" Martha asked.

"I heard something. In the bushes."

"Do you think it's a bear? They're waking up now."

Sarah tugged Martha's arm and backed away from the sound, which came again.

Closer.

"Run to the car," Sarah said. "Fast!"

As they reached the car, she heard someone shout a greeting. Unless she was losing it, that wasn't a bear talking to them. She halted with her hand over her pounding heart and looked toward the trees.

A man emerged from beneath the low branches. His stocky build was emphasized by his thick parka. The hair sticking out from under his knit cap was pure white, and his blue eyes sparkled. He set a stack of wood by the cabin before walking over to where Sarah and Martha stood next to the car.

"Can I help you ladies?" he asked in a surprisingly high voice for such a big man. "If you're looking for directions, the only way out of here is the way you came in." He gave them a friendly smile. "I guess I must have left the gate open."

"Yes," Sarah said. "That's why we thought it wouldn't be a problem if we drove in."

He took off his knit cap and stuffed it into the pocket of his parka. "Most folks don't realize there's a cabin up here. I kind of like it that way. Now that you've had a chance to look around, do you mind heading back out?"

"May we ask you a question first?" Sarah asked.

"Go ahead."

"We're friends of Ella Buttonwood," Martha said. "She's talked a lot about the hunting camp, so we thought we'd see if she was here. Have you seen her in the past week?"

"The only time she comes up from Maple Hill is when she cooks for me during the fall hunting season," he said. "This is my hunting camp. I'm Jed Perry."

That name was familiar, but Sarah couldn't remember from where.

Martha's eyelashes practically fluttered. "Mr. Perry, I'm a big fan of your paintings."

Sarah nodded. Jed Perry was well known for his paintings of scenes that would have been commonplace in the late nineteenth or early twentieth century. His works were set in locations around the Berkshires. She hadn't realized that he owned the hunting camp.

Mr. Perry said, "Thanks..."

"Martha," her friend supplied.

"Thanks, Martha," Mr. Perry said. "Anyhow, you were asking about Ella. Is there a problem?"

Sarah exchanged a glance with Martha. As wrapped up as Maple Hill had been in quilt fever and its aftermath, it was remarkable to realize the rest of the world hadn't been riveted by what was going on.

"Have you heard anything lately from Ella?" Sarah asked.

He shook his head. "Usually the only time I hear from her is when she calls in September to find out if I want her to come up to cook for deer hunting season. I don't know why she calls every year. She knows we couldn't get along without her." He gave them a worried look. "Has something happened to Ella? I got a call from the police asking if I'd seen her, and now you two are here asking the same question. Are Ella and her family okay?"

Martha said, "E-Ella is—"

"Out of town," Sarah said before her friend could say too much. Neither of them knew Mr. Perry, other than his work. She didn't want to be sharing more than she should with a stranger. "She didn't say where she was going."

"But why would the police call me?"

Sarah thought quickly. She didn't want to lie. "It's right after Maple Hill's town meeting. Maybe there's some town business she needs to deal with right away."

"Ella usually takes the kids somewhere nice for a few days," Mr. Perry said, "before the diner opens. I've told her that she's welcome to use the cabin if she wants. She has a key, but she never comes up other than to work. I've never met anyone who works as hard as she does."

"She loves cooking," Martha said.

"It's more than that." Mr. Perry pulled up his collar as a gust of wind rushed through the trees. "She wants to make sure her niece and nephew have everything they need. In fact, she started working for me right after the kids came to live with her. She dotes on them like they were her own."

Sarah couldn't help thinking of Chelsea's indifference toward her aunt's disappearance. Was it teen rebellion or something else? Ryan seemed pretty upset, but Chelsea acted as if she didn't care if her aunt ever came back.

"Thanks." Sarah opened the car door. "Sorry to intrude."

"No problem. Though I do like to keep visitors down to a minimum when I'm painting here."

Sarah recalled the canvases and the easel. "This is a nice place to work."

"Yes, but I have to be careful. I don't want my originals stolen. That's one of the reasons I hired Ella. I like having someone I can trust in the cabin when there's a crowd hunting in the woods up here."

Sarah thanked him again and Mr. Perry waved good-bye.

Neither Sarah nor Martha said much as they went past the gate and along the road pitted with potholes.

When they reached the main road, Martha asked, "Why didn't you want me to tell Mr. Perry about her disappearance?"

"Because of you."

"Me?"

"You don't believe that Ella took the money. If that's true, there's no reason to spread rumors about her. Mr. Perry seems to genuinely care about Ella, and I didn't want his trust in her to be misplaced if someone else took the money."

"Oh Sarah. I could just hug you right now. And you heard Mr. Perry!" Martha said. "He trusts Ella enough to leave her alone with his valuable paintings. Will you believe me now that Ella is too honest to take the money?"

"I didn't *disbelieve* you before, but right now, all the facts are pointing to Ella taking the money."

"Then we need more facts."

"I agree."

"So what do you suggest we do next?" Martha asked.

Sarah eased the car into a tight curve and slowed as a driver in a hurry passed her on a double yellow line. "If Chelsea could find a key to the diner, I'd like to get in there."

"Chief Webber must have gotten in there somehow. Maybe he could let you in."

Sarah shook her head. "You know he wouldn't want us interfering with his investigation."

"But he asked for help this time."

"With the quilt. Nothing else." Sarah said. "I have faith, Martha, that some clue will turn up, and it will lead us to the truth."

Sarah heard the phone ringing as she opened her front door. Hurrying to the hall table, she picked the phone up. "Hello?"

"Sarah, it's Vanessa. I've only got a sec, but I got the information you wanted," Vanessa said.

"Oh thank you!"

"My sales rep called," Vanessa went on, "and he told me that he placed that flashy red flowered fabric in three shops in his sales area. Got a pen?"

Sarah went into her sewing room and over to her computer. She picked up a pen out of the cup next to it. Taking a piece of paper from the printer, she said, "Go ahead."

Vanessa slowly read off the stores' and owners' names, the addresses, and the phone numbers of three shops. Two were in Pittsfield and one was in Williamstown near the Vermont border.

"Thanks," Sarah said as she finished writing down the third shop's information. "I really appreciate your help on this, Vanessa."

"You're welcome. I hope this helps, Sarah. Got to go."

Sarah barely managed to say good-bye before Vanessa hung up.

"Thank you, Lord, for guiding me around brick walls," she said. "And I know you know what's causing Vanessa's heartache. Remind her, please, that I am with her in friendship no matter what."

Feeling better with the prayer on its way, Sarah switched on her computer to get directions to the shops. She picked up the phone and called the number of the first shop on her list to see if it was open late on Friday night. This could be exactly the breakthrough she'd been praying for.

CHAPTER FOURTEEN

Martha was babysitting a few of her grandkids that evening, so Sarah set off by herself to visit the three shops where the garish flowered fabric was available. She promised herself she'd update Chief Webber in the morning whether she found anything or not.

Sarah struck out at the first two shops, both in Pittsfield. No customers had been interested in the tacky fabric. The first shop owner had put it on a discount rack in hopes of recouping at least some of her investment. The owner of the second shop had given up on selling it and planned to donate the fabric to a local 4-H club for its sewing projects.

By the time she got back in her car to drive to Williamstown, it was getting late. The third store would be closed by the time she got there. Sarah reluctantly returned home, though she didn't mind crawling into bed a little early. The day had been exhausting.

The next morning when Sarah woke, winter had turned to spring as if God had flipped a heavenly switch. The temperature was soaring into the sixties, and the sun shone. Even the remaining snow covering the ground had melted overnight. She knew it would be only a tantalizing taste of warm weather because winter didn't surrender easily in the Berkshires in March. But she didn't want to waste a moment of the sunny day.

The store in Williamstown didn't open until ten, so Sarah had plenty of time to get some things done around the house.

She scrambled an egg and made toast while coffee brewed. She took her breakfast out to the front porch and sat on one of the Adirondack chairs. She had a good view of the street and enjoyed seeing some of her neighbors up and around on this beautiful morning.

She called a greeting to her neighbor Elmer Dowling, who was carrying his fishing rod and creel from his car. Elmer hadn't let his seventy-four years slow down his fishing. He put an ice fishing house on one of the frozen ponds in the winter. As soon as the ice melted, he was in his hip-waders in some cold stream or squatting by the side of a shallow and rocky brook.

"How's the fishing?" she asked.

"Got my limit," he said.

Sarah smiled. Elmer always got his daily limit, whether it took him half an hour or half a day.

"Took some smallmouth bass and a northern pike to-day," Elmer said. "I'll be glad when the streams are open for trout fishing next month. Much better eating than the farm-grown ones." He added as he reached his door, "I'll bring a few over. Native trout's the best eating, in spite of the bones." He waved and went into his house.

Sarah's good spirits dimmed as she realized trout season in the streams began April first. That was the day Ella should be opening her diner. Would the truth be known by then? What would happen to the kids and the diner if it wasn't?

Sarah finished her breakfast and put the dishes in the dishwasher, but couldn't shake off her agitation. She pulled out her vacuum and ran it upstairs in the bedrooms, her own at the back and the two rooms she rented out to boarders. The twins would be using the rooms tonight, and she wanted to make sure no stray dust bunnies had moved in under the beds. By the time she had things ready for the girls' visit later that day, it was time to head to Williamstown.

The fabric store was in a row of shops along the Mohawk Trail. It wasn't far from the elegant buildings and the famous theater on the Williams College campus.

Sarah looked at the colonial-style sign on the front of the store as she got out of her car.

Linda's Laces and Sundries.

Sarah hoped the third time was the charm as she opened the door and went inside. The shop sold a combination of fabrics and souvenirs from Williams College. Purple and white football jerseys hung next to bolts of cloth and rolls of lace. Mugs and T-shirts with the college logo took up one whole wall. Several customers were browsing. Their voices and laughter made the store seem instantly welcoming.

Sarah walked over to the counter to the left of the door. A slight woman with bright red hair sat behind it, looking over some order sheets and twiddling a pencil between her fingers.

The woman looked up. "Oh hi! Can I help you?"

"Hi. I'd like to talk to Linda, please."

"That's me. Linda O'Reilly."

"Linda, I'm Sarah Hart—"

"*The* Sarah Hart?"

"Excuse me?" asked Sarah, taken aback at the woman's sudden enthusiasm.

"I've read your new column in *Country Cottage* magazine. It's great! Lots of information, but easy to understand."

Sarah felt heat climbing her cheeks at Linda's gushing praise. "That's kind of you to say."

"I'm a big fan." She pointed to a bulletin board at the end of the counter. "I made a copy of both of your columns and hung them up for my customers to enjoy too."

"That's so sweet," Sarah said. Not knowing what else to say, she skipped to the purpose of her visit. "I was wondering if you could help me. My friend Vanessa Sawyer owns the Wild Goose Chase fabric store in Maple Hill."

"I know that shop," Linda said, smiling. "And I've met Vanessa. She's a savvy lady and a very nice one too."

"She is, and she said a fabric salesman you both use might have sold you a fabric that I'm looking for."

"Do you have a swatch?" Linda asked.

"No, but I can describe it. The material is fine-grained cotton, and it's a very bright and odd red. A pattern of cream colored flowers—small ones—are scattered across the fabric. It became available for the first time about six months ago?"

"I know which fabric you're talking about. Really loud, right?"

"Yes."

"We had it in stock, but I don't think I've got any left."

"You sold it?"

Linda nodded. "Yes. Would you like me to order more for you?"

"I'm not looking for the fabric. I'm looking for someone who bought the fabric."

"Oh."

"I'm trying to track down information on a specific quilt," she hurried to reassure Linda that there was a legitimate reason for her questions. "Is there any chance that you have a record of who bought the fabric?"

"I do keep records of which fabrics my regular customers buy. That way, I can remember the colors and styles they like. Let me look." Linda bent to pull out a book covered in sprigged muslin. Opening it, she paged through it. Each page had a fabric sample and information on ordering it. "This one, right?"

Sarah nodded when she saw the garish fabric. It was the one that was in the quilt. "Right."

"Hmmm...let me check my records." She tilted the book so Sarah couldn't see the page she turned. "Yes. Just as I thought. I sold only a few yards of it to one customer. I can't give you the person's name without checking with her first."

"I understand," Sarah said. "Would you mind contacting the person who bought the fabric and finding out if she is willing to speak with me?" She reached into her purse and pulled out one of her business cards and handed it to Linda. "Please let her know that I'd really like to talk with her. It's very important."

"I will." Linda put the card in her apron pocket and then patted the pocket. "I'll call her as soon as I get a chance."

"Thank you." Sarah moved away from the counter as a woman approached with a tall stack of shirts and a pair of coffee cups with the Williams College logo on them.

Sarah owed Vanessa a huge thank-you. One of the brick walls Sarah had been running into might be cracking.

As Sarah returned to her car, she saw two familiar people strolling in front of the stores. Neither Chelsea nor Ryan noticed her because they were intent on the displays in the stores' windows. They carried several bags with the logo of a clothing store that was popular with teens.

"Chelsea!" Sarah said. "Ryan! I didn't expect to run into you here."

When neither of them responded, Sarah gestured toward Linda's shop. "Do you know if your aunt ever came to this store to buy fabric?"

Chelsea gave another of her indifferent shrugs and peered at her reflection in the closest store's window. Hastily, she shook her head to bring her bangs back over the tiny scar above her eyebrow. Her brother glanced at her, then away. Neither of them looked at Sarah.

"We're finding out," Chelsea said, "that we don't know as much about our aunt as we thought."

Her words reminded Sarah that she hadn't told the Palladino kids about the quilt yet. "Do you want to go somewhere and get a coffee or a soda? My treat."

Ryan shifted the bags he carried to his other hand. "Sorry. We need to get going. Chelsea, don't forget you told Eric that you'd meet him."

"This will take only a minute," Sarah said.

"What is it?" asked Chelsea in a tone that suggested she was bored with the whole conversation.

"Why don't you walk over to my car with me? I've got your quilts."

Ryan looked at his sister, who nodded. They followed Sarah to her car. While Ryan stuffed the quilts into his shopping bags, Sarah explained about examining the quilt they'd found in the cellar and how it couldn't be an antebellum quilt. She watched their faces closely. Ryan's seemed to turn gray, but Chelsea's expression didn't change.

"That's no surprise," Chelsea said as soon as Sarah was finished. "Aunt Ella lied about everything else. Why not the quilt?"

"Are you okay, Ryan?" Sarah asked.

He hunched his shoulders. "Guess so."

"Could I bring dinner over for you two tonight? You must be sick of trying to figure out all your meals yourselves and I'd feel so much better knowing you're getting a home cooked meal."

The question was directed more at Ryan, but Chelsea took a step in front of him to answer. "No, thanks, Mrs. Hart. There's plenty of food at the house. Plus, I'm going out tonight with my boyfriend and Ryan is going over to a friend's house, so we won't be home."

Sarah was puzzled more and more by the teens. She looked at the number of bags they held. Ryan had three, and Chelsea must have had at least a half dozen.

Sarah was tempted to ask them about their apparent shopping spree, but before she could think of a delicate way to ask that wouldn't disturb the kids more, Ryan walked past her and across the parking lot to the far side. Chelsea followed without a word.

Sarah got into her car. The nagging feeling that she had missed something returned.

Sarah made it home with plenty of time to grab a quick bite for lunch and whip up a batch of brownies and another of peanut butter cookies. She could never have too many sweets when her granddaughters came for a sleepover. She gave Chief Webber a quick call to let him know she was still following up on the fabric.

As she hung up, she heard a car pull up and car doors slam before the door opened, and the twins rushed in. She gave them each a hug. Looking past them, she saw Jason trailing just behind.

"Which room should we use, Grandma?" asked Audrey.

"Use both if you want. It'll be just the three of us gals here tonight." She smiled as the girls ran up the stairs, their backpacks flapping behind them. "How are you doing, Jason?"

"Not bad." He unzipped his tan windbreaker. "How's your investigation going?"

"I've got one answer. The quilt is definitely a fake."

"This is getting more and more complicated. Why would Ella go to such lengths to cook up a scheme like this?" Jason asked.

"I don't know." She put the last of the cookies into a container. "With Vanessa's help, I may have tracked down the person who pieced together the quilt top." She told him about her visits to the fabric shops.

"I'm impressed." He grinned. "Though I shouldn't be surprised any longer that you can look at a quilt and have it tell you a story while the rest of us see only colors and a pretty design."

"You're right. Every quilt tells a story." She poured a cup of coffee and handed it to him. "The story isn't just in the pattern, but in the stitches and the colors chosen and the fabrics themselves. I like studying quilts and learning their stories."

He took a sip and smiled. "You make great coffee, Mom." He leaned back against the counter. "And does this quilt tell you why a well-respected woman would ruin her life and the lives of her niece and nephew?"

"Mostly it's suggesting that there's more to the story than I've discovered yet." She refilled her own cup.

"But, Mom, if you want to get to the bottom of this, you're going to need more than a storytelling quilt."

"I'll need facts. I learned that from you and Chief Webber."

Footsteps pounded on the stairs as the twins raced down. Amy burst into the kitchen, carrying a baseball glove and a softball. "It's not too muddy in the yard. We checked on the way in. Can we borrow Grandpa Gerry's bat and play some ball?"

"Why don't you use the wiffle ball and bat?" Sarah asked. "It's safer here where the houses are close together." She stepped aside to let the twins go past her to the cellar door. "There's also a set of bases down there from when your father was younger. Bring them up if you want."

"Shouldn't we show them to Mom first?" asked Audrey, her lips twitching. "If they were Dad's when he was a kid, aren't they antiques?"

Jason let out a "Hey!" and pretended to chase his daughter to the cellar stairs while everyone laughed.

Amy started for the door, then paused to ask, "Can we use your side yard, Grandma? If we play there, there's no danger of us hitting a ball through someone's window."

"Of course, you can play there, but still with the wiffle ball please."

"I can't hit one of those as far as a softball," Amy argued.

"That's the point." Sarah smiled at her granddaughters.

Audrey had returned from the cellar, hefting the sporting equipment along with her. She asked, "Can we call a few friends to come over and play?"

"Go ahead." She smiled. "The more the merrier."

More quickly than Sarah could guess possible, the twins had texted their friends and invited them to play. The first kids began arriving before Jason finished his cup of coffee. Teams were selected, and the game began.

Sarah sat on the front porch with Jason to watch the game and enjoy the unseasonable weather. Each time someone got a hit, shouts filled the yard. Cheers rose even higher than the ball when Amy, despite her claims otherwise, sent the wiffle ball sailing toward the back fence and then over. Jason jumped to his feet to applaud. Congratulations followed Amy around the bases, and her team swarmed around her when she jumped onto home plate.

The game hit a lull after the ball was retrieved. Batters struck out or hit fly balls. Nobody made it home.

Jason yawned. "Excuse me," he said.

"Still working long hours?" Sarah asked.

He nodded.

"How's work going?"

"Don't ask."

"Oh dear. I hope it's not that bad."

"Not bad." He rested his elbow on the chair's arm and propped his chin on his hand. "Frustrating. I knew it'd be tough to get Phyllis's aunts' adoption files unsealed, but it's going to take a miracle."

"You believe in miracles."

"I do, but I'm not sure the judge does," he said. "It's all about the facts."

"I was visiting your grandfather yesterday, and he told me that Mrs. Bennett went to the post office every day in hopes of getting a letter from her daughters or about them. Every day! But she never heard a word." She clasped her hands on her knee. "Doesn't that count for something?"

"I wish it did. But the judge doesn't want a nice story. He wants proof. Don't worry, Mom. I'm down, but I'm not out. I'm going through the court decision that led to the children being taken away. Word by word. And I'm not giving up until I find some way to prove that the decision to remove the youngest girls was made in error. I'm determined to get this family back together." He smiled. "Since we moved to Maple Hill, I've discovered how important it is for families to be close."

The words filled Sarah's heart and warmed her more than the sunshine. She sent a silent thank-you up to heaven before she said, "That's nice to hear."

"It's true. We loved living in California, but there always seemed to be something incomplete about our lives. Something missing. Wouldn't it be great if Jenna and David and the kids moved to Maple Hill too?"

Sarah laughed. "Jenna's a real Texan now. I don't know that she'll ever come back to New England. She hates snow."

"I know, but she misses having family around. She'd hoped that we'd move to Texas when we decided to leave California."

"Really? I don't remember either of you mentioning that."

"I never considered it worth mentioning," Jason said, "because Maggie wanted to get away from the heat, and Texas wouldn't have helped with that."

A cheer came from the game, and Sarah looked up to see another hit by Amy arcing over the fence.

"I think this calls for a celebration," Sarah said, getting up.

"Can I help?" Jason asked.

"Enjoy the game. I'll be right back."

Sarah hummed as she went into the house. Having kids playing in the yard was such a blessing, one she had taken for granted when her own children were young.

She came out onto the porch a few minutes later. She put a tray with the sweets she'd baked earlier and a pitcher of juice on a stump near one of her flowerbeds. She didn't have to call the kids. They saw the treats and swarmed over like a flock of multicolored birds, all chattering at once.

"Brownies and peanut butter cookies," Sarah said in answer to questions from every direction. She poured juice into plastic cups and passed them out to the eager kids.

"Why don't you kids sit down before you spill everything?" Jason asked. He took two cookies and a cup. "We'll call it our seventh inning stretch, even though we're in the bottom of the fourth."

Still talking nonstop, the ballplayers found spots along the porch and on the steps while they discussed hits, catches, strikes, and near misses. Laughter filled the air.

The rumble of a powerful engine coming down the street somehow managed to drown out the chatter.

"What's that?" asked Jason. "A jet landing on your street?"

"I certainly hope not," Sarah said.

Every head swiveled to stare at a cherry red car, low in front, its back arched like a track star in the blocks. Everything about it spoke speed.

"Wow," Jason said. "The last time I saw a fancy car like that was in Hollywood."

The horn beeped as the window rolled down, and an arm waved toward them.

"That's Fred!" Sarah said.

"Fred who?" asked Jason.

"Fred Daniels. Remember him from high school?"

"Oh sure. He's teaching now, right?"

"Yes, he teaches history. What's he doing driving a car like that?"

"I wonder whose car that is." Jason stood and helped her to her feet. "And I wonder if he'd let me have a turn behind the wheel."

Laughing, Sarah wound her way between the kids and down the steps. She saw several of her neighbors staring at the car from their yards.

"Good morning, Fred," Sarah said.

He grinned. "Not much like my rusty old car, is it?"

"No, not at all," she said. "I have to say I didn't expect to see you driving a car like this on my street today."

"Think of it as the bookmobile making a delivery," he said.

"Bookmobile?" she asked.

"I was returning some books to the library, and Spencer mentioned you were waiting for them. I don't know if you're still interested. I guess most of the people took their names off the waiting list when Ella took off, but I figured I'd drop them off with you and save you a trip to the library."

"That's very kind of you, Fred." She took the four thick books he passed out the window. She called to the twins. When they ran to the curb, she handed two books to each of them and asked them if they'd take them inside for her. She'd skim through them. Just in case.

"Where do you want them, Grandma?" Audrey asked.

"Put them on the dining room table please." Sarah looked back at Fred as the girls ran up the steps. "Can I ask you something?"

"Sure."

"Have you spoken with Martha Maplethorpe?"

He shook his head. "We've been playing telephone tag. Do you know why she wants to talk to me?"

"Yes, it's about the petitions your students have started to recall Ella. Martha and Ella are good friends, and Martha's really upset about this."

"She did sound upset in her message. I'll try to reach her again, but if you see her first, please tell her—it's just a class project. A civics lesson for those too young to participate in town meetings."

"So you're not going to do anything with the signatures?"

"No—that is, not unless it's necessary," he said.

Sarah hoped that wasn't a threat she heard in Fred's voice. He might not realize the petitions would be a dividing line for the community. Martha couldn't be the only one upset by them. And on the other hand, the people signing them wouldn't be happy to find out nothing was going to be done with them.

She was about to caution Fred when he looked past her. "Hey, Jason, how are you doing?"

"Good, except for being a bit envious of your wheels." Jason chuckled. "Whose are they?"

"Mine. I picked the car up this morning." He grinned like a little boy with a new bicycle. "Pretty slick, isn't it?"

The car must have cost a bundle. How could a teacher afford even a down payment on such an expensive car?

Easily…if he'd stolen the charity money from the Buttonwood house.

CHAPTER FIFTEEN

W hen Fred had left, the street resonating with the car's ear-splitting decibel level, Sarah had gone inside and booted up her computer. She typed in the make and model of the car and discovered that the missing fund-raiser cash would have covered about half of the manufacturer's suggested retail price.

She'd reluctantly asked Jason to keep an eye on the ball game and take the girls home after it was over. She hated to miss this fun time with her granddaughters, but they were involved with the game and she'd pick them up later for the rest of their sleepover date. Jason had agreed, but she'd seen his curiosity. She told him she'd explain later, not wanting to turn Fred into a suspect until she had a few more facts.

She needed to find out what Fred had said and done while in the Buttonwood house.

Sarah was hesitant to visit Chelsea and Ryan after their markedly stilted conversation earlier in the day. But she steeled herself against the teenage apathy and knocked on the front door. No one answered, but she heard a faint "Come in."

She walked in and was buffeted by loud cheers from the TV. The kids must have it on whenever they were home. She knocked on the parlor door's molding.

"Hi!" Sarah said.

Chelsea was stretched out on the couch, her gaze focused on the TV screen. She was wrapped in a quilt since the house was still chilly inside even though the day was warm. Several more quilts were bunched up on the chairs, and Sarah wondered if anyone else had been at the house last night. Would the Palladino kids party with their friends now that no adult was in the house? She hoped not.

Chelsea's eyes focused on Sarah before sliding back to the TV. "Oh Mrs. Hart, I didn't realize it was you."

"I heard you say, 'Come in,' so I did."

"I was expecting Eric."

"Well, I'll make this quick. I don't want to intrude on your boyfriend's visit."

"How did you know he's my boyfriend?" she asked.

"Just a hunch." Sarah glanced at the TV. The noise and voices were distracting. She was surprised. It appeared to be the same show Chelsea had been watching the other night. Not only the same show, but the exact same episode.

"You must really like this show," Sarah said.

"It's *Hollywood Hopefuls*." Chelsea gazed at the screen like a dieter staring at a chocolate cake. "Aren't they the luckiest girls in the world?"

"Do you mind turning it down?" She wished Chelsea would turn it off completely. "This will only take a minute, but it's important."

Chelsea lowered the volume and sat up. "Okay, what's so important?"

"I was wondering if you could tell me about Fred Daniels's visits here."

"Mr. Daniels?" Chelsea shrugged. "There isn't much to tell. He spent time down in the cellar, and he talked a bunch to Aunt Ella about the quilt exhibit. Didn't you ask me this before?"

"I was wondering if you ever heard what he and your aunt were talking about. Or if you remember how many times he came to see the cellar."

"I have no idea. Half the town has been in and out."

"I understand that Mr. Daniels was going to have his classes help with the exhibit," Sarah said, trying not to be irritated when Chelsea's attention kept going back to the show.

"I don't know. I have Mr. Lundgren for history." A commercial came on, and Chelsea focused more on Sarah. "I did hear kids complaining about the work he had planned for them to do. But he hasn't been back since Aunt Ella left. Neither has Mr. Krause. I guess they couldn't see the point now that there won't be a museum."

Sarah sat. She'd wanted to believe she was mistaken about Fred, but, if Martha was right and Ella hadn't taken the money, someone else had.

"Who has been back?" she asked.

"You and Abby McCormick." Chelsea twirled a strand of her hair around her finger.

"How often?"

"Like you, she seems to find any excuse to drop in once a day to interrogate us."

Sarah took a deep breath. "I just want to help find your aunt and learn the truth."

"Yeah, that's what Ms. McCormick says too. Blah, blah, blah about finding the truth and feeling sorry for us, but you just ask question after question even when we can't tell you anything."

"I'm sorry it seems that way, Chelsea. Honestly, I want to help."

"Why?"

Sarah was taken aback. "Because I believe your aunt may be in a lot of trouble, whether she took the money or not."

"But she did," Chelsea said. "She saw an easy way out of her troubles, and she left. She doesn't care about us. All she cares about is getting away from here. Away from us. Well, good riddance."

"I'm sure you don't mean that, though I understand you must be very angry with your aunt."

Chelsea set the remote on the sofa within arm's reach. "Okay, this is going to sound lousy, because Aunt Ella did take Ryan and me in after our parents were killed." She reached up self-consciously and checked that her bangs covered the scar on her forehead. "But the truth is, Mrs. Hart, that even though Aunt Ella's intentions may have been good, her money management wasn't."

"You did mention that she wouldn't be opening the diner this spring."

"It's not just that."

"Oh?" Sarah didn't want to be nosy, but she sensed Chelsea wanted to talk. She couldn't help wondering what it was like for the two teens living all alone in the big, creaking house. They'd already lost their parents, and now their aunt had disappeared.

"I didn't say anything because I didn't want to embarrass Aunt Ella," Chelsea said. "But what does it matter now? She's ruined her life as well as ours."

"No one blames you and Ryan for what's happened." Sarah reached out to put her hand on Chelsea's arm, but drew it back when the girl shifted away from her. "If I can, I'd like to help. I'd be glad to ask my pastor to speak with you too."

"It's not that." Chelsea shoved herself to her feet. Walking over to a window, she kept her back to Sarah. "It's about not having enough money to go to college. Not the college I want to go to. I worked for more than a week on my admission essay, and I was accepted at Williams College. I was set to go this fall. Now there's no money because Aunt Ella spent it trying to keep the diner afloat."

"Are you certain of that?"

"Yes." Chelsea turned to look at Sarah. "Mrs. Hart, I've been taking care of the household budget for the past couple of years. Aunt Ella was overwhelmed with the diner's books, so I offered to help out around the house. I learned about bookkeeping from my mother. She was a CPA." She barely took a breath as she continued. "I figured Aunt Ella would let me do that instead of waiting tables at the diner. I hated waiting tables. It's awful to have to take orders from classmates and watch them having a good time while I'm working for the measly tips they leave me." She shrugged. "Oh well, I don't have to worry about that anymore."

For that moment, Chelsea had let down her guard and Sarah had seen pain and fear in the girl's eyes. She walked over to Chelsea and put her arms around the girl, surrounding her with a warm hug. Chelsea stiffened for a minute, then wrapped one arm around Sarah's back.

Knowing Chelsea might be a little uncomfortable with this display of feeling, Sarah stepped back and asked, "Are you positive that there isn't enough money for you to go to Williams? Nothing left from your parents?"

"Their insurance money and everything left over when their estate was settled was supposed to be set aside for Ryan and me to go to college." She waved her hand. "But it's gone. Gone into that diner and now that's going to be gone too."

"Surely there's financial aid you could get."

"I didn't apply because I thought there was plenty of money. The deadline had passed by the time Aunt Ella told me the truth." She walked around the couch and sat. "So that's that. I guess I need to start looking for a job."

"You should call the college financial aid office on Monday and explain what's happened," Sarah said as she stood. "I'm sure that they'll be able to help you."

"Maybe."

Sarah thought she heard a door slam upstairs. "Is that Ryan?"

"Ryan's not here."

"Where is he?"

"He went to meet Aunt Ella."

CHAPTER SIXTEEN

Sarah stared at Chelsea in disbelief. They'd been talking all this time, and Chelsea hadn't said a word.

"You know where she is?" Sarah asked.

Chelsea looked away. "We know where we *think* she is."

"Where?"

"We got this from her today." She pulled a badly wrinkled and cracked postcard out of the back pocket of her jeans and held it up. Sarah got a quick glimpse of a photo of a gray obelisk reaching above trees. "Recognize that?"

"The Washington Monument?"

"No, the Saratoga Battle Monument in New York." She shoved the card back into her pocket. "She told us she's at a hotel in Saratoga."

"Which one?"

"The Isaac Schuyler Inn."

The large hotel that sat within Saratoga Spa's parklands was a luxury resort. Rooms there weren't cheap, but if Ella *had* taken the money, she'd have plenty to spend on a fancy hotel.

"Ryan went to meet her there?" Sarah asked as she began to calculate how long it would take to drive from Maple Hill to Saratoga. At least an hour and a half. "When did he leave?"

"Right after the mail came. Once he saw the postcard, he was gone."

"Did you let Chief Webber know about this?"

"No. Should I have?"

Sarah pulled her car keys out of her purse. "Call him now! He'll want to know that you've heard from your aunt."

"All right. I will." She pulled herself to her feet with the enthusiasm of a student on her way to the principal's office.

"Tell him that I'm driving over too." Sarah didn't want to get in the police's way, but she had a promise to keep. If she could convince Ella to come back to Maple Hill, Martha's heart would be put to ease.

"Okay." Chelsea pulled her cell out of another pocket.

"Are you going to be okay?"

With another shrug, Chelsea said, "I guess so."

Footsteps came from the back of the house. "Hey, Chelsea!" called an unfamiliar voice. "Whose car is that out front?"

"There's Eric," Chelsea announced. "He'll be here with me. I'll be okay."

"Call Chief Webber."

"I will as soon as ..."

Sarah got the message. Chelsea wanted Sarah gone now that her boyfriend had arrived.

Sarah got into her car and called Martha. When her friend answered, Sarah said, "I need your help."

"You've found a clue?" Martha asked.

"We may have found Ella!" She explained about the postcard. "She is—or at least was—in Saratoga. Come with me. You and Ella are such good friends, she might listen if you tell her she needs to come back to Maple Hill and explain."

"And if she won't come?"

"If she won't come, you can stay with her while I talk with Chief Webber. We don't want her to give us the slip. Not again."

Sarah drove west along the Mohawk Trail. In the summer, it was filled with tourists coming to see the views from the top of the mountains. Now the trees were bare and the rock cliffs seemed extra sharp in the sunshine.

"I wonder why Ella would go to Saratoga," Martha said from the passenger seat. "It's not that far from Maple Hill. If I were trying to hide out, I think I'd find a place a lot farther away from home. Or a familiar but remote place like Mr. Perry's cabin."

"Me too," Sarah said. She edged around a car suddenly pulling out of a side street. The road was busier than the ones around Maple Hill.

"Do you think Ryan's already there? What do you think he'll do when he finds her?"

Sarah shook her head as she drove around the rotary in Williamstown and headed toward the New York border. "I have no idea. I guess we need to pray that he'll say the right things and that Ella will listen to him."

Almost an hour later, they merged with the traffic going north on the highway. It was another twenty miles before they reached their exit. By that time, they'd left the urban sprawl of Albany's Capital District behind, and the highway was edged by trees. They exited and followed a secondary road, passing small houses sitting on broad lawns. Most of the grand Victorian mansions and hotels were in downtown Saratoga, closer to the race track.

Except for the Isaac Schuyler Inn. It had been built in the luxurious style of the fancy hotels that once had been the pride of Saratoga, where the elite had come to sample the waters many years ago. It wasn't far from the Saratoga Performing Arts Center.

Sarah remembered a particularly hot summer drive from Maple Hill when she and Gerry had gone to the Performing Arts Center to watch one of the New York ballet companies perform. Neither she nor Gerry had enjoyed opera or concerts, but Gerry had indulged her love of the graceful storytelling of a ballet.

"Wow," Martha said as Sarah turned the car onto the long, meandering road leading up to the front entrance of the Isaac Schuyler Inn. They drove for nearly half a mile between wide lawns before they could see the inn itself. The lawns would be beautiful in the summer, but now were a dreary brown. The huge white-clapboard building was already surrounded by groundskeepers, cleaning out some of the flower beds around the building and trimming the bare hedges that lined the sidewalks.

Martha kept saying, "Look at that!" She was thrilled by the tidily trimmed landscaping and the various pergolas and trellises tucked into the neatly lined landscape beds.

Sarah wanted to look around too, but she kept her eyes on the narrow road. If Ryan had arrived much before them, he could already be on his way out—with or without Ella.

As they approached the inn, cars were parked along both sides, and a large white limo waited under the porte cochere at the very center of the building.

"Oh it's a wedding!" Martha exclaimed. "There's the bride. She's beautiful."

Sarah edged her car past the limo, careful not to hit it or the thick white columns that held up the porte cochere's roof. The parking lot was almost full, which explained the cars parked along the road. As they drove up and down the rows trying to find an empty spot, Sarah asked Martha to keep an eye out for Ella's car or Ryan's. Sarah pulled her car into a space in the row farthest from the hotel.

"I didn't see either car," Martha said as they got out.

"Neither did I. This is a huge hotel. They may have more than one parking lot," she said. "Let's stick together. It wouldn't be hard to get lost in this gigantic place."

"If we get separated, look for me in the spa," said Martha.

Sarah was glad when Martha continued to joke as they walked toward the hotel. She guessed Martha's silliness covered her anxiety. Now that they were here, Sarah didn't have any idea what she should say to Ella. She prayed for the right words to say, and she trusted God to guide her when the time came.

The wedding party was still gathered under the porte cochere. A harried photographer was trying without a lot of success to herd everyone to the spot by some potted bright red tulips where she could take pictures.

"Over here, ladies," she called to Sarah and Martha. "Oops! You're not with the Branson wedding, are you?"

"Excuse us," Sarah said as she and Martha hurried toward the inn's front door.

Sarah and Martha went into the hotel. The foyer was as impressive as the hotel's facade. Creamy marble floors were laced with gold streaks. Overhead, ornate medallions on the ceiling were connected by garlands carved from plaster. Pale yellow walls held paintings of scenes around the city. Overstuffed sofas in chocolate-colored leather were grouped in front of a fireplace. The fire crackling there offered a pleasant welcome.

"Wow," Martha said. "It looks like a mansion. Was it someone's home?"

Sarah shook her head. "I don't think so. I've heard that it was built during the Depression as a work project to give people jobs."

They walked to the front desk that was set in an alcove to their right. The counter was topped with more marble. Cherry panels beneath it glowed with care and plenty of polish. A rack of guidebooks and postcards were set next to a plate of cookies waiting for guests.

Behind the reception desk stood a young woman. Her blonde hair was pulled back in a sleek chignon, and her navy blue suit was without a speck of dust. A cameo closed the collar of her white blouse and shone as brightly as her polished name tag that read "Debbie."

With a warm smile, she said, "Welcome to the Isaac Schuyler Inn. How may I help you today?"

"We're here to see Ella Buttonwood," Sarah said. "Could you let us know what room she's in?"

Debbie smiled. "I'd be happy to ring her room for you. One moment." She tapped a few keys on her computer, then clicked the mouse. A faint frown lined her forehead when she looked up. "Did you say Buttonwood?"

"Yes, Ella Buttonwood," Martha said. "It's spelled like it sounds. Button wood, but it's one word."

"We don't have an Ella Buttonwood registered here."

"Could you tell us when she checked out?" asked Sarah.

Debbie looked down at the computer again, then up at them. "I'm sorry. No Ella Buttonwood has stayed here in the past year. Our records go back that far, and we haven't had a single guest with that surname. Could she be registered under a different party's name?"

Sarah turned to Martha. "I didn't think about the fact that she might use a fake name."

"She couldn't use a fake name," Debbie said. "For security purposes, we ask for some form of identification with a photo on it or a credit card in the guest's name when anyone checks in."

"Has anyone else been here asking for her?" Sarah gave a quick description of Ryan. "Has he been here?"

"Not that I've seen, and I've been working on the desk since eight this morning. Would he have been here before then?"

"No, I don't think so," Sarah said.

Sarah and Martha thanked Debbie for her help and walked back toward the chairs in the center of the lobby. Sarah slumped into a cushy chair. "I'm sorry, Martha. I shouldn't have dragged you all the way out here when I didn't even know for sure Ella was here. We should have at least called before we left and asked if Ella was registered."

"Oh don't blame yourself. I was just as excited as you were at the possibility of finding her." Martha sat next to her. "Are you sure Chelsea said this hotel?"

"Positive."

"Sarah, I've been thinking about something." Martha said. "Everything we've been told about Ella and the money has come from Chelsea. What if she hasn't been completely honest?"

Sarah could see why Martha was hesitant to bring it up. The idea of Chelsea lying didn't sit well with Sarah either.

"I'm not trying to persuade you that Ella didn't do it, Sarah. Really I'm not," Martha said. "She's my friend, and I'll stand by her whether she's taken the money or not." She brushed her hands through her hair. "Oh I wish I'd never even thought of this."

Sarah reached over and took one of Martha's hands. She said, "Martha, you're a good friend and a good person. If you weren't a good person, you wouldn't be trying so hard to help Ella."

"And blaming some poor kid instead."

"You're looking at the facts and trying to figure out how they add up. Sometimes, the answers are ugly, but that doesn't mean we shouldn't check to make sure."

"Check how?" Martha asked.

Sarah took out her phone. "First by finding out if Chelsea called Chief Webber as I asked her to."

"Maple Hill Police. How may I help you?" It sounded like the female officer who had worked at the counter when Sarah went in to see the quilt.

"Hello. This is Sarah Hart. May I speak with Chief Webber please?"

"Let me see if he's available."

Sarah leaned back in the chair and waited. Through the phone she heard faint voices, and she wondered if whoever had answered the phone had left it on the counter.

"Chief Webber," came his strong voice. "How may I help you?"

"Chief, this is Sarah Hart."

"Hi, Mrs. Hart. Did you find out anything about who might have made the quilt?"

"I'm actually not calling about the quilt." When two guests took the chairs opposite her and Martha, Sarah stood and walked over to a door that overlooked the courtyard. "I was wondering if Chelsea Palladino called you a couple of hours ago."

"Yes, she did. Twice, in fact."

"About the postcard from Ella? They thought their aunt was staying at the Isaac Schuyler Inn in Saratoga."

"Yes, she told me that," Chief Webber said, "but then she called me back less than five minutes later to let me know that Ryan had returned home."

"He went to the hotel?" She glanced at the girl behind the registration desk.

"That's what Chelsea told me," Chief Webber said. "I had one of my officers call the Inn and confirm that Miss Button-wood had never stayed there."

"I see." Sarah couldn't think of anything else to say. "Thank you Chief Webber. I'm sorry to bother you."

As she ended the call, Sarah continued to stare out over the courtyard. Ella must have sent a postcard to misdirect her niece and nephew, even when they were worried about her and their futures. This did not improve Sarah's impression of Ella. All along, Sarah had hoped she could do as she'd promised Martha and prove that Ella hadn't taken the money. That it was a misunderstanding, and the truth would come out.

Now, for the first time, she doubted she'd be able to keep that promise.

CHAPTER SEVENTEEN

S arah had tried to reach Chelsea and Ryan by phone several times on the way home from Saratoga. Each time she called, she got the answering machine.

She picked up her granddaughters, dropped off Martha, and headed home. After a supper of roasted chicken and ziti, Sarah and her granddaughters selected a movie to watch. She did the dishes and popped some popcorn while the girls changed into their pajamas and slippers. Sarah finally relaxed as they laughed together over the hilarious movie. When the movie was done, Sarah left the mess of popcorn and bowls for the morning and followed the twins up the stairs.

It had been, Sarah thought, one of the nicest evenings she'd had in a long time. She guessed from the way the girls chattered, they'd had a great time as well.

Amy and Audrey stopped in the comfortable sitting area that she'd set up for her boarders to use to watch TV or read. They each flopped on one of the overstuffed chairs, and

Sarah sat on the love seat with a Flying Geese quilt hanging over the back.

"Grandma, will you read to us for a while?" Amy asked.

Sarah smiled. "You haven't asked me to read to you in years. I hope this isn't a delay tactic, so you don't have to go to bed on time."

Amy looked innocent, but Audrey wore an impish smile. "Ah, c'mon, Grandma. We had MCAS tests this week. Don't we deserve a reward for surviving that?"

"What did you have?"

"Language Arts," Amy said.

"Composition," Audrey explained. "And *poetry*."

"I thought you liked poems," Sarah said.

"Not on tests." Amy draped her legs over the chair's arm. "Which word best describes the feeling of the poem? A–Happiness. B–Misery. C–"

Audrey said, "C–Hunger, or D–Who cares?"

"D!" Amy laughed.

Sarah went to the bookcase and selected a book of Shel Silverstein's poetry. "How about some poems you do like?"

"As long as there isn't a test at the end," Amy said.

"I promise."

Sarah began to read. Audrey and then Amy cuddled next to her on the love seat. It was cramped, but Sarah didn't care. She read about the crazy creatures that rollicked through the poems and laughed along with the girls. When she finished with the story of Noah and the unicorns who missed their chance to escape the flood by getting on the ark, she closed the book.

"I think," Sarah said, standing and putting the book on the shelf, "it's time to go to bed. Why don't you girls get ready and I'll come tuck you in. And don't forget to brush your teeth."

"We won't," said Amy.

"Won't forget or won't brush your teeth?" Sarah asked.

The girls giggled, and after they'd washed their faces and brushed their teeth, Audrey went into the bedroom on the left. She'd put her backpack on the chair earlier, staking a claim on the room for the night.

While Amy stood in the doorway, Sarah pulled the covers up to Audrey's chin and said prayers, thanking God for their day and their family and friends. She bent forward and gave her granddaughter a kiss on the forehead.

Sarah stood looking at Audrey for a minute. She couldn't help thinking of how Chelsea kept brushing her bangs over the barely visible scar on her brow. The girl acted as if it were something shameful.

"Grandma," Amy asked, "do you think *this* house could have been a stop on the Underground Railroad?"

Audrey sat up. "Didn't you listen when Mrs. Jefferson said in history class that she doesn't think the Underground Railroad came through Maple Hill?"

"I asked Grandma," Amy said.

"Okay, girls. No arguing."

"Would you have worked on the Underground Railroad if you had the chance, Grandma?" Amy asked.

She smiled. "At least you didn't ask me which side I fought on in the Civil War. That's what your father asked Grandpa William."

The girls giggled.

"No way," Amy said.

"Yes way." Sarah laughed. "And let me tell you. Grandpa William did not think it was funny."

That made the girls laugh harder.

As Sarah reached for the light switch, Amy said, "But, Grandma, you didn't answer my question. Would you have worked on the Underground Railroad?"

"I hope," Sarah said, "I would have been the first in line to help."

Sarah tucked in Amy too, and went down the stairs, pondering what the girls had said. If she was willing to step up to help strangers, she must be as willing to do the same for a neighbor. It didn't matter if Ella was guilty of taking the money or not. What mattered was that Sarah had a chance to be a friend to someone in need.

She wouldn't forget that again.

Sunday morning dawned as warm and sunny as the previous day. Sarah hummed while she made pancakes for the twins' breakfast. The girls came downstairs and dug into their pancakes as if they hadn't eaten in a month.

Sarah savored the simple joy of spending time with her granddaughters. She listened when they started talking about activities and friends at school. Audrey had won a part in the spring play, and Amy was trying out for softball in a couple of weeks. Sarah was pleased how well they'd settled in after the cross-country move to Maple Hill.

She cleared the table and put the dishes in the dishwasher while Audrey and Amy went upstairs to dress and brush their teeth and hair. How many Sundays had she waited for Jason and Jenna to get ready for church? In those days Gerry had cooked breakfast and done the dishes, giving her time to supervise the children so Jason didn't end up with his nose in a book instead of changing his clothes. Or Jenna didn't hog the mirror while she got her hair perfect.

Sarah's smile stayed with her as she drove the twins to Bridge Street Church. Their backpacks were on the passenger seat, and they rode in the back, listening to music on a shared MP3 player.

She parked in the lot beside the church and took each girl by the hand. They swung their arms as they strolled up to the door that was thrown wide to invite in everyone and the warm spring breeze.

The box pews were filling up as they went down the center aisle. Organ music drifted to the high ceiling above the gallery that ran along three sides of the church. Bright sunshine glistened through the clear glass windows.

Sarah nodded and smiled to her friends and neighbors as she walked toward where her son and his wife sat.

She paused by the Diamonds' pew and asked if she could speak with them after the service. Dave nodded, and his pretty wife Liz smiled as she bounced their baby son on her lap.

"Good morning," Sarah said as she reached where Jason and Maggie sat. "You look as fresh as a spring day, Maggie."

Her daughter-in-law brushed her hands against her vivid, flowered skirt. "It'd be difficult not to wear something bright today."

"I agree." Sarah herself had chosen a lively green blouse.

Sarah let the twins slide in first, then sat next to Amy. Closing the door on the pew, she flipped the latch. She reached for the hymnal on the back of the pew in front of them.

"Did you have a good time with Grandma?" asked Maggie.

Both girls began to speak at the same time, then looked at each other and smiled. Before they could answer, the organist hit the first note of "Holy, Holy, Holy." The congregation rose and joined the choir singing the beloved hymn.

As they sat, Pastor John stood up at the pulpit. He put his hands on either side of the pulpit and greeted them.

"Let us begin with Psalm 31," he said. "In you, oh Lord, do I put my trust; let me never be ashamed: deliver me in your righteousness. Bow down your ear to me; deliver me speedily: be my strong rock, for a house of defense to save me. For you are my rock and my fortress; therefore for your name's sake lead me, and guide me. Pull me out of the net that they have laid for me: for you are my strength."

Sarah drew the words close to her and savored them. While she searched for the truth, she must never forget the one guiding her. He had a plan for her. She simply needed to be patient enough to let it unfold.

When they sang the last hymn, Pastor John spoke the benediction. "May the God of hope fill you all with joy and peace in believing, so that you may abound in hope by the power of the Holy Spirit."

Again Sarah took the words to heart. She must hold onto hope. It wouldn't be easy, but she couldn't give up.

At the doorway of the church, she smiled at their pastor. "Thank you, John, for such a relevant sermon. This one was particularly on target for me." She thanked him again and went out into the sunshine.

The last mounds of snow piled in the parking lot were surrendering to the warmth. As the kids ran about the churchyard, Sarah looked for Dave and Liz.

They were waiting by their car. Both smiled when she walked toward them, but Dave's smile faded when Sarah asked him about how Ella had been the last time he saw her.

"She acted fine," Dave said. "She was frustrated because her bad knee didn't let her go up and down the cellar stairs as much as she'd like, but otherwise, she seemed normal."

Liz asked, "Didn't you say something about her running around like a chicken with her head cut off?"

"That's true. She was going in a dozen directions at once. She was taking calls, answering questions, working with everyone who wanted to help." He opened the car's backdoor so Liz could put the baby in his car seat. "But I certainly wouldn't have guessed she was planning to run off with the town's money."

"If she did."

Dave nodded. "I know how dangerous it is for people to jump to conclusions about someone else, but who else could have taken the money?"

A list of names ran through Sarah's head. Abby, who hated the museum idea. Fred, who had an expensive new car. George, who cringed at the mention of a credit check and was getting lots of calls that certainly seemed to agitate him.

"I don't know," she said, rather than pointing a finger when she didn't have conclusive proof.

"I'm going to need to get into the cellar one of these days soon to get back the supplies I ordered," Dave said. "I didn't want to intrude right away, but the lumberyard will want either money or the materials back."

"Can you wait any longer? It's going to upset the kids, especially Ryan, because it'll be another sign that their aunt isn't coming back."

Liz and Dave exchanged a look, then he said, "I probably can talk to Clint over at the lumberyard and ask if he can give me a few extra days before I have to return the supplies. He might be willing to wait three or four days, but probably no more than a week."

"Even three or four days is better than nothing."

"I'll try to talk him into a week."

"Thanks." She smiled as she looked into the car at the baby they'd named for his father. "How's Dave Junior doing? He's growing by leaps and bounds."

"He's started saying something," Liz said with a smile, "that Dave is convinced is Da-da. He's crawling around on his belly. We've started calling him 'Wiggle Worm.'"

"I hope that nickname doesn't stick." Sarah laughed and couldn't resist giving the baby a little tickle on his tummy before she walked to her own car. She was glad that things were going well for the young family, and she wished the Buttonwood family could find the same happiness and contentment.

Lord, you know the paths of our lives, and you steer us along the path of righteousness. Be a rock for Chelsea and Ryan now when their family has splintered again. And remind Ella that you are her strength.

Taking the comfort of the prayer with her, Sarah got into her car. She knew God had a plan for Ella and her niece and nephew too, and she hoped that she could be an instrument in God's hands to bring it to a happy fruition.

It was dark when Sarah returned home from Jason and Maggie's. She yawned as she drew her car into the drive-way. One of her neighbors must have company because there were several unfamiliar cars parked along the street.

She switched off the lights and the car. She'd enjoyed Sunday dinner with Jason's family, but the thought of tumbling into her bed and falling asleep was even more delicious than Maggie's strawberry-rhubarb pie with gobs of whipped cream.

She started to open her car door but paused when she saw a motion at the edge of the light on her porch. Someone was on her porch! Was the person looking into her window? Why would anyone be looking in *her* window?

Pulling out her cell phone, she held it with her finger over the first button. A quick press, and the phone would call 911. She got out of the car. When she slammed the door shut, the person on her porch froze in the porch light.

It was Abby!

CHAPTER EIGHTEEN

H i Abby," Sarah said. When she thought about it, she shouldn't be rattled to find the reporter on her porch. Abby had proved to be quite the dogged investigator.

"I bet you're surprised to see me here," Abby said.

"A little."

"I wanted to see what sort of hooks you use to hang your plants in warm weather." Abby smiled, but she watched Sarah closely. "I've been thinking about getting some hanging plants for my back patio this summer. They'd be easier to take care of than a full flower garden."

"As you can see, I use plain old metal hooks."

"I can see that now, but I couldn't tell when I was walking past. I guess I'm going to have to break down and get glasses so I can see more than five feet in front of my face." Abby sidled toward the steps. "Well, see you around, Sarah."

"Bye Abby."

Sarah stood on her porch as she watched Abby continue down the street. That had to be the oddest conversation she'd had in a long time. Was Abby looking for something? Sarah had no idea what Abby hoped to find at her house.

Before midday on Monday, Phyllis called to confirm lunch the next day with Sarah. Phyllis sounded excited about the chance to catch up after so many years. Sarah was too.

The phone rang again soon after, and Sarah hoped it was Linda O'Reilly from the fabric store in Williamstown.

It wasn't, but Sarah was pleased to hear a familiar baritone voice. "Chester, what are you up to?"

"Trying to stay out of trouble." Chester Winslow's laugh was as warm as the man himself. She hadn't seen him since before she went to Texas, and she missed his company. He had a way with his jokes and compliments that made her feel young again. He was a lot of fun. "How about you?"

"I'm trying to stay out of trouble too."

"Are you succeeding?"

"It's still undecided." She didn't want to go into all the details of the missing money with Chester.

He laughed. "I'm planning to be over in Maple Hill a week from Saturday. I thought I'd pick up your next column in person. We could have dinner."

"That may be a problem."

"Dinner or picking up the column?"

Sarah carried the phone over to the kitchen table and sat. "The column. I hate to say I haven't even started writing it yet."

"Out of ideas already?"

Before Ella and the money had vanished, Sarah had thought about writing a column on the quilt code controversy. Now she felt it was too touchy an issue.

"No, ideas aren't a problem," Sarah said.

"I have one I think would be great for your column."

"Really? Let me get a piece of paper." She got up and went into her sewing room. She opened the notebook where she kept column ideas and picked up a pen. "Go ahead. What's the idea?"

"Ever hear of *Bargain Squad?*"

"I think so." She wrote *Bargain Squad* at the top of the page.

"It's a reality show," Chester said. "They send out two teams of people to yard sales. Each team has a hundred dollars to spend. A few weeks later, they sell what they've bought at an auction. The ones who make the most money get to keep it. They did a really interesting show last month about someone who made a fortune with an old quilt they'd found at a garage sale."

Sarah lowered her pen to her desk. She wondered if Ella could have seen the same show and realized that an antique quilt could be worth a lot of money. An antique quilt with the cachet of the Underground Railroad attached to it would be even more valuable. It was a good theory, but Sarah would need proof.

"What do you think, Sarah?" Chester sounded as if he'd asked the question already.

"It sounds great."

"The idea or dinner or both?"

Sarah smiled, again feeling that quiver in her stomach. Chester was so charming, and she found she liked being charmed. "Both."

"Great. I'll call you later in the week, and we'll figure out where and when. Till then..."

"Till then." She clicked off the phone and leaned back in her chair. How long had it been since she'd thought of anything but the puzzle of the missing money? She was going to enjoy the respite...for a minute.

Sarah tried to concentrate on baking an apple pie, but her ears kept listening for the phone. Linda had promised to call as soon as she'd spoken with the customer who'd bought the gaudy flowered fabric. Clearly she hadn't gotten in touch with the woman yet.

Sarah was taking the pie out of the oven when the phone finally rang again. She set the pie on top of the stove and rushed to get the phone.

"It's Linda O'Reilly," came a cheerful voice. "I've finally connected with my customer."

"Did she use that fabric to make a quilt?" asked Sarah, trying not to let her excitement build too quickly.

"Yes."

"Did she give you permission to let me have her phone number?"

"She did. Her name is Gwen Winters." She gave Sarah the woman's phone number. "She said she'd be glad to talk with you anytime you want to drop by. As I suspected, she reads your columns in *Country Cottage* magazine too, and she's excited to meet you."

Sarah looked at the number she'd written down. "Where does she live?"

"Stockbridge." She quickly read off Gwen's street address.

"Wow. Gwen drove quite a ways to get fabric from your shop. It's got to take almost an hour each way."

"From what she's said, I think she visits every shop within a fifty mile radius. She's always looking for something unusual for her quilts. When I saw that new fabric, I knew it was unique enough for her to like it. I ordered some especially for her."

"Thank you, Linda, for calling her. I really appreciate it. I hope I can return the favor some day."

"I hope you can too," Linda said. "We have a quilting circle that meets at the shop the first Monday of each month. Maybe you could stop in some Monday and do a program for our members. They'd love to hear you speak about your restoration work."

Sarah smiled. "I'd enjoy that. Why don't you call me in a couple of weeks, and we'll set a date that works for both of us?"

Linda thanked her and hung up.

Taking the phone with her, Sarah went into her sewing room and booted up her computer. She called Gwen Winters at the same time she was typing the quilter's address into a site for driving directions.

As soon as Sarah identified herself and explained that she wanted to speak about a quilt, Mrs. Winters said, "Oh I'm glad you called! Linda said you wanted to talk about a quilt I made with fabric from her store."

"Yes," Sarah said. "Would it be possible for me to come down this afternoon?"

"I've got a couple of errands that I need to run, but I'll be home after three. Will that be okay?"

"Perfect. I'll be there between three and four."

"I'm looking forward to it."

So was Sarah. She thanked Mrs. Winters and said good-bye. After setting down the phone, she pushed the button to print out a map from Maple Hill to Stockbridge. It would take her fifty minutes to make the drive. That meant she had about half an hour before she needed to leave.

Sarah went into the kitchen and set the pie on a cooling rack. By the time she got home from Stockbridge the pie would be cool enough for her to enjoy with supper. She considered trying to reach the Palladino kids again, but it was still too early for them to be home from school and later she might have more to tell them.

Someone knocked on her door. She paused. What was George Krause doing here?

Opening the door, she said, "Good afternoon, George."

"Hi, Sarah," he said, smiling like an eager schoolboy. His clothes, she noted, weren't as wrinkled as the last couple of times she'd seen him. "Do you have a few minutes?"

She glanced at her watch. "A few. I've got to leave in about half an hour." She motioned for him to come in.

"That should be long enough." His phone rang as he stepped into the house, and he held up one finger. "One moment." He picked up the phone, pushed a key to silence it, and put it back on his belt. "Sorry about that."

Sarah smiled but wondered if the call had been one of the people hounding him. George clearly had money problems as bad as Ella's. Maybe worse, if the calls truly were from impatient creditors. That was a good reason for taking the money, but, if he had stolen the museum funds, why was he still hanging around? Was he staying to keep people from thinking he had a reason to hightail it out of Maple Hill? That was dangerous, when Ella could come back home at any time.

Unless he knew where she was and how long she'd be away.

"What can I do for you today?" she asked.

"Could you show me the details in the quilt that tipped you off that it wasn't what Ella said it was?"

"The police have the quilt."

"I know, but Ella mentioned that you'd taken some pictures of it. Will you show me those?"

"Sure."

He took off his coat and handed it to her. "I hope I never run into another situation like this, but, if I do, I'd like to be prepared."

"I can't teach you everything in a half hour," Sarah said as she put his coat over the banister. "I'll give you some basics. Maybe when I have a free day and you've got the time, you can come back over. I'll go into more detail with you then."

"That sounds like a good plan."

"Let me get the photos." She looked at the dining room. "Why don't you go in there? The light's best in there right now."

"Thanks." He gave her another kind smile.

George was paging through one of her quilting books when Sarah came into the dining room with the photos of Ella's quilt.

"I had no idea," he said as he slid the book back onto the shelf, "how much there was to know about quilting. I hope you don't mind me looking at your books."

"Not at all."

"I know so little that I don't even feel I can ask the right questions at this point."

Sarah set the photos on the table. "Let me show you a few of the basics I look for in an antique quilt."

Spreading the photos, Sarah pointed out the most obvious anachronisms in the quilt's construction. George asked only a few questions, but they were ones that showed he knew quite a lot about preserving museum-quality textiles. He was an attentive student. Again and again, the buzz of his phone vibrating barged in on their conversation.

Finally Sarah asked, "Do you want to check who's calling?"

"I *know* who's calling." He pushed back from the table. "You don't have to be polite, Sarah, and act as if you don't know what's going on. I know Irene has been annoyed about the calls coming in at the historical society."

Sarah began stacking up the photos. She wasn't certain how to reply. Anything she said could sound overly nosy or overly condemning. She didn't want to be either.

"I know how these calls sound," he said. "But they aren't exactly what they seem. My ex-partner left my name and number with his creditors. They call me in hopes of finding him."

"Well, I'm glad to hear you're not in financial trouble." And she was. George wasn't so desperately deep in debt that he'd take the museum money to soothe his creditors.

"That's not quite true. My ex-partner ruined my credit along with his when he ran up hundreds of thousands of dollars on the company credit cards." He looked down at his cell phone as it vibrated again. "Getting all these calls has made running what's left of our business pretty tough, and finding a place to stay here even tougher when nobody will give me a credit card. I'm learning to deal with it, though, and I'm determined I won't pay a penny of what he owes."

"I don't blame you," she said.

He sighed as his phone grew silent. "I'm glad you don't. Maybe that's why I found another job here in Maple Hill. I want to see how the mystery of the missing money turns out, and I want to make sure someone innocent doesn't suffer. I told the cops that I didn't believe Ella took the money. She was excited about the exhibit, and she worked hard to get the nonprofit paperwork completed in record time. She would have had it all done even faster if her kids hadn't kept interrupting her."

"Interrupting her how?"

George raised his hands, palms up. "To tell you the truth, I didn't pay much attention. Every time I came up from the cellar, one or the other was keeping her from working on the forms. I'm not sure how she managed to get them done." He lifted his coat off the banister and pulled it on. "Maybe when Chelsea was out with her boyfriend and Ryan was somewhere with his friends. Maybe when they were in school or asleep. I don't think Ella slept more than a few hours each night. She went above and beyond to get those forms finished. I would have sworn in court that she was behind the project one hundred and ten percent." He shook his head. "Guess it goes to show that you never really know what anyone else will do."

Sarah sighed. Everything she was told, everything she learned seemed to point to Ella taking the money. Everyone believed it, except Martha, and even Martha was beginning to waver.

"You know what I find the oddest about this whole thing?" George asked.

"What?"

"It's almost as if the entire scheme was timed exactly when you couldn't be there to blow the whistle right away. By the time you were back, everyone in town was gaga over the museum, and you couldn't have stopped it, even if you'd had a chance to look at the quilt closely."

Why hadn't she considered that before? Because she couldn't have imagined that the whole plot to defraud the town might have been triggered by her trip to Texas. Who had known she was going to visit Jenna?

Maple Hill was such a close-knit community, she wouldn't be surprised if Ella, Fred, and Abby all knew about her trip. One of them must have taken advantage of the fact that the local expert on quilts was away and couldn't study the quilt in more depth. Then he or she had set the whole plan into motion. But which one?

CHAPTER NINETEEN

Stockbridge was one of Sarah's favorite towns in western Massachusetts. Its Main Street was edged with colonial houses, quirky restaurants, and fun shops, and the town offered enough entertainment to spend a full day there.

Gwen Winters's house was a small cottage on a quiet street away from the tourist commotion on Main Street. It was light gray, and its shutters were painted a warm cranberry. A carved wooden sign in the front yard advertised *Winters' Quilts—Good for Every Season*.

Sarah parked next to the driveway that led to a shed set to one side and behind the cottage. She held her purse with the photos close to keep it from snagging on the hedges flanking the front walk. She shivered as she hurried toward the house and rang the doorbell. The weekend's warmth had left just as quickly as it had come.

A very short woman with long black hair opened the door. She could not have been more than thirty. "You must be Sarah Hart. Come in." She held the door open. "I'm delighted to meet you."

"I'm so glad you were willing to speak with me, Ms. Winters." Sarah held out her hand.

"Please call me Gwen." She shook Sarah's hand. "Come in before you freeze. I know the old saying is something about April being the cruelest month, but I think it's March in New England."

Sarah stepped into a tiny foyer. Her hostess offered to hang up Sarah's coat and motioned for Sarah to go through a door into a room on the left.

"Make yourself comfortable," Gwen said. "I'll get us some tea and a snack to enjoy while we talk."

"You don't need to go to all that trouble. It sounds as if you've had a busy afternoon." Sarah looked around at the small print wallpaper in blues and pinks. The staircase had a small braided rug on each riser. Primitive paintings of people in colonial dress decorated the walls. It was a house that instantly felt like a home.

"It isn't any trouble. I can't wait to talk to you about my quilting and some ideas I want to share with you."

"Ideas?" asked Sarah. "About what?"

"Let me get the tea, then we can talk." With a smile, she walked past the staircase and on toward the back of the house.

Rafters crisscrossed the low ceiling of the living room. It was bright with sunshine coming through the large window. A large brick fireplace held a snapping fire. The furniture arranged on the polished oak floor looked to be as old as the house, but the pieces had been newly upholstered in soft pinks and gentle greens.

Sarah sat on the sofa, putting her purse on the floor beside her. She stood again when she noticed a framed collection of ribbons near the bookcases at the far end of the room. She wasn't surprised to see that each one had been won for quilting or other needlework. The two largest ones had been given for "Best of Show" at the Eastern States Exposition. The Big E, as everyone called it, was the largest fair in New England and was held every fall in West Springfield.

"These are impressive," Sarah said as Gwen entered the room, carrying a tray with a teapot, cups, and cookies. "To win at the Big E is a real accomplishment."

"I first started exhibiting when I was a teenager. I always won ribbons at the county fair and, when I thought my quilting was ready, I entered at the Big E. Do you go?"

"I try to go every couple of years."

"It's such fun, isn't it?" Gwen set the tray on a table by the sofa. "Would you like to see some of my quilts? We need to let the tea steep."

"Sure." Sarah wanted to ask right away about the quilt Gwen had made with the bright red flowered fabric, but she was eager to see more of the talented woman's work.

Gwen smiled. "C'mon. They're in the den."

The tiny den was past the stairs. One whole wall was built of fieldstone, and a quilting frame and love seat took up most of the space. On a built-in desk, a sewing machine was surrounded by fabric scraps. Snipped threads were scattered across the dark green rug.

A gray tiger cat was curled up on the braided pad on the desk chair. It opened one yellow eye, glanced at them, and then went back to sleep.

"Never mind Horatio," Gwen said. "He believes he's the master of this house, and we're necessary inconveniences that disrupt his naps." She went to a Williamsburg yellow door and opened it to reveal an old-fashioned cupboard. "The den used to be the summer kitchen. This cupboard must have been a sort of pantry, but it makes the perfect place to store quilts because it's deep."

Sarah took several quilts as Gwen lifted each one out of the cupboard. They smelled of lavender and lilacs.

"What a lovely scent!" Sarah said.

"My sister makes potpourri, and she always gives me a big container of it for my birthday and Christmas." Gwen took out a final quilt and closed the cupboard door.

Opening up the quilt she held, Gwen draped it over the love seat. Sarah recognized the Broken Star pattern. The central star was bright yellow and orange. The blocks surrounding it looked like pieces of an exploding star and were the same colors.

Sarah bent closer. The stitching around each block was taut and accented the shape of each block. A sawtooth border had required Gwen to sew many small triangles precisely together. It was artfully done.

"No wonder you have those 'Best of Show' ribbons!" Sarah said with candid admiration. "Your quilting is exquisite."

Sarah's respect for Gwen's needlework grew as her hostess showed off several more quilts. A mosaic quilt portraying a fox stalking a goose had almost eight thousand pieces of fabric. A quilt that had been made from a pattern from the thirties was an appliquéd rainbow of sweet peas, the blossoms looking as if a breeze teased them.

"This one is my favorite," Gwen said.

Sarah smiled as Gwen placed a Tree of Life quilt over the others on the love seat. It had an intricate pattern of twenty trees that looked like pines. Each tree had been pieced with tiny triangles in a variety of colors. Set on a light green background, the five rows of four trees looked like a forest.

"It must have as many pieces as the fox and the goose quilt," Sarah said in awe.

"Actually more." Gwen smiled. "I gave up counting them because I decided I really didn't want to think about how many pieces I'd cut."

Sarah helped refold the quilts and handed them to Gwen to put back in the cupboard. "Thank you for showing these to me."

"Do you think they're worthy of being in one of your columns in *Country Cottage*?" Gwen asked. "I thought since I was helping you with your mystery fabric, you could help me with your column. My business is new and ... well, to be honest, I could use some publicity."

Sarah was unsure of her response. She'd never done a column on one specific person's quilts. It might give her readers the impression she was biased. Plus, there were so many wonderful quilters out there, it seemed unfair to feature only one. Mark, her editor, would not be happy about Sarah trading favors for a mention in his magazine.

There was her answer, Sarah realized. She smiled at Gwen and said, "I really do appreciate your helping me, Gwen. And your work is exquisite. But I'll have to talk it over with my editor first."

"Excellent," Gwen said. "Why don't we have a cup of tea and take care of your business?"

Sarah followed Gwen out of the den and into the cozy living room. Gwen switched on a couple of lamps as the daylight was turning gray with thickening clouds. When Sarah was sitting on the sofa again and Gwen in a chair facing her, her hostess poured two cups of tea. She handed Sarah one, then offered the plate with homemade chocolate chip and oatmeal raisin cookies. Sarah took an oatmeal one.

"Linda told me that you were interested in a quilt made with a specific fabric I bought from her," Gwen said after taking a sip of tea.

"That's right. I was asked to evaluate a quilt that had that same fabric. Now I'm trying to find out who made it." Sarah put her cup on the tray. She reached down to retrieve the photos from her purse and handed them to Gwen. "Did you make this quilt?"

Gwen nodded. "Yes."

"Do you remember when?" Sarah asked.

"Let me get my quilting journal."

Finally—*finally*—she was getting to the truth.

Gwen came back in, paging through a journal-like book. "Ah, here it is." She tilted the journal toward Sarah. "This is the quilt you mean, isn't it?"

Sarah took one look at the picture attached to the page. The now familiar Log Cabin quilt had been photographed while draped over the sofa where she was sitting. "Yes, that's the quilt."

Gwen turned the book back to read. "According to this, I was hired to make it last September. I finished around Columbus Day. I can look up the exact date if you need to know."

"No, that's all right. But could you tell me who hired you to make this quilt?"

"You know, he never told me his name."

Sarah relaxed a little. If the quilt had been made at a man's request, that should shift suspicion away from Ella. Martha would be so happy. Still, Sarah could almost hear Chief Webber reminding her that she needed hard evidence.

Gwen flipped back one page in her book. "I only saw him twice, and he wasn't very talkative. He had a picture of the pattern he wanted and gave me half of my fee up-front to pay for materials. He paid the rest when I finished the quilt. He paid with cash."

"What did he look like?" Sarah asked.

"He was tall with dark hair."

"Was he thin or heavy?"

"He was really thin."

That description fit Fred Daniels. But she had to be careful. He wasn't the only tall, very thin man with dark hair.

"Do you remember anything else about him?" Sarah asked. "Young? Old?"

"Not too old. Probably early twenties at the oldest." Gwen sighed. "I only saw him twice."

"How did he know when to come pick up the quilt? Did you call him?"

"Nope. When he dropped off the old quilt for the inner layer, he just asked me for an estimate on when I'd be done. Said he'd come to pick it up then."

"I knew there had to be an older quilt under the new top," Sarah said. "Do you remember what the pattern was on the old quilt?"

Gwen picked up her cup. "It was a strippy quilt done in very dark colors with a crisscross quilting pattern."

A strippy quilt, Sarah knew, could be more than two hundred years old. The pattern was found in some of the earliest quilts made in America. The quilts were made from strips of different fabrics, which were sewn together and then quilted. Some were constructed from blocks made from joined strips of fabric, but many were simply created from strips of scrap material cut to various widths and pieced together.

"Do you know how old the quilt was?" Sarah asked.

Gwen's nose wrinkled. "It stank from mildew. There was a pattern to the dirt stains that made me think it had been folded for a long time and not moved. My guess is that it'd been in an attic or a cellar, but not stored in a box. It got dusty, and then the layers of dust became dirt. I tried airing it, but I couldn't get the smell out. When the guy dropped it off, I suggested that it might be too soiled to use, but he wouldn't hear of it. He insisted that I put the old quilt beneath the new top without doing a thing to it. Does any of this make sense to you?"

Actually it did. If Ella wanted to pass off a brand-new quilt as an antique one, odors of mildew from the quilt inside would fool people, as Sarah had learned firsthand.

"Did you see anything distinctive about the old quilt?" Sarah asked.

Gwen reopened her quilt journal and paged through it. "Yes. There was a small symbol sewn in red thread on the back in the bottom left-hand corner. It might have been the way the quilter signed her quilts."

"Red thread?" Mrs. McEvoy, Ella's great-grandmother, had put a small red emblem on her quilts. If the quilt inside Ella's quilt had the same mark, it would be proof positive that the old quilt inside the one found in the cellar belonged to Ella's family. "Was it an acorn?"

Gwen closed her journal and held it to her chest. "Maybe we could talk more about it later. I'm sure you'd like to do an interview with me for the column about my quilts. I could let you know then if I remember what was on the quilt."

The sudden pressure about the column bothered Sarah. "I promised that I'd talk to my editor, but I can't promise that he'll okay the column."

"Why don't you get your editor's okay for the column on my quilts and shop? Then we can talk again."

Sarah couldn't believe Gwen's audacity. "All right. Thank you for your help thus far. I'll let you know what I hear from my editor."

She left, determined not to be blackmailed into doing a column she wasn't completely comfortable writing. She'd just have to track down the man who had commissioned the quilt herself.

Night had fallen by the time Sarah returned to Maple Hill. Downtown was deserted, and most of the shops were dark. Even Liam closed early on Mondays. She drove straight to the police station to tell Chief Webber what she had discovered about the quilt. Maybe now that she had confirmed there was another quilt inside the Log Cabin quilt, the DA would let her open the top quilt to prove it.

Inside the police station, it was almost as quiet as out on the street. Sarah recognized the young officer by the counter. She'd talked to Officer Hopkins several times before. When he greeted her by name, she asked if Chief Webber was in.

"Let me check," the young policeman said.

Sarah waited by the counter, stepping aside when a pair of officers went past her. They were talking about the Boston

Red Sox spring training in Florida. She couldn't help smiling as she imagined her father discussing exactly the same topic at the nursing home.

"Mrs. Hart?" Chief Webber snapped her out of her reverie. "What can I do for you tonight?"

"I have further information on the quilt, and I think it will be enough for the DA to grant permission to open a couple of the seams."

"C'mon back, and let's talk."

Once Sarah was seated in front of the chief's desk she explained what she'd learned in Stockbridge. Chief Webber listened without comment until she was finished.

"How sure are you that what Mrs. Winters saw is the same symbol you saw on the quilts from Miss Buttonwood's house?" he asked.

"I can't be. That's why I want to check it."

Chief Webber became silent again, and Sarah waited. She was familiar with how he considered every possible solution to a problem. She'd learned that badgering him for an answer before he was ready to give one was futile.

The clock on the wall ticked around an entire rotation before he said, "All right, Mrs. Hart. Here's the bottom line. I'm going to offer the DA two options. First, we could ask Mrs. Winters to come in and describe what she saw. She would not be compelled to be honest, but most people are when they're being questioned by the police. On the other hand, we could open up the quilt."

"Even if Mrs. Winters tells you what she saw, you'll still need to confirm it," Sarah said.

"Exactly." He smiled. "You're really getting the hang of this investigation business, Mrs. Hart. Let me call the DA." He glanced at his watch. "I'm not sure I can talk directly to her tonight, but I'll leave a message with one of her aides. If she agrees to let the quilt be opened, I'm assuming you'd be willing to help."

"Yes."

Chief Webber got up. "I'll let you know if we get the go-ahead."

"It may give us the answer we've been looking for."

"One of them at least."

Sarah's excitement faded a bit. He was right. Even if they connected the old quilt to the ones at Ella's house, they still wouldn't know where Ella was.

CHAPTER TWENTY

As Sarah walked into her house that evening, she heard a car slow in the street. She turned as it stopped beneath the streetlight in front of her house and recognized it as Vanessa's. She stepped out onto the porch to greet her friend. She wondered why Vanessa was stopping by. Vanessa tried to spend every evening with her children.

"What a nice surprise!" Sarah said when Vanessa came up the walk. She gave the younger woman a hug as soon as Vanessa stepped up onto the porch.

Vanessa hesitated for a moment, then returned the hug. She stepped back and said, "Can I talk to you for a minute or two?"

"Of course." She held open the door. Taking off her coat, she offered to hang up Vanessa's.

Sarah led the way into the living room. Vanessa perched on the sofa while Sarah settled into her rocking chair.

"Have you found out anything more about the quilt?" Vanessa asked.

Sarah began rocking, the squeak of the rockers against the floor a comforting sound. "I still have a lot of questions, but I did find the woman who made it."

"I'm glad." Vanessa smiled, then stared at the fireplace for a long moment. "When I was in grade school, we had to do a family tree project. I spent hours asking my parents and grandparents about our family's history. Every kid wants to hear fascinating stories about their great-great-grandparents, right? Before the Civil War, one branch of the family were freemen who lived close to one of the Underground Railroad routes north of the Ohio River. But they weren't conductors and they never offered a safe house to fugitives." She sighed and looked down at her folded hands. "It wasn't that they didn't have the chance. They chose not to because they were afraid for their children. There were stories of slave owners taking revenge against those who helped escaping slaves. Revenge that went beyond the law."

Sarah thought of the question the twins had posed the night they slept over: Would Sarah have worked to help fugitive slaves? It was simple to answer that now, when there was no chance she'd actually have to risk her life and her family's lives to get others to freedom. It hadn't been that simple when the choice was a reality, and getting caught meant paying a high cost.

The fugitives had risked everything. Not because they had nothing to lose, because they could be killed or separated if they were caught, but because they had so much to gain. Freedom and knowing that their families would remain together. The conductors on the Underground Railroad had had everything to lose.

Getting up, she sat next to Vanessa on the sofa. "They did what they had to in order to protect their children. As a mother and grandmother, I understand that."

"So do I, because I'd never do anything that could put my kids in danger. But I've always wondered, still, if it was the right thing that they did. If they regretted it. If they were ever ashamed."

"There's no reason to be ashamed of protecting your family. And hey, everyone has branches of their family tree they'd rather forget. And surely there are other wonderful stories in your family."

Vanessa's smile returned, brightening her face and her eyes. "Thanks for reminding me of that, Sarah."

"That's what friends are for."

When Vanessa stood, Sarah did too. They shared a hug before Vanessa left. Sarah knew Vanessa would be okay, and she was grateful for their friendship.

Sarah huddled into her winter coat while she walked along the sidewalk toward Liam's. She hoped the weather would take a turn toward spring again. Their one brief taste had been tantalizing, and now the March cold seemed even drearier.

Everyone she passed had their heads down, trying to protect themselves from the wind and cold. Scarves were pulled up and hats down.

Sarah opened the door to Liam's and stepped inside. Warmth and Murphy greeted her. She bent to give the dog a pat on the head, and he rewarded her with a wagging tail and a silk-soft lap of his tongue on the back of her hand.

Sarah recognized Liam's soft brogue and looked into the bookstore area. Fred Daniels stood by the cash register, and from the other side of the counter, Liam reached into a cardboard box set between them. Fred was writing hastily. Both men turned to look at her. Each wore a guilty expression.

"Caught in the act," Liam said with his usual smile. "Don't worry, Fred. Sarah can keep a secret."

"I hope so, because you definitely have caught me, Sarah," Fred said.

"I did?" She glanced from one man to the other. "What did I catch you doing?"

Fred picked up a book and handed it to her.

It was a mystery. She read the title and then the author's name on the cover of the book. "Ricka Lyons? I don't understand."

"Oops. Maybe I should recommend the book to my regulars more," Liam said with a smile and turned to Fred. "My apologies, Ms. Lyons."

Sarah opened her mouth, then closed it as she looked from Fred's shy smile to Liam's broad one.

Fred opened the book and turned to the title page where the book was autographed with best wishes from the author. On the table another book was open to the same page and the name was partly signed.

"*You* are Ricka Lyons?" she asked.

Fred put his finger to his lips. "Don't spread it around, okay?"

"Why not? It's wonderful that you're a published author." She closed the book and looked from the name on the front cover to him.

"I'm happy being known as a history teacher. That's why I've got a pen name."

"Tell her," Liam said, "how we came up with your name."

"It's kind of silly," Fred said. "Ricka is from the female version of Frederick, and Lyons came from Daniels. Like Daniel in the lion's den."

"We thought it was funny." Liam laughed again. "And nobody's suspected Fred is the real author."

"Have you read any of my books?" he asked.

"I...I don't think so."

"Don't feel bad. They aren't really best sellers." He picked up the pen and finished signing the book with a flourish. Handing it to Liam, he said, "Though my royalties are paying for a few nice-to-have things." He held out a book to Sarah. "Here. On the house. Let me know if you love it—and if you don't love it, find Ricka Lyons and tell *her*." Liam and Fred laughed.

Sarah smiled and thanked him for the book.

As he continued signing books, Sarah put the book in her bag and walked away to look along the bookshelves. It all fit together. A fancy sports car definitely came under the heading of nice-to-have things, so Fred *hadn't* needed to take the money for the Underground Railroad exhibit to pay for it. She was glad he wasn't involved with taking the money. He'd always been a good kid and now seemed to be a good man. Her smile faded as she realized that left only Abby and Ella on her list of suspects.

The front door opened, and Phyllis walked in. She was dressed in a black suit under her thick coat. Sarah gave her friend a hug and introduced her to Liam and Fred. Phyllis glanced with curiosity at the box of books, but Sarah steered her toward the café section.

"Sit wherever you wish," Liam called after them. "Karen will be with you in a moment."

Sarah selected a table near the window where they could watch the comings and goings around the green, even though few people were out in the frigid wind. Phyllis sat across from her and picked up one of the menus waiting there.

"How was your trip to visit your sister?" Sarah asked.

"We had a wonderful time," Phyllis said. "Though it would have been better if we'd had good news from Jason."

"He's working hard to help you."

"I know, I'm sorry. That sounded like I was complaining about his work. I'm not." Phyllis picked up a napkin and began folding it into smaller and smaller squares. "We're meeting this afternoon. He was supposed to talk with his contact at the Department of Children and Families again this morning. I hope it goes better than the last conversation did."

"He told me he's run into some roadblocks."

"More like a mountain of red tape. Grandma Grace wouldn't hurt a fly, but the judge doesn't seem willing to believe that. She loved her children so much I can't believe she was ever able to smile again after they took her two girls away. If someone had taken away one of my children, I don't know what I would have done."

Sarah looked down at the menu between them. She hadn't guessed her conversation with Phyllis would mirror her thoughts last night about the Underground Railroad. Families torn apart forever. Sarah sent up a grateful prayer that her family had never suffered such a loss and that Jason had the courage and determination to tilt at bureaucratic windmills.

"Phyllis," she said, "Jason won't give up as long as there's a chance to clear your grandmother's name."

"Do you think he can?"

Sarah wouldn't give her friend false hope. They'd been friends for too long not to be honest with each other. "I know he'll try everything. He'll contact people at DCF and family court and anyone else he needs to."

"Sarah, you don't know how much I needed to hear that." Phyllis stopped worrying the napkin. "There's a piece of my heart missing, and I know my mother feels the emptiness even more than I do."

Sarah took her friend's hand. "Trust in God to bring you back together when the time is right."

"I do." She wiped her eyes on the napkin and smiled. "But I keep praying that the time will be right soon."

Someone cleared her throat, and Sarah looked up to see Karen Bancroft waiting to take their order. Liam's part-time waitress was tall and slender and moved gracefully. She always wore a friendly smile. Her fashionably short hair was black, but she'd recently added some red highlights that matched the rickrack on her apron.

"Sorry to interrupt," Karen said. "Are you ladies ready to order?"

Phyllis ordered a cup of coffee and the corned beef sandwich special. Liam had decided to have an Irish special on the menu every week in March to honor St. Patrick's Day.

"I'll have the sandwich special too," Sarah said, "and—"

"A spiced chai latte with whipped cream?" Karen smiled when Sarah nodded. "As you always do."

They laughed, and Phyllis changed her order to a spiced chai latte as well.

As soon as Karen left to take their order to the kitchen, Phyllis asked, "Did Jason tell you how long it would take to get approval to open the adoption records?"

"No, but he'd tell you before he'd tell me," Sarah replied. "You're his client. I'm just his mom."

That brought a quick smile from Phyllis. "Let's talk about something else. Jason mentioned he has twin daughters and that Jenna has two boys. Tell me all about them."

That was the only invitation Sarah needed to reach into her purse and pull out the photos she'd taken in Texas. Phyllis went through them and asked dozens of questions before she showed photos of her own grandson. Soon it was as if no time had passed since they'd been young mothers, sharing all the ups and downs of raising young children and nurturing good marriages. They laughed together, finished each other's sentences, and kept asking, "Do you remember when…?"

A deep voice interrupted them. "Excuse me ladies, are you registered voters in Maple Hill? Would you like to sign a petition to recall Ella Buttonwood as town meeting moderator?"

A clipboard with a piece of paper with dozens of signatures was set in front of Sarah. She looked up at a young man, who was enveloped in a thick, puffy black parka while a heavy knit cap covered his hair. He was about Liam's height, she realized, when Liam came toward their table.

"No, thank you." Sarah pushed the petition away.

"But," he said, "after what she did, don't you think she should be removed from her position?"

"I said, 'No, thank you.'"

"But—"

Liam interceded by saying sternly, "Young man, I think you should stop bothering these ladies. You're welcome to collect signatures outside the café." He pointed to the front door. "You can ask my patrons to sign your petition on their way in or their way out, but not while they're inside enjoying their lunch or looking at books."

The young man muttered something before walking out the door. The wind slammed it shut behind him. Voices buzzed through the café in his wake.

"I'm sorry," Liam said. "I didn't realize what he was up to until he asked you to sign."

"Thanks," Sarah said. Even though Fred said he didn't intend to use the petitions for an actual recall, she wondered if someone else would pressure him to take advantage of all those legal signatures.

Karen brought their order over. "I didn't expect to see *him* with one of those petitions to recall Miss Buttonwood."

"Why not?" asked Sarah.

"Don't you know who that kid is?"

"No."

"That's Eric Janowski. He's dating Chelsea Palladino."

"Are you sure it's Eric?" Sarah asked.

Karen set a cup topped with whipped cream in front of Phyllis, then reached to her tray for Sarah's. "I'm sure."

"Why would he be collecting signatures to recall her aunt if he's dating Chelsea?"

"I have no idea," Karen said. "Seems a real lousy way to treat your girlfriend." She went to take orders from another table.

"She's right," Phyllis said. "Families are too precious to let anything divide them. I keep thinking about the letters my grandmother wrote to the children taken from her. They explained why she chose to give them up when the social worker insisted that it was the only way to keep her other children. At one point, my grandmother feared she would lose all her children because they were so poor."

Sarah remembered her father talking about Grandma Grace coming into the post office every day in hopes of receiving word from her children. "Did she mail the letters to the social worker?" Sarah asked.

"She never mailed them because she didn't know where to send them. She wrote them and put them away. We found them after she died."

"Do you still have them?" Letters written by a grieving mother...was that the kind of proof Jason was looking for? They wouldn't be considered hearsay, would they?

"Yes. Mother saved them to share with her sisters if we ever found them."

"I think you should show them to Jason. I can't imagine a better testament to your grandmother's love for her children than those letters." Sarah asked, "Did you bring the letters here with you?"

"No. They're in Chicago. But I can have them overnighted here." She picked up her purse. "I'm going to call my husband right now. Do you mind?"

"Not at all." Sarah said. "We're pretty much done with lunch. In fact, why don't you see if he can fax some over to Jason's office?"

"Oh Sarah, that's brilliant! I'll let you know what happens. If we find my aunts, it'll be because of you and Jason."

"And you! You're the one who's never given up."

Phyllis got up and walked away, already dialing. She paused at the counter where she handed Karen money for lunch.

Sarah smiled. Jason would be excited to get his hands on the letters. She wasn't sure how he'd use them, but she knew her son was resourceful and stubborn. He'd find a way.

When Phyllis went outside, shrugging on her coat and talking rapidly into the phone, Sarah saw through the open door several people gathered on the sidewalk. Abby was among them, writing rapidly in a notebook. She must be interviewing Eric about the petition. Abby glanced into the café, and her gaze met Sarah's briefly before the reporter looked swiftly away.

Sarah mulled over the reporter's role in Ella's disappearance while she slowly finished her spiced chai latte. Abby was still on Sarah's suspect list, despite the fact that a young, dark-haired man had been the one to ask Gwen to make the quilt. Abby was smart enough to use a proxy if she was going to try to scam a member of her community.

Finding Abby hanging around her porch still bothered Sarah. The excuse Abby had given was weak, but Sarah couldn't figure out why the tenacious reporter would be snooping at her house. Abby did seem to be covering every possible angle of the story, but Sarah couldn't tell her anything new. The quilt was out of her reach, and the trail in Saratoga had run cold.

Sarah finished her lunch, even though she didn't feel like eating. She went up to the counter to pay. Liam came over and, with a smile, told her that her friend had paid for her lunch.

"Told me that it was the least she could do to thank you," Liam said.

Phyllis's kindness eased the frustration Sarah had been feeling. Not because Phyllis had paid for her lunch, but because Phyllis had known that Sarah would be touched by her thoughtfulness.

"What a blessing a good friend is!" Sarah said.

"I have always thought a good friend is about the best blessing there is."

She patted his hand. "Must be why you're such a good friend to everyone who comes in here."

"All a ploy," he said, his eyes twinkling, "to keep you pretty colleens coming back."

Sarah laughed as she went to the door and out into the cold afternoon. Between Phyllis's kindness and Liam's teasing, her heart felt refreshed. She couldn't let herself get too ground down by the lack of progress in discovering the truth. She needed to be like Phyllis and keep looking. No matter how long it took.

CHAPTER TWENTY-ONE

Sarah had to knock several times before Chelsea answered the door at the Buttonwood house later that afternoon. Chelsea came to the door draped in a ragged quilt. She pulled the quilt closer, holding the ends around her.

"Oh, it's you." Chelsea said by way of greeting.

"Can I come in?" Sarah asked. "It's cold out here."

"It's cold in here too." She stepped aside to let Sarah in. "The furnace stopped last night."

"Did you run out of fuel oil?"

"Ryan's called the oil company, but they want to be paid before they'll fill the tank." Chelsea walked into the parlor, then looked back at Sarah. "And you know how much chance we've got of that happening."

"Would you like to stay at my house?" Sarah asked. "I've got two empty bedrooms. You could just stay temporarily until you get things with the oil company figured out."

"No thanks." Chelsea sat gracefully on the sofa, tucking her feet and the quilt beneath her. Luckily the TV wasn't on this time, but Chelsea still didn't make eye contact.

"Chelsea," Sarah said, "I wanted to talk to you about the postcard your aunt sent you. Did you give it to Chief Webber?"

"No. But one of his officers came by that day to pick it up. I didn't think he'd be interested since Aunt Ella wasn't in Saratoga."

Sarah tried another tack. "Would you mind if I looked down in the cellar again?"

Chelsea sat up straighter. "Yes. It's bad enough that I'm cold. I don't want to be cold *and* damp."

"You don't need to go with me. I can find my way around." Sarah went to the cellar door.

"Mrs. Hart, there's nothing down there. You'd probably find more looking around the diner. If you want to poke around there, knock yourself out."

"I thought you didn't know where the keys were," she said.

"I didn't. Ryan had them. He left them on the counter yesterday, and I found them. They're hanging on the peg."

Going to the pegs near the staircase, Sarah saw one key ring had a label with "Diner" written on it. She lifted the key ring with two keys off the peg, noticing that another key ring's tag had "Camp" on it. She guessed it was for Mr. Perry's hunting camp.

"Do you want to go over to the diner with me?" Sarah asked. "Maybe we can find a clue to where your aunt is."

Chelsea shook her head. "I can't. I've got homework."

"All right," Sarah said. "I'll let you know what I find at the diner."

Chelsea didn't even turn around. "Whatever."

Sarah went to the front door, wishing there was something she could say to reach Chelsea. She couldn't imagine what words would help. She asked God to reach out to Chelsea and take her in his hands and bring her peace.

No cars were in front of the closed diner, and the unlit neon sign looked tired. Parking in the space closest to the door, Sarah got out. She climbed the steps. She was pleasantly surprised when the key slid into the lock and turned with a satisfying click. She wouldn't have been surprised if Chelsea had just slapped a "Diner" label on some random keys only to get Sarah out of her hair. Chelsea's glacial attitude made everything she said and did suspect.

The diner was silent, completely the opposite of when Sarah had last been there. In fact, she'd never been in the diner when it was quiet. Usually there were competing conversations and the sounds from the kitchen as well as the waiters and the jukebox and the frappé machine.

She flipped a switch and was glad when the lights came on. With the heat off at Ella's house, she hadn't been sure they would. She looked out the window, and saw that the neon sign on the diner and on the big sign at the other end of the parking lot remained dark.

Her footsteps sounded too loud on the black-and-white square tiles. She went along the counter, then stepped behind it. The grill and the deep fryer were covered with stainless steel lids. The shelves under the counter were empty, except for a stray straw that someone had forgotten to throw out.

Pushing through the swinging doors at the back, Sarah groped along the wall in the prep area until she found the switch. Hard fluorescent light burst on. The floor was red concrete, and the color was wearing down in the well trafficked areas. The doors of two freezers and a three-doored refrigerator were propped open to reveal bare shelves. A drip into a deep sink made a steady thump. Counters were clean and empty. Above them, shelves held cooking pots and fry pans.

Sarah went through another door at the far end. It led into a storage room where cases of straws and napkins were stacked to the ceiling. Cardboard boxes of paper plates and cups in various sizes leaned high up against the walls. Everything looked ready for the diner to open in a few weeks.

There was a second storage room as well. Sarah peeked in and saw boxes of sugar packets and ketchup bottles placed beside soup mix and jars of mustard. Large crates were labeled "Salt" and "Pepper." More nonperishables were stored along with them.

Both Ryan and Chelsea had insisted that Ella didn't plan to open the diner because she couldn't afford to. Yet hundreds of dollars of supplies sat on these shelves.

Sarah froze when she heard a man say, "Turn around slowly. Keep your hands in the air."

Sarah obeyed, holding her hands above her shoulders, fingers wide.

"Mrs. Hart!" Officer Hopkins stared at her. The Maple Hill policeman stood rooted with his hand hovering over his gun belt, the safety snap on the holster already undone. "What are you doing in here?"

"I was just looking around." She reached toward her coat pocket, then paused. "I've got the diner keys in my pocket, if you'd like to see them."

"Where did you get them?" he asked.

She withdrew the key ring. "Chelsea lent them to me, so I could see if there were any clues here about where her aunt might be. Why are you here?"

"A passing motorist saw the lights on and called it in." Officer Hopkins took the key ring, examined it, and then handed it back to her. "I better radio in the all clear." He stepped out of the room, already speaking into the radio piece on his shoulder, assuring the dispatch operator that everything was okay and he was on his way back to the station.

When Sarah went with him out into the front of the diner, Officer Hopkins switched off the lights in the back.

"Have the police checked the diner since Ella was reported missing?" Sarah asked.

"You know we can't answer questions about an ongoing investigation."

"Maybe you could just tell me if I'm wasting my time here."

He grinned and held open the front door for her. "Your efforts probably would be better spent elsewhere. That's my opinion, of course. Nothing official."

"Of course." She smiled back. "Thanks, Officer Hopkins."

"Any time, Mrs. Hart. Do you need help closing up?"

She shook her head. "I want to hang around here for a while and think." Despite the fact that Officer Hopkins had implied the police had already searched the diner, Sarah might recognize something they had missed.

"Make sure you lock the door behind me, then. When I came in, it was unlocked. Good luck with your search." He tipped his cap and left.

An hour later, Sarah switched off the last lights in the diner. Her hopes that she might find something the police had missed were dashed. She relocked the door behind her and went out into the chilly darkness.

She drove back through town. It was quiet. The grocery store and the gas station were open, but every other business had closed up for the night. Light shone out of the windows of Ella's house, but nobody answered when she knocked on the door. She tried the knob, and the door opened easily. Both Abby and Chelsea had said the door was always locked. Or had that only been when they believed valuable artifacts were in the house? Again Sarah was bothered that she couldn't remember for certain whether Chelsea had unlocked the front door the day they discovered Ella and the money were gone.

"Chelsea? Ryan?" she called as she walked in.

The house was silent.

Sarah went to the rack and hung the keys to the diner on an empty peg. She looked from the cellar door to the front parlor. Twice now when she had spoken about looking around again in the cellar, Chelsea hadn't wanted Sarah to go. The first time Chelsea had brought up the postcard from Ella, then this afternoon out of the blue she'd mentioned the diner keys.

Chelsea wanted to keep Sarah from going into the cellar. What was Chelsea trying to hide?

Sarah opened the cellar door and pulled on the cord for the bare bulb. She picked up a flashlight from a shelf in the stairwell and turned it on. She walked slowly down the uneven steps.

The cellar smelled even worse than she remembered, and the chill cut through her coat. Without the furnace's heat, there was nothing to chase away the damp.

Sarah walked to the large black oil tank. She raised the flashlight to aim it at the gauge. The fuel tank was half-full. Had Chelsea been lying to her, or had Ryan misread the gauge? It seemed more likely that it was the latter, because Sarah doubted the teens would let the house get cold if they had a choice.

The problem must be with the furnace. She went to the behemoth. She remembered a similar one from her childhood. Even then, it had been antiquated. She looked at the glass tubes along the sides. In neither of them was the small ball visible. That meant the boiler was out of water. Old steam furnaces had to be refilled by hand. Some had a fail-safe so that if the water was used up, the furnace turned off before the boiler cracked.

Sarah was surprised that Ella hadn't taught her niece and nephew how to check the furnace and add water to it. She twisted the small dial by each furnace gauge and watched as water slowly rose in the tubes. Filling the boiler took several minutes, but when the tiny balls rose in the gauges about two-thirds of the way to the top, she pushed the button to restart the furnace. It came alive with a muted groan deep within its massive bulk.

She'd show the kids how to put water in the furnace later. Her hand tightened on the flashlight. If they came home while she was down here, they'd have every right to be furious. She needed to hurry up.

She walked around the furnace and toward the debris where the wall had come down. She winced when she stepped off the concrete and into a cold puddle. The water splashed up her leg to soak her pants.

She squatted and sprayed light across the floor. A spider scurried away into the shadows. The rotted wood fell apart as she picked up one slat. She dropped it and frowned. Why hadn't she realized, after her first visit here, that the quilt wasn't dirty enough? If it had been here since the Civil War, it should have been stained all the way through instead of only on the folds.

She shifted the light toward the stud wall. She still didn't understand why a stone wall had two-by-fours behind it.

Was *that* what had been bothering her? She bent to look more closely at the carvings on the wood.

A trio of curvy lines were set between two rows of inverted vees. It did look like a map of a route through the mountains, but it could have been any mountains or any river. There were no other landmarks to identify which way to go. Two other symbols—a circle with a hole in the middle and a triangle that looked like one of the vees with a line on the bottom—were set to the right side of the curvy lines. She had no idea what they were supposed to represent.

She reached out one finger toward the deepest carving. It was one of the trio of lines. She ran her nail lightly along the bottom. Lifting her finger up into the light, she saw the undeniable fuzz of sawdust.

It was light in color, so it must be fairly fresh. She had Gerry to thank for knowing that. Her husband had spent hours on his woodworking projects, and he usually hadn't cleaned up until he was ready to start varnishing his finished project. She'd accused him of leaving piles of sawdust around for months. He'd shown her how sawdust changed and darkened as it mixed with other dust and dirt.

What was recently created sawdust doing in a carving that was supposed to be a hundred and fifty years old? She remembered Chelsea saying that the experts had warned them not to touch the carvings. Any investigation could have ruined the supposed old carvings.

Maybe the house had termites. That was possible, but the only bits of sawdust were in the carvings. That made her believe that someone had carved the diagrams not too long ago. They'd managed to dispose of the rest of the sawdust, but missed some of it. Caught up in quilt fever, no one had noticed the few flakes remaining in the grooves.

She looked up at the rafters to check that nobody had been cutting into them. They were solid. Not even a sign of dry rot. Had Chief Webber's men noticed the sawdust too? Sarah took out her phone, but the signal was too weak in the cellar. She climbed the steps, turned off the light, and slipped through the cellar door. At least now, if the kids came in, she could honestly say that she'd let herself in to return the diner key.

A creak resonated in the house. She flinched and looked up the stairs. No one was lurking in the coffin corner. She held her breath and waited for another sound. There wasn't any. It must have been the house settling in the cold. She reached for her phone.

"Chief Webber, please," Sarah said as soon as someone picked up.

Again there was a pause while the call was transferred. She waited for the chief to answer, then outlined what she'd found in the cellar. "I wanted to make sure you knew," she said as she finished.

"Fresh sawdust?" he asked, his voice all business.

"Yes."

"Stay there, Mrs. Hart. I'm sending a patrol car over. I want you to show my officers what you've found."

CHAPTER TWENTY-TWO

Officer Hopkins and another policeman spent almost half an hour in the cellar. Sarah stood to one side, staying out of their way, as they collected evidence and took photos.

"You've got good eyes, Mrs. Hart," Officer Hopkins said. "Nobody else noticed the sawdust."

"It was more a feeling that something wasn't right," Sarah said. "What do you think the fresh sawdust means?"

Officer Hopkins just gave her a look that didn't require any words.

"I know." She smiled in spite of herself. "You can't tell me anything when it's an open investigation."

"Sorry," said the other officer, "and thanks for calling us in. Do you have a key for the house? We can lock up for you when we leave."

"There should be one on the pegs in the front hall."

"Thank you, Mrs. Hart," said Officer Hopkins.

She took the hint. "You're welcome. Good night."

Her cell rang as she passed the parlor door. She fished it out of her purse and was surprised to hear Chief Webber's voice again so soon.

"The DA just gave her okay to open up the quilt," he said. "I know you'll want to get started on it right away."

"I do." She glanced at the sofa. A quilt was tossed over it. She walked in and tilted the lower right-hand corner. The red acorn that Mrs. McEvoy had embroidered was vivid on the fabric. "Can I come in tonight?"

"Sure. Let me grab a quick supper, and then I'll have the quilt ready for you. Say, in an hour?"

"I'll be there."

When Sarah walked into the police station, an officer escorted her back to the room where she'd examined the quilt before. Chief Webber stood inside, his hands clasped behind his back as he stared at the quilt as if waiting for it to give him the answers he needed.

Beside him stood a very pretty dark-haired woman who appeared to be in her midthirties, dressed in a stylish off-white suit with a coral camisole. She wore a tasteful, simple gold necklace and hoop earrings. A pair of stiletto heels made her look even taller, and Sarah guessed the woman was almost six feet tall in her stocking feet. She carried an aura of authority and intelligence.

Sarah understood why when Chief Webber said, "Mrs. Hart, I don't believe you've met Brenda Choi, the district attorney. Brenda, Mrs. Hart is our quilting expert."

Ms. Choi extended a well-manicured hand to Sarah. "It is a pleasure, Mrs. Hart. Chief Webber has told me about your clever ability to follow clues to a solution." She smiled at the chief of police. "Sometimes even before his officers can."

Chief Webber took the ribbing with a smile.

"He has also assured me," the district attorney went on, "that you understand the importance of keeping evidence as pristine as possible."

"I do," Sarah said quietly. "And I appreciate the opportunity you're allowing me, Ms. Choi."

"I hope you won't be bothered by my questions," Ms. Choi said. "I know next to nothing about quilting."

After Sarah urged the district attorney to ask whatever she wanted, Chief Webber quickly outlined what Sarah was and wasn't allowed to do with the quilt. "You still have to wear gloves while you rip out the seams. I know it'll be awkward, but we must insist on that."

"You explained that I might need to rip out seams in each corner?"

"He did," Ms. Choi said. "But let's hope you get lucky and don't have to alter the evidence any more than necessary."

Chief Webber stepped back from the table. "Mrs. Hart understands that."

Sarah couldn't help feeling pleased that Chief Webber had defended her to the district attorney. She put her quilting bag on the second table. "Do you want me to sew the seams closed again?"

"No," the district attorney said.

"That would suggest *we* were hiding something." Chief Webber smiled as he sat on the chair by the door.

Ms. Choi stepped back from the table to give Sarah room to work. She leaned one shoulder against the wall, but there was nothing casual about the way she watched every move Sarah made.

Sarah took a seam ripper and a pair of small scissors out of her bag. *Lord, I know there's a time to rend and a time to sew and a time for every purpose under heaven*, she prayed as she pulled on a pair of gloves and carried her tools over to where the quilt was spread out on the table. *And this is my purpose tonight, Lord. Rending this quilt.*

First she picked up the scissors. She clipped some of the knots that Gwen had tied with such precision in the lower right-hand corner. That was where Mrs. McEvoy had sewn her red acorns.

The work was very slow because Sarah didn't want to damage either quilt. Ms. Choi asked a few questions, then became as silent as Chief Webber when she saw how Sarah had to focus.

After Sarah had finished cutting off the knots, she drew out the threads that had tied the quilt top through the old quilt to the backing. That was the easy part.

Reaching for her seam ripper, Sarah slid it beneath the first stitch in the corner and yanked it upward with just enough pressure to snap the stitch. Working her way along the seam, she winced when she caught the tip of the seam ripper in the inner quilt's fabric, then slowly pulled it back so as not to actually rip the material.

A half hour later, she had torn out enough stitches to flip back the corner. Her eyes were tired, and her back ached. Gwen's tiny stitches made the work frustratingly slow.

Chief Webber stood and came over to the table when she set down the seam ripper. Ms. Choi moved closer too, as Sarah peeled back the fabric carefully. She could see a pattern on the binding of the inner quilt. Blackbirds had been pieced together back-to-back. Rubbing the fabric carefully, she determined it was linen.

"Anything?" Chief Webber asked.

"The quilt hidden beneath this Log Cabin top might actually be antebellum." Sarah looked up at him. "Wouldn't that be ironic?"

"But no red acorn?" asked Ms. Choi.

"Not yet," Sarah said.

"I thought you said it was in the bottom right-hand corner." Chief Webber pointed to where Sarah had drawn back the fabric.

"If the inner quilt is laid out in the same direction as the top piece."

He chuckled and ran his hand back through his hair. "Good catch, Mrs. Hart."

Moving around the table, she said, "Let me try the opposite corner. I'm sorry this is taking so long."

"Take all the time you need." He returned to his chair, and again Ms. Choi moved back from the table to give Sarah room to work.

Sarah nodded, then blinked hard several times. The stitches were beginning to blur in front of her as she concentrated on breaking the stitches. Tearing each thread without damaging the fabric was tedious work. Again, it took almost half an hour before she'd loosened enough that she could draw back the fabric to reveal the inner quilt's binding.

The same blackbird design was visible on the top of the quilt. She saw a few red stitches on the back of the inner quilt. Could it be part of the embroidered symbol that Ella's great-grandmother had put on her quilts?

Sarah tore out a few more threads and edged back the quilt top as far as it would go. "Chief Webber! Ms. Choi!"

They rushed over to the table.

"Look at this!" She turned the quilt over so they could see the tiny red acorn with initials in its center. "It's the symbol Mrs. McEvoy used."

"Good work," Ms. Choi said. "Nate, can I use your office to make some calls? I don't want my cell fading out while I report this back to my staff."

"Yes, go ahead." Chief Webber walked over to the door and, as soon as Ms. Choi had gone past him, called out to one of his officers. When a woman came to the door, he asked, "Has Hopkins returned yet from the Buttonwood house? If he has, tell him I want to talk to him now. If he hasn't, tell him to wait there. I'll be right out."

Sarah's joy at her discovery faded. By finding the embroidered acorn, she'd focused the suspicion on Ella again. The quilt had come from Ella's house. But nobody who lived there matched the description Gwen had given her of the man who'd ordered the quilt. Had Ella arranged for someone to act as a go-between?

Every step forward brought her back closer to the place she didn't want to be. She'd wanted to help Martha prove that Ella hadn't taken the money.

But who else would have done all this to mislead the town and steal all the money? She was missing a piece of the puzzle.

Again she wished Gerry was here so she could talk it over with him. She could use his calm point of view. She thought back to the psalm that John had preached on Sunday.

My rock and fortress, she thought. *Guide me.* She needed that guidance more than ever tonight.

Sarah was deep in a dream when she was jolted awake by the phone ringing. Rolling over, she groped on the night stand for the phone.

"Good morning?" Sarah asked groggily.

"Sarah, it's Martha!" came her friend's excited voice. "You'll never believe what I just got in the mail."

"Don't make me play guessing games before I've had my coffee," she said, only half-joking. She glanced at her clock. It was past nine. She couldn't remember the last time she'd slept that late. It had taken her a long time to get to sleep last night as she arranged and rearranged and arranged again all the facts she had. She still hadn't come up with any answer other than Ella had stolen the money.

"I got a postcard from Ella," Martha said.

Sarah sat up. "Ella Buttonwood?"

"Of course, Ella Buttonwood."

"What does it say?"

"Why don't I bring it over so you can see it?" Martha asked.

"Good. I've got a lot to tell you too. About Ella's quilt."

"Put the coffeepot on. I'll be right over."

Sarah hung up the phone. She quickly dressed in a pair of dark slacks and a bright-colored blouse. She hoped the brilliant yellow would keep her awake until she managed to drink some coffee. After brushing her teeth and her hair, she hurried downstairs.

The coffee had finished brewing by the time Martha arrived, waving a postcard. "I couldn't believe it when I saw this in my mailbox. Ella sent it from Bennington, Vermont." She held it out for Sarah to read.

Martha,

Having a great time here at my retreat. I'm learning so much, and I think it's going to be a great help.

"Retreat?" Sarah said.

"I've been wracking my brain trying to figure it out, but I can't. She must have told me about it at some point in time and I just don't remember. The memory isn't what it used to be, you know. But she wouldn't have sent me a postcard if she was hiding out with the money!"

"It does seem that way." Sarah turned her attention to the Bennington postmark on the card.

Bennington wasn't much more than a half hour north of Maple Hill. Flipping the postcard over, she saw a picture of a stone obelisk. The words, "Bennington Monument," were printed at the bottom right of the card.

"Look at the postcard," Sarah said. "Do you see what's on the front? It's the *Bennington* Monument."

"I saw that. Do you think she went to Bennington after she left Saratoga?"

"Martha, I'm not sure Ella ever went to Saratoga." She poured two cups of coffee and handed one to Martha. "When Chelsea showed me the postcard, she said it was from Saratoga. I didn't look that closely at the picture on the postcard. The two monuments resemble each other, especially the tops of the obelisks." She picked up her coffee cup and took a sip. "C'mon. Let's look at some pictures of the two side by side."

Picking up her coffee cup, Sarah led the way into her sewing room. She switched on her computer. While it was booting up, she told Martha about what she'd found in the cellar and with the quilt.

Martha sat heavily on the desk chair. "But that doesn't make any sense. Why would Ella go to all this trouble to run away and then send me a postcard?"

"I don't know what to think at this point, Martha. I know there's something that we've all overlooked. Something that's been staring us right in the face."

It didn't take long for Sarah to find images of the Saratoga and Bennington monuments. The upper third of the Saratoga obelisk was almost identical to the upper third of the Bennington Monument. Both looked like miniatures of the Washington Monument with small windows near the top. But the lower portions of the monuments were very different. The Saratoga Monument had pointed and rounded gothic arches cut into the sides of the obelisk. At the bottom, doorways were set between stone risers that climbed up to support the largest pointed arches. The Bennington Monument was far simpler. Only a pair of slit windows interrupted the simplicity of the lower third of the monument.

"The postcard Chelsea showed me was definitely the Saratoga Monument," Sarah said. "The one you got is definitely the Bennington one." She pushed back from the computer. "But how do we know if Ella's really in Bennington? Saratoga turned out to be a wild goose chase."

"We know she's at a retreat." Martha turned the card over to the writing again. "But she doesn't say what kind or where."

"Okay, let's search some more." Sarah opened a search engine and looked for retreats in Bennington, Vermont.

The results tended toward general listings for cabins and hotels in the Green Mountains, not specific retreat events. Beginning again, she tried multiple different word combinations, trying to get more specific information. Martha alternately leaned over Sarah's shoulder and walked back and forth to the kitchen to refill their coffee cups.

It was slow work, but finally Sarah said, "Okay, Martha, here's what I've found. A retreat for collage artists at Bennington College. A retreat for collectors of Bennington Pottery at the Paradise Inn. There's a retreat for descendants of Ethan Allen at the Four Chimneys and another at Southern Vermont College for memoir writers." She looked up from the list. "But here's the one I think we should check out. It's a retreat for financial planning at the Bennington Inn. If the stories about Ella's money troubles are true, then she might be there."

"That has to be it!" Martha said. "What are we waiting for? Let's go and find Ella."

Sarah smiled. She was starting to get just as excited as Martha was that they might actually be on Ella's trail. But she didn't want to waste another afternoon in the car.

"Let's call first and see if Ella is registered." Sarah read off the inn's number for Martha, who punched it into her cell phone.

Sarah listened closely to Martha's end of the conversation, but couldn't tell if it was good news or bad news. She leaned forward, as if the physical movement would allow her to piece the conversation together better.

"Well," Martha said after she ended the call, "that wasn't much help. The woman at the front desk said all the reservations were paid by the retreat organizers, so they don't know the names of the people attending. Then when people signed up, they just had to pay one fee to the organizers for their meals and the sessions. Apparently the attendees aren't staying at that hotel. When I asked if she could direct me to the retreat organizers, she said they were teaching all day."

Martha looked so defeated, there was only one thing to do for her friend.

Sarah stood. "Then it looks like we're going to Bennington!"

CHAPTER TWENTY-THREE

The Bennington Inn was in the northern part of the city, not far from Bennington College. Smaller than the Isaac Schuyler, the inn was set among thick pine trees. The road leading up to it showcased its colonnade of white pillars across the front. Tall windows were set in precise rows on each of the five floors facing the road. Every window was divided into twelve small panes of wavy glass.

Sarah wondered, while she parked the car in the nearly empty lot, if they had done the right thing in not calling Chief Webber. She didn't want to send out the cavalry if this was a dead end just like Saratoga. In the end, she thought it was best to wait to call the police.

"Ready?" Sarah asked.

Martha nodded, but she looked much less gung ho than she had when she had burst into Sarah's house that morning, waving the postcard. She knew Martha now shared her uncertainty about finding Ella and what they'd do if they did. They'd spent a good portion of the half hour drive north

discussing how to confront Ella without sending her fleeing. They had a few ideas but nothing concrete. They would
have to wait and see how Ella reacted to them showing up
at her retreat. That is, if she was here.

As they walked to the front steps, Sarah glanced behind
her. The tip of the Bennington Monument could be seen
above the trees. Beyond it, the mountains rose, their white
tops blending with the low clouds.

"Looks like it's snowing hard up on the mountains,"
Sarah said.

"That'll keep the ski resort owners happy," Martha said.
"And they're welcome to it. I'm ready for spring."

The interior of the hotel was tastefully decorated with
clean lines and muted colors. A color-blocked runner ran
the length of the brightly polished oak floors. The ceiling
was laced with thick rafters hung with pierced tin lamps, the
light making entrancing patterns on the blue walls.

"This way," Sarah said, seeing a sign for the registration
desk. The registration area was far simpler than at the Isaac
Schuyler. It was around the corner in a generous space with
bleached wainscoting. A dark-haired man wearing a gold
vest beneath a navy blue coat stood behind the high counter.

He looked up and smiled as they approached. "Good afternoon, ladies. Are you checking in?"

"No," Sarah said. "We're looking for the financial planning retreat. Can you tell us where it is?"

"That's being held in the Monument Room." He pulled
out a map and opened it on the counter. "We're here," he

said, pointing to a spot in the very center. "The Monument Room is down the left corridor. Go to the end of the corridor and turn right. It will be the third door on your right."

"Thank you."

The clerk nodded and, excusing himself, turned to answer a ringing phone.

Sarah and Martha followed the clerk's directions along a pretty corridor. The lower part of the wall had the same wainscoting as the registration area. The upper was decorated with photographs of various scenes around Bennington. The local colleges, the monument, the sign in front of a landmark fish fry, the museums.

"Turn right here," Sarah said when the corridor merged with another. Chairs lined the wall, and a table held sodas, bottles of water, and a coffee urn.

Next to a closed double door, an easel held a poster board sign that read "Make Your Future What *You* Want It to Be: Retirement Made Simple" printed in bold black letters.

"This is it." Sarah slowly opened one of the double doors, trying to make as little noise as possible.

The retreat must have been between sessions, because no one stood by the microphone at the front. She opened the door fully. People milled around and talked in small groups.

"There she is!" Martha said. "Over by the windows."

Martha quickly crossed the room, Sarah only a step behind. Ella, dressed in the suit she'd worn to the museum fund-raiser, was talking with a man near to her age. The same suit and, Sarah realized, her family's heirloom pearls.

The man paused in what he was saying as he realized Martha and Sarah were approaching them. Ella did too.

Sarah held her breath. What would Ella do?

"Martha! Sarah!" Ella asked with a puzzled smile. "What are you doing here?"

"Ella, you've got no idea how happy we are that *you're* here." Martha hugged her friend. "We've been looking everywhere for you."

"Why didn't you ask Ryan or Chelsea? They know where I am. In fact, they talked me into attending this retreat." She smiled more genuinely. "They even suggested I leave my cell at home, so I could have a nice quiet vacation before I open the diner next month."

"You're opening the diner?" Sarah asked.

"Of course I am. I always open on the first day of April. First thing in the morning, so all the fishermen have a place to have breakfast. Why wouldn't I this year?" Ella laughed. "Oh you saw the sign outside. I'm not retiring. I'm *planning* what I need to do when I retire. I want to figure out how to arrange for my retirement while still making sure the kids have everything they need for college."

When Martha opened her mouth to ask another question, Sarah glanced around at the other people attending the seminar. She said, "Maybe we should talk out in the hall."

Martha seconded the suggestion, and Ella went with them.

Once they were out in the deserted corridor and the conference room door was shut behind them, Sarah said,

"Ella, you need to come back to Maple Hill with us right away."

"Right away?" Her face grew pale. "Is there something wrong with the kids?"

"No, but the police need to talk to you."

Ella sighed deeply. "Ryan and Chelsea promised me that they wouldn't have any parties while I was away. I hope they didn't disturb the whole neighborhood."

"It's not that." Sarah took Ella's hand and sat down, Ella following her lead.

"What's going on?" she asked.

"Ella," Sarah said, "the Maple Hill police are looking for you and the money from the fund-raiser for the Underground Railroad exhibit."

"What?" Ella looked from Sarah to Martha and back again. "Why?"

"When you left town, no one knew where you went. They thought you took the money."

"But the money's in the bank."

Sarah shook her head. "No, it isn't. That's why the police are looking for you. Do you know where the money is?"

"I thought it was in the bank. Where else could it be?"

Sarah asked, "Ella, did you take the money to the bank yourself?"

She frowned. "I think so. I dropped off several things at the bank the day after the fund-raiser. I had so much stuff between the fund-raiser and getting ready to open the Miss Maple, I had to use a couple different cash bags to take it all in. And then Chelsea had banking to do for our household account, so we ended up splitting the work. She and Ryan went to the bank again that afternoon."

"But you aren't sure if you put the money into the bank?" asked Martha. "Good heavens, Ella! It's thousands of dollars! How could you not double-check that it was in the bank?"

"Everything was so chaotic that day," Ella said. "I was so exhausted from the fund-raiser, I let the kids persuade me to leave early for the retreat. That way, I could do some sightseeing and shopping to relax before it started. I knew I wouldn't have a chance to go anywhere for the rest of the year, especially with the work we'll be doing on the museum, so I tossed some things in a suitcase and left."

Sarah sighed and glanced again at Martha. How could she have forgotten that Ella didn't know that the quilt and the carvings were both fake?

"I have something to tell you," Sarah said as she gently patted Ella's hand. "It's not going to be easy to hear."

"Are the kids okay?"

"The kids are okay, but the museum isn't." Sarah went through the events of the past week.

As she listened, Ella kept repeating, "I can't believe this! I can't believe this!"

"It's true," Martha said.

"I was so certain the quilt was real and that my grandmother's stories were true too," Ella said. "I wanted those stories to be real, but she must have just told them to entertain me when I was a kid. I was stupid to be that naïve. What do we do now?"

"Come back with us to Maple Hill," Sarah said, "and help us sort this out. Will you?"

"Yes." Ella stood. "I want to know what's going on too."

CHAPTER TWENTY-FOUR

||||||||||||||||||||||||||||||||||||||||||||||||||||||||||||||||||||||||||||||||||||||||||||||||||||||||

B y the time Sarah stopped in front of the Buttonwood house an hour later, her back ached with the stress of the day. She wished she had been able to ride back to Maple Hill with Ella. The car ride home would have been the perfect time to hear Ella's side of the story about her finances. But she understood Martha's need to ride home with Ella. Sarah was sure the two friends had a lot to catch up on, and she knew that Martha would share any important information as soon as she could.

Ella and Martha pulled up right behind Sarah's car. Sarah waited on the sidewalk until the other ladies joined her.

"Will you ladies mind waiting with me until the kids get home from school?" Ella asked. "I think I'm going to need some moral support when I confront the kids about what you and Sarah told me."

"Of course," Martha said.

Sarah would have preferred to go to her own home and fix herself a lunch full of comfort food. It would be so hard to watch Ella ask Chelsea and Ryan to explain the stories they had told.

And why.

That's what worried Sarah the most. Why had the kids lied about their aunt's whereabouts?

Sarah said, "If you want, I can call Chief Webber now, so he can come and hear your side of the story before you talk to Chelsea and Ryan."

"No!" Ella shook her head. "I don't want the cops here now. Maybe it's just a terrible misunderstanding."

"We'll need to contact the police eventually."

"I know, but let me talk to the kids first. Please."

Sarah just nodded.

They followed Ella up onto the porch and stood back as she fumbled in her purse for her key and unlocked the door. They went inside.

"I hope the kids come right home from school," Ella said. "I don't want to keep you here waiting too long."

"I don't think you'll see them here anytime soon," said Abby as she stepped out of the shadowy front parlor.

"Abby! What are you doing here?" Ella asked.

Instead of answering, Abby said, "I guess I was right all along."

"What do you mean?" Sarah asked.

"Sarah, was the idea to use a quilt to fool Maple Hill yours or Ella's?" She glanced at Martha. "Or was it hers?"

"None of ours," Ella said. "Abby, why are you here, and what did you mean about the kids?"

"I don't know where they are, but I know they're not at school. And I sure would like to know where you've been and why you're back now."

Ella pulled off her coat and tossed it over the quilt on the back of the sofa. "I'm back because I live here. Tell me. Why are *you* here, Abby?"

"For the same reason I've been here all along. To get the story." Abby turned to Sarah. "The police won't tell me what you found in the cellar. What was it?"

"You'll have to wait for the police to release that information," Sarah said, taking off her own coat.

"And do you deny being a part of this plan from the beginning?"

"Me?" Sarah asked.

"Sarah?" Ella asked at the same time.

"Why not?" Abby flipped a page of the notebook and scanned her notes. "You were the one, Sarah, who first said the quilt could be authentic, which set the fund-raising in motion. Suddenly Ella is being handed big bucks."

Sarah sighed. All the guilt she'd felt because she'd let herself get caught up in the quilt fever came back. She sat on the sofa and shook her head. "Abby, the only thing I'm guilty of is a bad case of quilt fever. I should have insisted that Ella let me examine the quilt more closely before I even made a guess about its age, but I didn't. I loved the idea of something wonderful like an Underground Railroad museum in Maple Hill. But I know you didn't."

Abby stopped writing. "Are you saying that you think I'm the thief?"

"No," said Sarah. "Not any longer. But you've got to admit that you acted strangely when I found you here after Ella was reported missing and we found the money was gone too. And you were sneaking around on my porch."

"I was following up on my story." Abby lowered the notebook and looked at all three women. "And I wasn't sneaking around your house, Ella. You know that I had a key." She looked at Ella. "Tell them that you gave me a key to the house."

"Yes, I did give you a key, and I told you to hang it right there when you were done taking photos." She pointed to the rack of keys by the stairs.

Sarah looked at the rack. One of the pegs was empty.

"Well, the money is missing," Abby said. "Who took it if Ella didn't?"

Sarah opened her mouth to reply, but she was interrupted by a heavy knock at the front door.

Ella got up and went to open it.

Two police officers, a man and a woman, stood on the front porch. Neither smiled as the woman asked, "May we come in?"

Ella stepped aside to let them into the front hall.

"We got a call that Miss Buttonwood's car was seen on the street," the female officer said. "Are you Miss Buttonwood?"

"Yes, I'm Ella Buttonwood." Ella's voice was unruffled, just as it was when she served as town meeting moderator. "How can I help you?"

"Miss Buttonwood, you need to come with us," The female police officer said. "We have a warrant for your arrest on grand larceny and fraud."

Ella's chin tilted up. For the first time, Sarah saw a resemblance between Ella and Chelsea. They both had that cool arrogance that implied they could remake the world in their own image. "I'm not guilty. I didn't take the money."

"Ma'am, you should listen to your rights before you say anything," the female officer said.

The male officer began to read Ella her rights. "You have the right to remain silent. Anything—"

"I don't have anything to hide because I haven't done anything wrong," Ella said, stubborn as always.

"Ella," Sarah said, "just listen."

Ella glanced at her and complied.

Sarah breathed a soft sigh of relief that, for once, Ella had heeded her.

"You have the right to an attorney," the male officer continued his litany until he had run through everything the law required him to say. "Do you understand your rights, Miss Buttonwood?"

"I do." Ella turned away from him. "Sarah, would you call your son? I trust him to help me."

"Of course," Sarah said.

"You can tell him we've brought Miss Buttonwood to the police station to book her," the female officer said.

Sarah hesitated, then gave Ella a hug. It didn't matter that they weren't close friends. Ella needed to know she wasn't alone. "I'll call Jason right now. Don't say anything until he gets there. Promise me."

"I promise."

Martha handed Ella her coat, then stepped back to sit on the stairs as the police officers guided Ella out of the house and to their car. Sarah saw neighbors gathering to watch. Next to her, Abby was taking notes.

Sarah opened her purse and pulled out her phone. Her fingers shook while she pressed the key to call Jason's work number. It rang once, then twice.

"Jason Hart," came her son's voice.

"Jason, it's Mom."

"Hi! What's up?"

"Jason, I found Ella."

"That's great!" he said. "I knew if anyone could find her, it'd be you, Mom."

Her words tumbled over each other in her haste to pass along the news. "She didn't take the money, but the police just arrested her."

Jason became serious. "Are you certain she didn't take the money?"

"Yes. Can you go down to the police station and advise her on what to do?"

There was a pause, and she heard him sigh. "I can't go immediately. I'm waiting for a call from a judge who may be able to help with opening the adoption files. He's supposed to call in about ten minutes. As soon as I'm done pleading my case with him, I'll go to the police station and talk to Ella. It shouldn't be more than half an hour. Do you think she'll be able to wait that long?"

"I'm sure she will."

"Good. Oh there's my other line. Got to go."

"Thank you, Jason," Sarah said, but he was already gone to answer his other call. Putting away her phone, she whispered a prayer that Jason would be able to help both Ella and Phyllis.

Abby asked, "Is your son going to represent Ella?"

"I don't know," Sarah said. "You'll have to ask him that. Let me ask you a question, Abby."

"Look," Abby said. "I've got to go. The story's at the police station now." She rushed out of the house, the door slamming shut behind her.

Martha stood slowly and went over to the door.

Sarah went into the parlor and got their coats. "Martha," she said as she put hers on, "one thing that Ella told us bothers me. She said that there were so many things to take to the bank, Chelsea and Ryan ended up taking a trip themselves. What if the fund-raiser money was with them and not in the original things Ella brought to put in the bank? What if whoever made the deposit—or even both of them together—decided to keep the money for themselves?"

"Oh dear! It certainly fits, Sarah."

"It does. It had to have been someone in this house who faked the carving and the quilt. All the heavy traffic didn't come through until after the plans for the museum started. And neither of the kids has acted really eager to have their aunt come back. Abby claims they aren't at school." She pointed to an empty peg on the key rack. "But I know where they went."

CHAPTER TWENTY-FIVE

Clouds rolled down over the mountains as Sarah drove up the narrow road. The day's light was sucked into the gray sky, and the trees edging the road stole what remained, leaving the road as dark as night.

Sarah was thankful that Martha was with her. Her friend kept her eyes focused on the road too, pointing out when Sarah was getting too close to the trees on the right side of the road. As they drove up the rutted road toward Mr. Perry's hunting camp, they bounced in and out of potholes. The thickening darkness seemed to swallow even the headlights.

If Martha hadn't called to slow down, Sarah might have driven right into the gate at the edge of Mr. Perry's property. Sarah turned the car to aim the headlights at the gate. It was partially open.

"That's a good sign," Martha said.

Sarah smiled at her friend. Martha's optimism was what she needed now when her thoughts were on what awaited them up the road.

Nosing her car slowly forward, Sarah got as close to the gate as possible so Martha could get out and push it the rest of the way open. When Martha opened the car door, the icy wind filled the car instantly. By the time Sarah drove through the gate and Martha hopped back in, her friend was shivering.

"I'm sorry, Martha, I should have offered to get out this time," Sarah said.

"Oh I don't mind." Martha said, though she held her hands up to the vents spilling warm air into the car. "I'm the reason we're out here in the first place. If I hadn't asked you to help me find Ella, we'd be snug in our houses right now."

Icy snow tapped against the windshield. It began to swirl in the headlights and the trees around them swayed like synchronized swimmers in a gray pool. Sarah switched to low beams and hoped the storm would blow past before it dropped much snow. Another gust sent a curtain of snow at the car.

Gravel rattled under the tires, and Sarah breathed a hearty sigh of relief. That meant they were getting close to the hunting cabin.

Suddenly they were in the clearing. Lamplight glowed from the cabin's windows, making the fresh snow sparkle. To her right, Sarah noticed a snow-covered car. She pulled her own up behind it.

"That's the right shape for Chelsea's car," Sarah said.

"Looks like you were right about where they'd be."

Sarah reached for the door handle and pushed the door open. The wind tried to snatch it from her hands. She got out, then grabbed the door and forced it closed. Snow stung her face, and she wished she'd brought a scarf. Shoving her hands in the pockets of her coat, she walked to the front of the car and waited for Martha.

Together, she and Martha struggled through the wind-driven snow to the cabin. Every few steps, Sarah raised her head to check that the lights were still on. She hoped, if the kids saw her and Martha coming, they wouldn't panic and run away into the storm. That could be a fatal mistake.

Sarah walked up onto the porch. She whispered a quiet prayer for God's help in saying the right thing and opened the door.

Two young men looked toward the door and froze. She recognized Ryan, who sat in front of the fire. Another young man, maybe a year or so older than Ryan, stood on the stairs. He matched Gwen's description of the man who'd ordered the quilt. Tall, very thin, dark-haired.

"Who are you?" she asked as she walked in.

He seemed taken aback by her question. He didn't speak, only stared at her and Martha, who closed the door.

"What are you doing here?" asked Ryan as he stood.

Sarah directed her question to him. "Who's that?"

"He's Chelsea's boyfriend," Ryan said as Eric walked down the stairs to stand next to him. "What are you doing here?"

Sarah remembered seeing Eric at Liam's when he had asked her to sign the petition, but Sarah hadn't gotten a good look at him. His thick parka and cap had hidden his skinny frame and hair color.

Now Eric was looking around, his eyes fixing on everything and nothing in particular. Sarah hoped there wasn't a back door. She and Martha stayed between the boys and the front door.

"Is Chelsea here?" Martha asked.

Both boys nodded.

"She's upstairs," Eric said.

"What are you doing here?" Ryan asked again.

Sarah kept her voice calm, but stern. "Ryan, your aunt has been arrested and is in jail."

Ryan's face lost all color. "No! That's impossible."

"We were there when the police took her to the station."

Eric hit Ryan's arm. "You said she wouldn't come back until next week. That we'd have time to figure out where we'd go."

"We don't know they're telling the truth," Ryan said.

"Why would we lie to you?" Sarah asked as she unbuttoned her coat. The heat from the hearth was powerful in the cabin. "From the beginning, I've only been trying to help you."

"You snooped around our house," Ryan fired back. "And you called the cops to snoop around our house. Don't you think—"

His cell buzzed. He reached in his pocket and looked at the screen. "Aunt Ella!"

"You'd better answer it," Sarah said.

Ryan flipped open the phone and sank to the couch, but didn't say anything. Eric looked from him to Sarah and Martha, but didn't move.

"Hello? Hello?" Sarah heard from the phone.

She took the phone from Ryan. "Ella, it's Sarah."

"You found the kids?"

"Yes."

"Where?"

She kept her eye on the two boys, not wanting them to know what Ella was asking. "They're safe. I know you're worried about them."

There was a pause. "Are you at the diner?" Ella asked.

She was glad Ella had understood her need to keep things quiet. "No."

"The hunting lodge?"

"That's right."

Ella paused, then said, "Chief Webber said to tell you that he's sending a couple of officers. Try to keep everyone there."

"Okay." Sarah clicked off the phone. She held it out to Ryan, but he didn't take it.

"We never meant for her to get arrested!"

Sarah was tempted to ask him what he had expected to happen, but she wanted to keep the boys talking.

"Why don't you ask Chelsea to come down?"

"She won't." Eric sat and slammed his fist against the sofa's arm. "She's locked herself in up there."

Martha asked, "Are you sure she's still there?"

"Her jacket and shoes are down here," Ryan said. "Plus, she wouldn't go without me and Eric."

Wind screeched around the eaves, and snow scratched at the windows. Sarah exchanged a glance with Martha. The storm was getting stronger. Would the police cars make it up the mountain... and back down?

"Why did you come up here?" asked Martha. "Didn't you know someone would look for you here?"

"Chelsea suggested that we come here to hide because you and the cops and that snoopy reporter had already been here." Ryan stabbed his toe against the space between two floorboards. "We thought we could hide out here and decide what to do next."

"With the money you stole?" asked Sarah.

Eric's head snapped up, but Ryan said, "Yes."

"What are you doing?" Eric asked. "Shut up."

"Why?" Ryan stood, his hands at his sides. "They know, Eric. Game over."

"It is if you don't shut up!" Eric got up and stepped closer to the younger boy.

Sarah tried to distract them. She didn't want the teens to come to blows. "I still can't figure out how you did it all. Whose idea was it to plant the quilt in the cellar?" She asked.

"It was my idea." Ryan clearly wanted to get everything out in the open. Sarah wondered how badly guilt had gnawed at him. "When Chelsea and I first saw the wall falling down last summer, I said there should have been a stash of treasure behind it. She said that maybe there was. All we had to do was pretend we'd found something that would get everyone excited. I put the stones back and we waited until we got everything ready to go this spring."

Eric glared at Ryan, but added his own take on the story. "Ryan's blabbed everything, but he's wrong. The idea was mine. When Chelsea told me about the wall, I asked her what she'd found behind it. She told me that she hadn't found anything, but wouldn't it be amazing if she had? Then she could get enough money to go to Williams College with me."

Both had believed the idea of bilking the town was his own, but Chelsea had prompted both of them to come up with the scheme. Sarah thought of how often Ryan had taken his cues from his sister. Had Chelsea manipulated them?

"We thought we'd gotten away with it." Ryan blinked rapidly, and Sarah saw tears in his eyes. "Now Aunt Ella is in jail."

Sarah felt sorry for them, but she had to know the truth. "Why did you use a quilt for your scheme?"

"We got the idea when we were watching *Bargain Squad* one night," Ryan answered as Eric muttered something and sat heavily on the sofa again. "It was Aunt Ella's favorite show."

"The show about the person who found a really valuable quilt at a yard sale?" Sarah asked.

"Yeah, and it got us thinking." Ryan stared at the toes of his boots. "If someone would pay that much money for a plain old antique quilt, how much would they pay for one that might be connected to the Underground Railroad? Eric—" He avoided looking at his sister's boyfriend. "He'd found out about the slave quilt code while doing a paper in history last fall."

Sarah heard a soft sound from overhead. Footsteps? She didn't look up, not wanting to distract the boys when they were spilling the truth. "Didn't you realize it would be examined by experts before it was accepted as legitimate?"

"We figured," Ryan said, "it would take some time. After all, a quilt doesn't have a serial number, and we didn't think anyone could trace it back to us." He grimaced. "We didn't count on you, Mrs. Hart, being so persistent."

"Yet you used one of your aunt's great-grandmother's quilts for the batting in the new quilt." Sarah rested her hands on her knees. Again she heard the soft sound. Martha must have too, because she looked toward the stairs.

"You think you're so smart," Chelsea said from the open area at the top of the stairs. "If Eric and Ryan hadn't made so many mistakes, you wouldn't have caught us."

No one spoke as Chelsea came down the stairs. She stopped only a foot from where Sarah sat.

Chelsea raised her chin and looked down her nose at Sarah. "I didn't make any mistakes," Chelsea said. "I was the only one who did anything to keep you from finding out the truth."

"By sending me on wild goose chases whenever I got too close to the truth?" Sarah met Chelsea's eyes steadily.

Chelsea's voice remained cool and composed. "I honestly thought you'd get tired and give up, but you didn't. How did you find Aunt Ella?"

"It's funny—she really did send Mrs. Maplethorpe a post-card," Sarah said. "We met your aunt at the financial planning retreat where she had gone to make sure both you and Ryan would have enough money for college."

"If she hadn't squandered our parents' money," Ryan said as he came to stand by his sister, "she wouldn't have to worry about it now."

"But she hasn't spent a penny of the money your parents left you," Martha said. She looked at Sarah, then back to the kids. "We had a good chat on the way back from Bennington. There's money for college. Enough for both you and Chelsea to attend any college you want."

"What?" asked Ryan.

Eric jumped up and stood right in front of Chelsea. "Is this true?" When she didn't respond, he leaned his face even closer to hers. "Why would you put us through this for nothing?"

"It wasn't for nothing. I've been handling Aunt Ella's accounts for the past two years," Chelsea said, "so I know every penny we'll get and where it is."

"Just the household ones," Ryan said.

"No, everything." Chelsea tilted her chin. "It started with the household accounts, but then I convinced her to let me take over the business ones too. I know every penny that comes in or out of the house or the diner."

"So if you knew you had enough money for college, why steal the money from the fund-raiser?" Martha asked.

Chelsea dismissed her with a wintry smile. "Because the money our parents left us is in a trust that can only be used for our education. I'm not going to college."

"You've got to be kidding," Eric said.

"I'm tired of being a waitress who nobody pays attention to," Chelsea said. "I want everyone to notice me when I walk by. As soon as I graduate from high school, I'm taking the money and heading to New York or Hollywood to start my acting career."

The two boys exploded into shouts that rang up to the room's high ceiling. Chelsea paid them no attention. She simply sat on the couch and pretended she couldn't hear them.

It took several minutes, but there was a moment of silence when the boys paused to take a breath at the same time.

Sarah heard someone knock on the door. She opened it to see Officer Hopkins and another policeman frosted with snow. She wondered how long they'd been knocking.

They came into the cabin, and the two boys took a step back.

"We don't have time to waste," Officer Hopkins said, holding up one hand. "We need to get you to Maple Hill while we can still get down the mountain. Get your coats and the money, and come with us."

Eric walked over to Chelsea. "Where's the money?"

She didn't answer.

"Chelsea! We've got to go."

"You go. I'm not," she said.

"Yes, you are." Eric took her arm and brought her to her feet. "It's over."

"Even us?" Her voice came out in a soft sob.

A real emotion or another act? Sarah wasn't sure, and she could see that Eric wasn't either.

"Where's the money, Chelsea?" he asked, but there was a quaver in his voice.

She said nothing.

"I know where it is," Ryan said quietly. He walked toward the stairs.

"No!" Chelsea shouted. "Don't tell them. I need that money." She ran at her brother.

Officer Hopkins grabbed her before she reached Ryan. The other officer went upstairs to follow Ryan's directions and find the money under a floorboard near the chimney. In just minutes, the officer came downstairs with a large shoe-box.

Chelsea lost it, screaming at her brother and her boyfriend as well as everyone else in the cabin. Neither policeman paid her any mind as they insisted she put on her coat and go with them. She resisted for a second before snatching the coat from Officer Hopkins's grasp and walking out between the two officers, her head high.

"Ladies, you'd better ride down with us too," Officer Hopkins said with a glance toward Sarah and Martha. "We've got four-wheel drive."

Sarah nodded. She'd have her son drive her up later to retrieve her car. They'd have no trouble in Maggie's Tahoe once the storm was over.

"We'll be right out." Sarah went over to the boys. Eric just hurried after Chelsea.

"We're going to jail, aren't we?" asked Ryan. His voice shook.

"I don't know." She put her arm around his shoulders and gave him a gentle squeeze. "But I know your aunt Ella will do everything to make sure you don't."

"But what if—"

Sarah stopped his question with another squeeze. "Trust God, Ryan."

"Why would he help me now? We've lied and we've stolen and we've hurt Aunt Ella." Two thick tears rolled down his cheeks. "She'll never forgive us."

She smiled gently. "Ella loves you, no matter what. Just as God does. Now let's go."

Ryan gave the cabin's key to Sarah, and she locked the door after she and Martha had turned off the lights. They went to the police car and climbed in. The kids were crammed in the large SUV's third-row seat, Ryan sandwiched between Chelsea and Eric. As Officer Hopkins drove down the mountain toward Maple Hill, the only sound above the steady rumble of the engine was Ryan's occasional sobs.

 EPILOGUE

Sarah gave Liam a wave as she came into the café. He smiled and waved back, then asked if she wanted her usual. She nodded, glad everyone was smiling today. The late winter storm that had swept over the town last week was long gone and with it, the last remains of the snow. Spring had returned, bringing with it a white carpet of snowdrops and crocuses.

Martha was waiting at a table by the window. She barely let Sarah sit down before she said, "I got a call on the way here from Ella. All the charges against her have been dropped."

"And the kids?"

"They're getting help."

Sarah picked up the menu and scanned it for the day's Irish special. She decided to have the colcannon soup, anticipating the flavors of cabbage, leeks, and potatoes.

"Social services will be stepping in to help Ella and Chelsea and Ryan." Martha said. "I'm sure they'll be spending time with Eric and his parents too."

"It's a shame that beautiful girl thinks she needs plastic surgery," Sarah said and looked up. Liam had come to take their order. "I hope they help Chelsea come to see how pretty she is."

"Pretty on the outside," Liam said as he set two cups in front of them. "But she needs to discover how to be as lovely on the inside." He took their orders, then said, "In case you haven't heard, Fred has stopped the recall petitions. He said he was sorry for allowing the lesson to get out of hand."

"He called and apologized for not reaching me beforehand," Martha said. "He didn't realize I was upset until you spoke with him. He should have realized that he was lighting a keg of dynamite when everyone was upset."

"I think," Sarah said, "he had other things on his mind." She didn't explain further. She'd promised Fred not to say anything about his secret career as a novelist.

Liam winked at her before heading back to the kitchen.

Sarah spotted Jason walking by the window. He waved, then came into the café. He wore a dark suit and stylish tie. Sarah could see his father in his smile. It was a beloved sight.

"I thought I'd see if you were here," Jason said as he gave Sarah a hug and greeted Martha. He sat between them.

"What's up?" Sarah asked. "You look pretty pleased."

He waited while Liam put two bowls of fragrant soup on the table. "Phyllis asked me," Jason said, "to tell you that your suggestion about her grandmother's letters paid off. She brought them to me as soon as they arrived from Chicago. After I'd read them over, I presented them to the judge. He reviewed the court record and agreed to unseal the adoption records. Phyllis just called me to say they're having a very special family reunion this afternoon."

"Phyllis found her aunts already?" Sarah asked.

"One lives in Pittsfield, and the other lives north of Saratoga. They're meeting at a restaurant in Williamstown. She wanted me to tell you that she can't thank you enough for helping bring her family back together."

Sarah reached for a tissue in her purse. She pulled it out and dabbed at her eyes. "I'm glad I could help, and I'm glad you could help too."

Jason gave Sarah another hug. "Since we've moved back to Maple Hill, I've really come to understand how important it is for families to remain connected. I thought I knew that before, but with every passing day, I'm more certain that every family—and their good friends—creates its own unique patterns of love."

"Yes," Sarah said, turning to Martha and squeezing her hand. "And you've proved that a good friend, as you've been to Ella, is a true gift."

"Hear, hear!" said Martha as she clinked her cup on Sarah's. "To friends and family."

ABOUT THE AUTHOR

Jo Ann Brown has published more than eighty titles under various names. Her most recent book was the novelization for Thomas Kinkade's *Christmas Cottage* movie. Raised in a small town, she served as a US Army officer. She has lived in New England most of her life along with her husband and her three children and two very spoiled cats.

BOUND IN LOVE

BY CAMY TANG

 CHAPTER ONE

"Come on, girls!" Sarah Hart called to her twin grand-daughters as she left the warmth of the spring sunshine to enter the Maple Hill Library.

The rich smell of books greeted her. There was something in the air in the library that made her feel complete. Maybe it was being surrounded by so much wisdom, so many stories told by so many people. Her granddaughters, Amy and Audrey, seemed oblivious to what was in the air. They immediately headed toward the teen section at the back of the library.

"Wait just a minute," Sarah said. "Didn't you girls say you had to work on your research papers?"

Audrey changed direction without even rolling her eyes, but Amy spoke up. "Grandma, can't we just go see what new graphic novels they have?" She absolutely adored the colorful novel-length comic books that Spencer, the Maple Hill librarian, had been ordering lately for the teen collection. "It'll only take five minutes, I promise."

"Your five minutes will turn into an hour before you know it. Research paper first, then you can go read the new graphic novels," Sarah said.

Amy turned to follow her sister toward the catalog computers so she could look up the books she needed for her school paper.

Spencer wasn't at the circulation desk. Sarah peered down the length of the library, but saw only the empty oak tables running down the center. She had hoped to ask him if the mystery novel she'd requested had arrived through interlibrary loan. She headed down the stacks, glancing left and right into the nooks made by the bookshelves standing perpendicular to the walls.

As she passed beside the staircase to the second floor, she heard a deep shudder, like something heavy being moved. "Spencer?" she called tentatively.

"Is that you, Sarah?" His voice sounded muffled and faintly out of breath. His head popped into view from around a bookcase. "Hello." A sheen of perspiration covered his reddened face.

"What are you doing? Running a marathon through the stacks?"

He smiled. "No, just trying to get to an old storeroom."

Sarah turned into the space below the staircase. A bookcase had been standing against the wall, but Spencer had removed all the books, laying them in stacks on the floor, and he'd angled the empty bookcase outward to reveal a glimpse of a small door in the wall.

"I didn't even realize there was a door there," Sarah said, "but I should have figured there would be a storage space under the stairs."

"Some kids were goofing around last week and accidentally broke a couple of chairs," Spencer said. "It was slow today, and I have some old chairs in the storage area."

"Do you need help moving that bookcase?"

"No, that's fine," he said. "You came about the book you ordered? Sorry, it hasn't arrived yet."

Sarah asked again, "Are you sure you don't need help? Amy and Audrey are here doing research for a school paper, so I have time."

"Well...."

She set down her purse. "Where are we moving this?"

He flashed a grin. "Just far enough so the door can open and we can move the chairs out."

They positioned themselves on either side of the bookcase and heaved. The noise of the wooden bottom scraping the floor echoed through the library, but Sarah found the empty bookcase was much lighter than she had expected. At Spencer's direction, they "walked" the bookcase completely out of the nook so they'd have room to open the door to the storage room, which opened outward.

He dug in his pants pocket and pulled out a key chain filled with a dozen small keys. Each key was labeled with a piece of colored tape and tiny lettering in Spencer's hand. "When I took over the library, I found these keys in the desk and had no clue what each one unlocked. I had to go through the library and figure it out." He found a key with a yellow label and inserted it into the lock on the tiny doorknob.

The door unlocked and swung open, revealing a wall of boxes.

Sarah eyed the boxes. "I don't know how you'll find anything in a room packed so full."

"Have no fear," Spencer said. "I put those boxes there the year I took over the library. Behind them, the room is actually rather empty."

Sarah soon discovered that Spencer's idea of "rather empty" didn't quite match with hers. They removed the boxes blocking the doorway and he flipped on the light switch to illuminate the room. Several smaller bookcases, with a couple more lying on top of them now stood in their way.

"Uh-oh," Spencer said. "I forgot about those. I'll need to move them aside. The chairs are close to the back wall."

They had to crouch to enter the room because of the low, slanted ceiling. The small bookcases stood only two shelves high and Sarah glanced over them toward the back of the room, looking for the chairs. There were a few old student desks, some low metal filing cabinets, and a couple of boxes that weren't stacked, leaving her a clear view of the back wall.

"Spencer," she said, "doesn't the room seem too small to you?"

"I would say so. You couldn't stick another piece of paper in there."

"No, I don't mean too full. I mean, the storage room seems smaller than it ought to be, considering the amount of space under the stairs."

"Really?" Spencer poked his head into the tiny room, then stepped out to look at the stairs. "You're right." The storage room was perhaps twenty feet long, but the area under the stairs seemed much longer, at least forty feet long.

Sarah entered the room and sidled in next to a rusted metal book cart, then climbed gingerly over a solid wooden desk. She picked her way through the student desks and managed to get within a couple of feet of the back wall, with several stacked wooden chairs in her way. "I found the chairs," she called to Spencer.

She leaned forward and knocked on the back wall of the storage room. A dull hollow sound echoed through the small space. She knocked in several places, just to be sure.

"You hear that?" she asked Spencer. "I think there might be another storage area on the other side of the wall. Do you know where the door could be?"

"I think I know." Spencer beckoned to her and, when Sarah rejoined him, led the way along the length of the library, following the wall under the stairs.

"It's got to be behind one of these two bookcases," he said, pointing. "When I took over the library a few years ago, I moved most of the bookcases, but I didn't move these away from the wall because they fit in with how I wanted to reorganize the library furniture. So they've probably been here since the renovation that happened about thirty years ago."

"I remember that. When they expanded the second floor, right? We could check the library blueprints to see if there really is another storage room."

"They're at the courthouse. It'll be faster to move these bookcases aside."

He had a point. "Why don't we each empty a bookcase, then the two of us can move them aside together."

"Sounds like a plan," Spencer said.

Sarah was careful to keep the books in order as she removed them from the shelves, stacking them neatly out in the pathway down the center of the library, where they were out of the way. Spencer finished before she did, and helped her with her remaining books.

They positioned themselves on either side of the first bookcase.

"Ready? One, two, three!"

Sarah and Spencer scooted the edge of the bookcase away from the wall a few inches. He looked behind it and shook his head. "Nothing."

"Let's try the other one."

They moved the bookcase back into place and shifted around the stacks of books that needed to be put back on the shelves.

Spencer got ready to move the second bookcase and smiled. "Ready to solve a mystery?"

Sarah laughed as she grabbed the edge of the empty bookcase. "There's a chance we moved all those books for nothing."

"Well, here goes nothing!"

This bookcase was a bit heavier than the other two, or perhaps Sarah's muscles were tiring after hefting all those books. They needed two heaves this time to get it away from the wall enough for Spencer to peek behind.

"There's a door!" Spencer said.

"Grandma, what's going on?"

Both girls peered into the nook at the two of them, the askew bookcase, and the books stacked against the sides.

"What are you doing?" Amy asked. The girls each held a small stack of books to check out.

"We found a hidden storage room," Sarah said.

"Did you find any bones?" Amy asked.

"Gross!" Audrey said.

Sarah couldn't help but smile. "I don't know what's inside. We have to clear the way to open the door first."

"We can help." Amy and Audrey set their stacks of research books on a nearby table.

"Good, we'll need all the help we can get," Spencer said. "Amy, you join your grandma on that side of the case, and Audrey, you help me. We're going to 'walk' the bookcase into the center aisle of the library."

It took them longer than Sarah had expected. Because this bookcase was heavier than the other ones they'd moved, all four of them were out of breath when they were done.

"I think that's enough," he said after their last heave-ho. He headed back to the wall and grasped the doorknob, but it didn't budge. "Locked."

He pulled out his key ring and found the same yellow-taped key he'd used for the other door. It inserted into the lock smoothly, but wouldn't turn to open the door.

"Aw," Amy sighed.

"There are still a few unmarked keys." Spencer flipped through the key ring. He tried four other keys before one slid in and turned.

Click. The door unlocked.

It opened to reveal a dark room. Spencer reached for a light switch on the wall and clicked it, but nothing happened. "I have a flashlight I left in the other storage room."

"I'll get it," Sarah said. She hurried there and back, her mind swirling with the possibilities of what might be in a room left unopened for at least thirty years. She handed Spencer the flashlight and followed behind him as he stepped into the room.

Unlike the other storage room, they didn't have to crouch because of a low ceiling. Here, the ceiling was high because it was directly under the highest point of the stairs. Sarah immediately spied some tables and old bookcases, smaller than the ones out on the floor and more ornately carved.

"These must have been in the library before the renovation," Spencer said.

"I'm not an expert—Maggie would probably know better—but some of these look like they may be antiques."

"I wouldn't be surprised. The library was dedicated in 1902. Maybe some of this is from back then."

A shriek from one of the twins echoed against the slanted ceiling.

"What's wrong?" Sarah asked.

"I think there are cobwebs in my hair! I'm outta here."

Sarah couldn't see but guessed it was Audrey who beat a hasty retreat.

Sarah, Spencer, and Amy continued to weave their way through a few broken chairs. "I'm surprised there isn't more dust," Sarah said.

"This room seems pretty well sealed," Spencer said. "If it hasn't been opened since the renovation thirty years ago, there probably aren't many cracks in the walls for dust to come through."

Sarah's leg hit the edge of a desk. "Oh." She stumbled, and her toe jammed into something a bit softer than wood, although still heavy and solid. "What's this?"

A cardboard box was hidden under the desk, only an edge peeking out.

Spencer maneuvered the box out with a grunt. "It's heavy." He flipped open one of the flaps. "Books!"

"Let's see if we can get this box out of here," Sarah said.

With more pushing and pulling, they dragged the box out of the storage area. Sarah was happy to leave the dark crowded space for the loftier main area.

"What did you find?" Audrey asked.

"Just books," Amy answered her.

Audrey looked in the box before turning around. "C'mon. Let's go see if there are any new magazines." Amy followed shortly behind.

"Let's sort through these." Spencer dragged the box to one of the oak tables that ran down the center aisle of the library floor.

Sarah and Spencer pawed through the box. It contained hardcover books bound in thick, plain fabrics with the titles stamped in block lettering and also locally printed pamphlets and booklets.

Spencer glanced through the unmarked hardcovers while Sarah laid out the pamphlets and booklets, most of which were literature about local sites. There were collections of essays from the local Rose Growers Society, some Circa-bound genealogies of a few of the oldest families in Maple Hill, and a few pamphlets on locally made ceramics. The publications were all dated 1981.

"I wonder if the historical society will want to look at some of these." Sarah flipped through a Circa-bound book made up of photocopies of the pages of a weather-beaten, handwritten journal, which looked like a personal reminiscence of General Nathaniel Bradford, a Maple Hill hero from the Revolutionary War. The words *Pamela Harders, 1760–1820, book printed 1981* had been printed on the card stock cover. If Irene Stuart at the historical society didn't already have a copy of this, she would be salivating to take a look. "Why were all these in the storeroom rather than in the stacks?"

Spencer shook his head. "I have no idea."

"This is odd—all the hardcovers have the same cover design," Sarah said. The hardcovers were green, red, blue, or black, and had the same kind of block lettering stamped on the covers and spines, although the titles were different. Sarah picked one up. The cover seemed newer than the pages. It looked like an old pulp fiction novel, copyrighted 1948. "The hardcover books I read have dust jackets."

"I think these are old books that had been damaged or books that needed more durable covers. The library sends them to a local book binder to remove the old cover and replace it with a new one."

"So why weren't they put back on the shelves?"

"Once the books are back from the binder, they have to be processed and the catalog number reattached to the spine before they're put back. But none of these were recataloged." He pointed to the clean spine of a book. "No Dewey Decimal number."

"You think these books have been in that storage room since the renovation?"

Spencer nodded. "Maybe they were put with the pamphlets and booklets because they all needed to be processed. If the library gets busy, things like that are a low priority. But I don't understand why the books were put in storage rather than cataloged."

Sarah picked up another book, a slim volume with a dark green cover. Strangely, this one didn't have a title stamped on it, although the cover looked like those on the other books. Inside, there was no publisher, no title, and no author.

How strange. Sarah flipped to the first page and read:

I'm telling this story because I can't get the picture of her face out of my mind. When I go to sleep, I can still see her eyes on the day the FBI came to Maple Hill to take her away.

Sarah read the paragraph over again, unable to fully comprehend the words. Was the book talking about *this* Maple Hill?

She kept reading.

I can't keep it bottled up inside anymore. I'm writing this anonymously because my hands are tied and I can't do anything for her. That somehow just seems like a weak excuse.

So, here's the story. It was spring 1960 when Debby Neely moved to Maple Hill. She was about nineteen or twenty years old, a pretty girl. She was quiet, but she was a sweet person.

Sarah drew in a sharp breath. She remembered Debby. Sarah had been about twelve or thirteen years old, with a hazy preadolescent's awareness of anything that didn't involve school. She dredged up a blurred image of a smooth oval face, dark eyes, dark hair, and golden creamy skin. She only remembered meeting Debby a handful of times.

A shiver ran across her skin. This wasn't a book like the others in the box.

Sarah kept reading.

I don't remember when she actually came to town because she kept to herself for much of the first few months. I only know it was spring 1960 because she later told me. I didn't even become friends with her until fall of that year. We started talking and seemed to connect.

When she came to town, she hadn't intended to stay more than a night or two, but Pleiter's shop needed help that year—Al Pleiter had broken his leg, and the only Pleiters able to help out at the store were still in middle school. Debby got a job within a few hours of arriving in Maple Hill, and she stayed for almost two years.

Even though she was in Maple Hill for that long, it was hard for her to form friendships in town. Not because people were unfriendly, she just had her own host of secrets to keep, plus she was a quiet person. She mentioned once how she had always been quiet because her brother was so outgoing and had such a strong personality.

It wasn't like she didn't have any friends, though. She was close to her co-worker and the woman she was staying with, and later with me. I wish I'd pushed harder to get past her reserve, to get to know her sooner than I did. I only knew her for two years, but she changed the way I looked at the world, at myself, at God.

One day, out of the blue, she was arrested by the FBI.

But I know that she went to prison for a crime she didn't commit.

A Note from the Editors

Patchwork Mysteries was created by the Books and Inspirational Media Division of Guideposts, a nonprofit organization that touches millions of lives every day through products and services that inspire, encourage and uplift. Our magazines, books, prayer network (OurPrayer.org), and other outreach programs help people connect their faith-filled values to daily life.

Your purchase of Patchwork Mysteries makes a difference. When you buy Guideposts products, you're helping fund our work, which includes ministry to military personnel, prisons, hospitals, nursing homes and educational institutions. To learn more, visit GuidepostsFoundation.org.

To find out about our other publications and to enjoy free online resources such as inspirational newsletters, blogs, videos, Facebook and Twitter links, visit us at Guideposts.org.